Darcy on the Hudson

A Pride and Prejudice Re-imaging

By Mary Lydon Simonsen

Quail Creek Publishing, LLC
http://marysimonsenfanfiction.blogspot.com
www.austenauthors.net

Printed in the United States of America
Published by Quail Creek Publishing, LLC
quailcreekpub@hotmail.com
www.marysimonsenfanfiction.blogspot.com
Peoria, Arizona

Chapter 1

Summer 1811

Fitzwilliam Darcy was dying. Even though his friend, Charles Bingley, and his sister, Miss Georgiana Darcy, his fellow voyagers, continued to insist that he was not, he knew differently. No one could be this ill for weeks on end and not hear the angels singing. The *Zephyr* had just rounded Holyhead near Liverpool when the first wave of seasickness had come upon him. By the time the ship had sailed out onto the open Atlantic, Darcy was unable to leave his cabin. His hasty decision to join Bingley on a visit to his uncle's farm in New York had been made with little thought as to the actual voyage. Even though he knew he was a miserable sailor, having barely survived a crossing of the Irish Sea to Dublin, he had decided to push on and damn the consequences.

"Fitzwilliam, you are *not* dying," Georgiana said for the fourth time in an hour.

"I am sorry to grieve you, my dear sister, but I *am* dying, and it would be a mercy if you and Bingley would help me up to the deck and just toss me overboard."

"Please stop talking like that!" Georgiana stated in a voice clearly indicating she was at wit's end with her overly-dramatic sibling. "Your misery will soon be at an end. The captain informed me that we are within a day of sighting Sandy Hook, a notable landmark on the New Jersey shore, and then we will turn north into the Narrows and sail into New York Bay. Fitzwilliam, we are so very close to our destination."

"Your sister is right, Darcy," Bingley said, trying to buck up his friend. "All you need do is hold on for another two days. Shortly after docking at Manhattan Island, we will take a smaller ship up the Hudson River to Tarrytown, and you will once again be on *terra firma*."

Darcy shook his head. "No, Bingley. If I make it to land, I am not getting on another ship. Not ever. I might very well have to remain in the United States because I do not know how I will get back to England." After making that remarkable statement, he gestured for both to leave him as he knew he would be sick again, and the two left him to the care of Mercer, Darcy's manservant, who, in their minds, was more saint than servant.

Even in his misery, Darcy believed he had done the right thing by leaving England. A most distressing situation had occurred involving his sister and a family friend, a friend who had betrayed both of them, and in doing so, had most particularly wounded Georgiana. But with Napoleon's armies wreaking havoc across the European Continent, a concerned brother had looked to America for a place where his sister could recover.

Because of their hasty departure, there had been no time to hire a lady's maid and companion for Georgiana to replace Mrs. Younge following her dismissal from service for failing to protect her charge. In her eagerness to put an embarrassing situation behind her, Georgiana had stated that having a lady's maid was a matter of little importance, but it had turned out to be a matter of great inconvenience as Miss Darcy had found it necessary to rely on the assistance of other female passengers who were completely unknown to her before boarding the *Zephyr*, a situation her brother regarded as nearly intolerable.

Then again, Georgiana was only responsible for the timing of the journey, not its destination, as a voyage had been planned for the spring when Darcy was to meet with a cadre of businessmen regarding the development of industries along a proposed canal linking the Hudson River to Lake Erie. For three generations, the Darcys had embraced technology and had provided financial backing for the Bridgewater Canal in Northwest England and development of Derbyshire's Derwent Valley's textile industry. But these projects were nothing when compared to the riches to be made if the vast interior of the United States could be opened by way of a great canal. But these things only mattered if Darcy lived to see them.

* * *

As soon as the party disembarked on the west side of Manhattan, they were met by Mr. Garvey, a man in the employ of Charles's uncle, Richard Bingley, and it was he who was to accompany them on the next part of their journey. No one had to tell Garvey that Darcy had had a rough journey. The gentleman looked as if he was suffering from marsh fever, and he recognized the look of a man who had never gained his sea legs.

"Mr. Darcy, there is Beacon Tavern nearby where we'll get you a pint of ale and some bread and that'll fix you up for sure," Garvey announced, trying to reassure the ailing man's party that their friend would live. "We'll be staying the night there and set out for Tarrytown first thing after breakfast."

At the Beacon Tavern, they were served a board of bread and cheese and a mug of ale, but after tearing off a piece of bread and washing it down with the strong ale, Darcy showed no further interest in eating—not so Bingley. Except for intermittent bouts of seasickness, his appetite had remained hale and hearty, and he proved it by ordering a beef pie.

Garvey explained that early in the morning they would be boarding a sloop owned by Mr. Tom Bennet that would take them to a landing a few miles from Richard Bingley's house. Darcy reiterated that he would not get on another ship for a king's ransom.

"Meaning no disrespect, sir, but that would be a mistake," Garvey said. "You would be looking at another one or two days' journey. Because the road to Tarrytown is also the post road to Albany, it's always crowded, and the cattle drovers use it as well. Seeing how you're already ailing, I wouldn't think you'd want to be bouncing around in a hired coach. Besides, the North River, or the Hudson River as some call it, *is* our road. That's how people hereabouts get around if they're going any distance."

To Darcy, the options of a bumpy coach or a heaving ship were clearly a matter of choosing one's poison. "I shall think about it," he told Garvey.

Garvey assured Darcy that the Beacon Tavern had the best accommodations to be found on the east side of the Hudson, and although its patrons looked rough, they were mostly pilots who steered the ships through the Narrows and up the Hudson, and not the tough deckhands or dock workers who favored some of the seedier bars clustered near the wharves. But it was a tough sell for Garvey. By Darcy's standards, the Beacon Tavern was primitive, and when he heard a roar of laughter from a group of rough-looking men who had swigged more than a tankard or two, that decided the matter. Not wishing to subject his sister to the possibility of a second night at roadside accommodations that might actually be worse than the Beacon, he agreed to go to Tarrytown by sloop.

The next morning, as soon as they boarded the *Tom B*, they were met by her captain, Mr. Sampson, a Negro.

Although all had seen blacks in London, they were usually servants, and none knew of any who were addressed as mister, which thrilled Georgiana as she delighted in the novelties of this diverse land, including listening to the sounds of a dozen languages, all being spoken at one time. America might very well be the most exotic locale she would ever visit, and she wanted to make the most of it.

As the ship slipped away from the dock, Darcy's nausea returned, and Georgiana went back to nursing her brother, refusing all pleas by Mercer that she go up on deck with Mr. Bingley. However, neither brother nor sister lacked for news. Whenever a landmark was sighted, Bingley returned to tell the Darcys of their progress and would regurgitate information he had learned on deck from Mr. Sampson.

"We are about to come up on Spuyten Duyvil Creek, which is where the Harlem River empties into the Hudson and is famous for its oyster beds. Spuyten Duyvil is Dutch for Devil's Spout. The pilot said they often encounter strong currents at this point. 'Hold on to your hat,' is what he said."

Hold on to your hat? More like, hold on to the contents of your stomach, Darcy thought.

The closer the sloop got to its destination, the more excited Charles became. He had wanted to visit his father's older brother since he was a young lad. Richard Bingley had left England more than twenty-five years earlier to see to the American operations of their growing global import/export business. Upon the death of Charles's father, it had been determined that his younger sons would continue to run the British mercantile concerns. However, the father had stipulated that his eldest would be a gentleman and never dirty his hands by becoming a member of the merchant class. An affable Charles was more than willing to go along with this decree.

"We have just passed Yonkers, which was named

after…" But that was all Darcy heard. He would have liked to have learned more, but he was concentrating on not embarrassing himself by losing his breakfast. "We will shortly be coming up on Hastings on Hudson," Charles continued. "The Philipse family owned 90,000 acres, but lost everything after the War of Rebellion because they sided with the British. Darcy, think about it! 90,000 acres! And the captain said it is nothing compared to the vast holdings farther up the river where the Livingston family owns more than one-half million acres on the west side of the Hudson alone. By Jove, that rivals the holdings of the crown."

Darcy missed Bingley's commentary about Dobb's Ferry, where Washington had once encamped, because he had fallen asleep and would remain so until the sloop reached Tarrytown Harbor.

* * *

At first glance, Tarrytown appeared to be a bustling enterprise with several taverns, at least two churches, a Quaker meeting house, hotel, and a goodly number of mercantile enterprises selling whatever the sloops plying their trade between New York City and Albany carried as their cargo.

From the many barrels being loaded onto the ships, it was obvious that the region was abundant in corn, apples, pears, and other types of fruit as well as wheat, hops, and barley, all the ingredients necessary to brew beer and ale. It was also rich in natural beauty with palisades jutting up from the river's west bank and enormous trees hugging the shores of the Tappan Zee, that part of the Hudson where the river was at its widest.

Richard Bingley's house was three bumpy miles from the Tarrytown landing, and although modest when compared to Darcy's Pemberley or Bingley's Netherfield

Park, it was a thing of beauty to the weary travelers. When the visitors passed through the split Dutch door, they immediately entered an all-purpose room that served as the dining room and parlor, and which, in the Dutch colonial era, had been the bedroom of the master and mistress of the house. All who came through the front door would have admired the four-poster bed and expensive fabrics used for the bed curtains and covers, both indicators of the owner's wealth.

Considering the size of Bingley's fortune, Darcy had been expecting to find his uncle living in an elegant house and dressed in the latest fashion. Instead, his host wore a pair of breeches that had seen better days and a waistcoat that was either shrinking or its wearer was expanding. He knew of rich men who squirreled away every penny, but this man was no miser as he had thrown open the doors of his house to two strangers and a nephew he had seen only once in his life.

Richard welcomed the visitors and quickly ordered that supper be served. It was a simple meal of beef stew, strong black coffee, rye bread, and peach cobbler, but it was eaten with gusto by all but Darcy, who barely managed to consume the broth.

"I know you must be exhausted, so we will visit tomorrow when you have had your rest," Richard said in an accent that was more American than English. "You will know when breakfast is being served because Mrs. Haas, my cook, prepares crullers, a Dutch specialty, and you will smell the cinnamon through the floor boards, and then you will bite into the best pastry you have ever eaten."

Richard Bingley's house was typical of colonial Dutch architecture in that there were no hallways, and a person must pass through one room to gain entry to another. A narrow staircase led to three rooms above, and for purposes of privacy, Georgiana was given the smallest room farthest from the stairs. Darcy and Mercer would be in the room next to Georgiana, and Charles would occupy the largest room, but also the noisiest, because of its location next to the stairs. But Georgiana would soon discover that there was an exterior staircase leading to a porch that wrapped around three sides of the house, a novelty the seventeen-year-old found delightful.

As soon as Darcy had said good night to his sister, he closed the door separating their rooms and sat on a wooden chair and stared at the small bed that was to be his place of repose for the next four months. The bed, when compared to his huge four-poster at Pemberley, looked as if it belonged to a child. After Mercer had removed his boots, Darcy collapsed on the bed, and with his feet pressed up against the footboard, stared at the ceiling.

"Mercer, I hope this sojourn in the New World doesn't prove to be a major mistake on my part," Darcy said, his hands crossed over his still queasy belly.

"Oh, I don't think so, sir. Tomorrow, you'll be out and about, walking the property, breathing fresh air, and looking at that pretty river, and you'll stop thinking about the ship and start thinking about all the new things you're going to see."

As far as Mercer was concerned, the trip was off to an excellent start. He was sitting at the same table as his master, eating the same food as his master, and enjoying the same conversation as his master, and Mrs. Haas had made such a fuss over him, insisting that he have a second piece of peach cobbler. No, Mercer had to disagree with Mr. Darcy that their voyage to New York might not have been a good idea. In his mind, it was already paying dividends.

Chapter 2

Richard was correct. The crullers were a delectable treat, but they were merely the appetizers as Mrs. Haas had prepared what she called "stacks" of pancakes served with maple syrup and a rasher of bacon. While Charles worked his way through a stack of six and eyed the three pancakes left on Darcy's plate, they were joined by Mercer and Mr. Garvey, both of whom made quick work of their own stacks.

After breakfast, Richard took his guests for a tour of the property, and the smell of rich earth and newly-mown hay filled the air. The laborers had been in the fields since daybreak, cutting the grass while the dew was still on it. Darcy and Bingley noted that the scene was little different from what one could observe in England: men moving quickly across the fields, slashing the grasses with long-handled scythes in gentle sweeping motions. Some laborers had stopped to whet their blades on grindstones scattered throughout the fields and gulped down a jar of rum to quench their thirst before returning to their work.

Although it was midsummer, it was a pleasant morning with a breeze coming in off the river, and Darcy was glad to be anywhere other than on a ship. They passed fields of rye, wheat, and corn waiting their turns to be harvested, orchards filled with apple, pear, and peach trees, and bales of the newly-hewn hay dotted the landscape.

"I lease my house from Tom Bennet, my nearest

neighbor, who has five lovely daughters, the prettiest girls in the county, but one," Richard said, looking at Charles, "and I am sure you know who I am talking about: your cousin, Caroline."

Darcy stiffened at the mention of Caroline's name. Caroline, whose mother had died when she was quite young, was one of two daughters of Richard Bingley, both of whom had been educated in France. Darcy had been introduced to Caroline at the wedding of her elder sister, Louisa, to a member of the English gentry, and she had left an indelible impression on him.

"Miss Bingley!" Georgiana cried. "She and I were introduced when she was in London last year, and I would so enjoy seeing her again. And I must agree, Mr. Bingley, that she is very beautiful, quite the prettiest lady of my acquaintance."

"You will get no argument from me on that point, young lady," the proud father answered, "but she might have some competition when *you* come of age." Georgiana smiled, reveling in the compliment. "But she is currently upstate at Saratoga Springs with her friends or, should I say, her second family, the Storms. I am afraid that living with a father who prefers reading a good book by his hearth to attending dances causes her to seek company elsewhere. She is good friends with their ward, Amanda Beekman, and spends a goodly part of the summer at their country retreat. Even though Caroline will not be here, you could not have come at a better time. In two days' time, the Van Tassels, one of Tarrytown's most prominent families, will be hosting a festival to celebrate the conclusion of the haying season— a place to kick up your heels and eat and drink heartily."

"Are you saying we shall be invited to the festival, Mr. Bingley?" Georgiana asked eagerly.

"Of course. There is no guest list here, my dear. When there is a festival, everyone is invited, and because there are two Mr. Bingleys, please call me Richard or Mr. Richard, whichever you prefer."

Georgiana was elated to learn that they would be attending a social event so soon after their arrival in New York. But when she looked at her brother's face, she could see there was a good chance that he would not allow her to attend.

"Mr. Richard, I have not yet come into society," Georgiana informed him.

"Oh, goodness me! That doesn't matter. These celebrations are very much a family affair. All are welcome."

The rest of the walk was spent with Richard waxing eloquent on the beauty of the countryside, and although he remained an Englishman, he now considered the United States to be his home.

"I have lived in America since 1785, twenty-six years now, representing the Bingley family's commercial interests on this side of the Atlantic, that is, until I retired two years ago for reasons of my health," he said, pointing to a gouty foot. "In 1786, I married Susana Post, a wonderful lady from a prominent Dutch family. My father-in-law owned a shop in Manhattan on Broadway or Breede Weg, as he called it.

"After Susana's death in '96, I wanted to get Caroline and Louisa out of the city and away from all the noise and dirt. Once I crossed King's Bridge into Westchester County, I started to look for property, but no one would sell land to an Englishman. To this day, feelings about the fight for independence from England are quite strong. I had all but given up finding a house to lease when I knocked on Tom Bennet's door. His tenant had just moved out, heading west, where opportunities are greater and land cheaper, and we agreed to terms right then and there."

"Is there still resentment against the British?" a

concerned Charles asked.

"Some. And it is a subject best avoided as well as any discussions about the British Navy taking sailors off American ships on the high seas, claiming they are British citizens. At a minimum, you will have a vigorous discussion, or if things really heat up, you could end up in the midst of a brawl. It *has* happened. But New York's lifeblood is trade, and its biggest trading partner is Great Britain and its colonies. In America, especially here in the Northeast, money trumps everything, except religion.

"But no more stories about war or impressments as you will hear enough of them from my neighbors during your stay. Many of them fought in the American Revolution, and after a pint of ale, they will be more than happy to tell you their tales. And I will warn you now, beware of the applejack. It is a potent apple brandy, but it tastes so sweet going down, that you are flat on your back quicker than you can say 'Jack Frost.'"

* * *

Upon returning to the house, Georgiana asked her brother if they would be attending the festival.

"Georgiana, I am still not completely recovered, so it would be difficult for me to enjoy such an event with my constitution still impaired. But I *do* want you to go."

"If you do not go, then I shall not."

"Charles is going, and he will be happy to escort you."

"All the more reason for me *not* to go as people will assume Charles is my suitor, and I could not bear such speculation. Besides, you asked Charles not to tell anyone that you suffered from seasickness. If I went and you did not, then there would be questions, so we shall have a quiet day here and go for long walks."

Darcy knew there was another reason for Georgiana's

reluctance. Three months earlier, without his knowledge, his sister had engaged in a secret correspondence with George Wickham, the adopted son of the steward at Pemberley, in which Wickham had encouraged the sixteen-year-old Georgiana to elope with him.

Because they were very nearly the same age, Darcy and Wickham had developed a close friendship during their youth at Pemberley. The amiable young Wickham had succeeded in securing the affection of the elder Mr. Darcy to the point where he had provided him with the same university education as his son.

After Cambridge, their divergent interests had separated them, and Darcy was unaware of the reputation Wickham had earned as a frequenter of public houses as well as his habits of expense and his relationships with women. As a result, when Wickham came to ask him for the full value of a living promised to him by his late father, he was surprised. Every effort to persuade his friend against such a course of action had been rebuffed, and a cheque drafted on a London bank was handed to George Wickham in settlement of all entitlements bequeathed to him by his late father. The unexpected request should have served as a warning that Wickham was prepared to take advantage of his friends. Unfortunately, the realization that his friend had changed or that the real nature of the man had been revealed came too late.

At a public ball during the London season, Darcy saw a very different man from the boy his father had embraced. To his disgust, Wickham engaged in an open flirtation with a young woman, putting the lady's reputation at risk. When confronted about his ungentlemanlike behavior, Wickham confessed he was experiencing great financial difficulties and was in search of a rich wife. The nearly £4,000 Darcy had given to Wickham after his father's death had disappeared into the ether.

When Darcy refused to advance any additional monies, Wickham launched a verbal assault on the Darcy family. Instead of feeling gratitude for the elder Darcy's generosity, he stated that he had been treated badly and that the amounts set aside for his education and living were miserly when compared to the son's yearly allowance. Before leaving, Wickham assured Darcy he would have his revenge for keeping him in his present state of poverty, and he had very nearly succeeded.

"Well, if you will not go without me, then I *must* go," Darcy said after seeing his sister's disappointment. "But I wonder what Richard's neighbors will say about a guest who does not eat or dance? Hopefully, they will be so overwhelmed by your beauty and Charles's charm that they will pay little attention to me." Georgiana, looking at her handsome brother, laughed at such a ridiculous notion.

Chapter 3

Lydia and Kitty came running into the house shouting, "He has come. He has finally come."

"Who has come?" their father asked, peering over the bifocals perched on his nose. Tom Bennet had been reading the *New York Packet* and the other newspapers that had arrived from the city on his sloop, *Tom B*, when his daughters had burst on to the scene.

"Mr. Bingley's nephew, of course. He was expected five days ago."

"Lydia, I see you have already grown accustomed to steamship schedules, but such things are for use on the river, not the open ocean. When you cross the Atlantic, your arrival date is determined by when you enter the Narrows."

"Oh, Papa, that doesn't matter," thirteen-year old Lydia answered. "What does matter is that Mr. Bingley's nephew is very handsome and a bachelor."

"And his Christian name is Charles," Kitty, Lydia's twin, added. "At least that is what Mr. Richard called him."

"Lydia and Kitty, the table needs to be set for supper, so please wash your hands," Mrs. Bennet said, "and during our meal, you may tell us all about the handsome Mr. Charles Bingley."

"But it is not just Mr. Bingley who has come," Kitty added. "There is another gentleman and lady with them, and I think a servant."

"I suspect that you two were up in Mr. Bingley's tree," Lizzy, the second eldest Bennet daughter, said.

"No, we weren't," Lydia insisted. "We stood on the boulder by the great oak, and from there we could see Mr. Bingley, who has reddish gold hair."

"I would say his hair is more red than gold," Kitty said, as if this made all the difference. "Because he had his back to us, we did not see what the other gentleman looked like, and because of the lady's bonnet, we could not see her face either. I wish we knew who they were."

During supper, the identities of the mystery visitors were revealed. Mr. Bennet had arranged for his guest's passage to Tarrytown on the *Tom B.* Because the patriarch loved drama, he frequently withheld tidbits of information so he might surprise his family and enjoy their reaction to his news.

"The gentleman is Fitzwilliam Darcy of Pemberley Manor in Derbyshire, and the lady is his sister, Miss Georgiana Darcy, who is about seventeen years old. Richard tells me the Darcys come from a distinguished Norman family with ties to the monarchy, and their grandfather was an earl. But I shall not hold that against them," he said with a chuckle.

"An earl!" Kitty exclaimed. "Isn't an earl the grandson of a king or something like that?"

"An earl is a member of the upper nobility, but dukes and marquises are above them in rank," Mary, the practical middle daughter, offered. "Although Mr. Darcy does not have a title, there is a certain cachet associated with families of Norman ancestry as many of them arrived in England with William the Conqueror."

"Oh, who cares about some boring old title or if they are Norsemen," Lydia answered.

"I said 'Norman' not 'Norseman,' although it is

believed that Normandy was settled by the Norsemen, thus accounting for the similarity in their names."

Lydia stamped her foot in frustration. She was always being corrected by someone, and that someone was usually Mary. "Norman! Norseman! I do not care about any of that. What we need to know is if Miss Darcy is intended for Mr. Bingley or if he is free to marry another."

"Before you consider marrying either of these gentlemen, please remember that Mr. Bingley is an Englishman," her father cautioned his daughter. "He should feel free to admire the local beauties, but he will return to his home country *alone*."

"I agree with Papa," Mary concurred. "So whether Mr. Bingley is interested in Miss Darcy should be of no interest to us."

"Oh, hogwash," Lydia said. "Just because he is English does not mean he cannot marry Jane or Lizzy."

"I thank you for my share of the favor," Lizzy answered, "but I have no intention of marrying anyone other than an American," and her father nodded his head in approval.

* * *

"Fitzwilliam, what am I to wear to the festival?" Georgiana asked her brother. With no female confidante to advise her, she had pleaded with him to come into her room so she might make this most important of decisions.

"Surely, you have something appropriate hidden in all those trunks you brought with us."

"But what is appropriate in England may be quite different from what is appropriate in America," and Darcy could hear the anxiety in her voice.

"I would suggest the green dress you wore when we dined with Aunt de Bourgh," Darcy answered with more certainty than he felt. "It is not too fine, but it is fine enough for a haying festival."

This little scene reaffirmed Darcy's commitment to find his sister a lady's maid as soon as they returned to England as he had no wish to serve as his sister's fashion advisor.

"Yes, that will be the perfect dress." She came over and kissed her brother on his cheek. "Someday you will make someone a fine husband."

When Georgiana and Darcy came downstairs, Charles was waiting for them on the porch.

"I think I may have had more than a case of *mal de mer*," Darcy told Bingley. "Although I am feeling better, jumping about doing jigs and reels might cause a regression. As a result, I shall not dance. Another thing, Bingley, I do not want my health to become a topic of conversation. Are we agreed on those two points?"

Charles, who was so eager to mingle amongst the Americans, heard little of what his friend had said and merely nodded his assent so they might arrive at the festival all the sooner.

* * *

Upon their arrival, the visitors gazed upon tables filled to overflowing with ham, turkey, carrots, peas, corn on its cob, tomatoes, huge slices of watermelons, breads, and other tasty treats. The aromas from the dessert table were particularly enticing: peach pies, cherry pies, quince pies, and best of all, apple pies. From the time he was a young lad lurking about the Pemberley kitchen, Darcy's favorite dessert was an apple tart, and he suspected that the pies with the golden latticework crusts hid a generous amount of apple filling. As much as Darcy wanted a slice, the queasiness in his stomach was still there, and he would not risk becoming ill and embarrassing himself in front of strangers. He would be here for four months. There would be time enough for pie.

After all had feasted, a fiddler struck a chord, and a cheer went up followed by a rush to a grassy area that had been cleared for dancing. By the time the last note of the first song had been played, Darcy was impressed by the quality of the music and the dancers, particularly the ladies, including a golden-haired beauty who had caught Bingley's eye. After seeking an introduction, he had learned that she was the eldest daughter of his uncle's landlord, Tom Bennet. But Charles would have to wait his turn to dance with her as she had already promised dances to three others. But Bingley, who loved to dance, would not stand idle, and he engaged the next eldest Bennet daughter, also a fine dancer, with dark curly hair, fine eyes, and a beautiful smile.

"I can tell you love to dance, Mr. Bingley, and you will find many willing partners here."

"I am very glad to hear it, Miss Elizabeth, as I *do* love to dance." Looking around, he continued, "Everyone here is so skilled a dancer, they could grace any ballroom in England."

"We have the benefit of being close to New York where there are excellent dancing masters, many from France. For those who choose not to go into the city for lessons, there is Dancing Master John Griffiths' book of dances. Except for the minuet, with all its complicated steps, the dances are easily learned."

However, such chatter could not divert the gentleman's attention from the prettiest girl at the festival. "Your sister is also an excellent dancer," he said while glancing in Jane's direction. "I asked Miss Bennet for a dance, but I was late to the party, so to speak, and I must wait. But I understand from my uncle that there are five Bennet sisters."

"Yes, but Mary, who sits over there in the yellow dress, has a malformed foot and does not dance. Kitty and Lydia are the two youngest and are twins," she said, pointing to her sisters who were already dancing. "They will gladly oblige you with a turn."

"Then after this set, I shall go and ask them directly."

With Bingley and Georgiana dancing, an uneasy Darcy drifted among the guests. He looked about for Richard, but Bingley's uncle had quickly sought out those men who wished to play cards. With the long days of summer providing ample light, other guests were also engaged in skittles and horseshoes. Darcy's preference was to be left alone, but it was not to be as Bingley was headed in his direction.

"Darcy, I must have you dance," Bingley called out as he approached his friend.

"As you know very well, I have no intention of dancing," Darcy answered while giving his friend a withering stare to remind him of *why* he was not dancing.

"But there are so many agreeable ladies here, many of whom are in need of a partner," Bingley pressed.

"Surely, the ladies of the neighborhood do not rely on visitors from England to supply their dance partners." But Charles continued to prod. "Bingley, I cannot be tempted to dance. Go back to the ladies and their smiles. You are wasting your time with me."

Darcy was unaware his comments had been overheard by Elizabeth Bennet and her dear friend, Charlotte Lucas, and both ladies exchanged glances.

"It seems as if that particular gentleman is very proud," Elizabeth said as she moved away from the gentleman.

"Yes, it would appear so, but I understand Mr. Darcy is from a wealthy and prominent family in England. We should not be surprised that a young man with family, fortune, and everything in his favor should think highly of himself. I daresay he has a right to be proud."

"A right to be proud! Based on what evidence?" Lizzy asked Charlotte. "Other than that he was born to wealth and privilege, we know nothing of him, and yet you say he has a right to be proud. Besides, how dare he not dance with me," Lizzy said, stamping her foot in feigned outrage.

Unaware of the consternation his remarks had caused, Darcy turned around and looked right at Elizabeth. He had earlier observed her dancing with Bingley and had noted how capable a dancer she was. He had also observed her fine eyes and luscious dark curls and would have continued to admire the lady, but even amongst Americans, a people who did not seem to stand on ceremony, it was rude to stare and so he moved in the direction of the card tables.

"Oh my goodness! He looked right into your eyes," Charlotte said.

"Yes he did and immediately turned his back on me and walked away."

"But, Lizzy, I am sure he was admiring you. Earlier, he had watched as you danced with Mr. Bingley. At the time I thought nothing of it, but now I wonder."

"Wonder what? Mr. Darcy was merely observing the rituals of the natives and has discovered that even savages can dance," Lizzy countered. "However, he does have a satirical eye. If I am again in his company, I will be impertinent or I shall soon grow afraid of him."

"*You,* afraid of a man! I should live so long," and the two of them shared a good laugh. Even so, Charlotte would not let go of the topic. "Perhaps, Mr. Darcy is being compared to *another* Englishman."

"Of course, you are referring to Edward Chamberlain, the great love of my life, except that he was not," an exasperated Lizzy answered as this topic raised hackles like no other. "But because no one will believe me, I shall be forced to make up some tragic story about Edward and me. Perhaps, my pretend lover will inspire my writing."

"But Jane said…"

"Yes, I know what Jane said. But when we were in England, my sister saw love everywhere we went. To my mind, Edward Chamberlain is ancient history and about as interesting."

"But you like history."

"Ah, here are Peter and Josiah Van Wart, late as usual. I think they intend to ask us to dance."

* * *

On the ride to Mr. Bingley's farmhouse, Georgiana, who was thrilled beyond measure to have experienced her first dance in America, was all praise for her company. "No one seemed to care that I had not officially come out into society. All that really mattered was that I was a capable dancer."

Not surprisingly, a young lady as beautiful as Georgiana had been engaged for every dance, including dancing a reel with Nathaniel Van Cortlandt, the scion of one of the Valley's oldest Dutch families.

"Mr. Van Cortlandt is to have a career in the army and is training at the military academy at West Point farther up the Hudson," Richard Bingley explained. "They have dances scheduled in the autumn and spring, and I believe the next one will be in late October. So, Miss Darcy, if you continue to grace us with your presence at that time, I shall see to it that you receive an invitation, if not from Nathaniel, then from Joshua Lucas."

"Joshua Lucas? Was he the one who danced the hornpipe?"

"Yes, indeed, his solo performance is expected at every gathering."

"I must say he dances with great vigor but is equally capable of executing some of the most intricate steps."

Darcy smiled at this exchange. Georgiana knew very well the name of the young man who had danced the hornpipe because Lucas had engaged her for two dances. Darcy recognized it for what it was: a harmless flirtation, but it might prove advantageous in helping Georgiana to regain her confidence after the unfortunate incident with George Wickham. This sojourn to America might be exactly what was required for her to put the Wickham business behind her.

"Mr. Darcy, I know the reason you did not dance, but what is your overall impression of our rustic festivities?" Richard Bingley asked.

Before Darcy could answer, Charles took the lead in praising everything: the food and beverages were delicious, the music excellent, his partners accomplished, the conversation enjoyable, and the weather perfect. The younger Bingley chose to ignore the drunks and rowdies, the flies and mosquitoes, and the humidity. For Charles, there was no dark side of the moon.

"Again, I must ask *you*, Mr. Darcy, what you thought of our humble celebration?"

"It reminds me of the harvest festival the Darcy family hosts every year at Pemberley and was equally enjoyable. Hopefully, before I leave, I shall have an opportunity to sample the local delicacies instead of enjoying them vicariously. However, I did savor a cup of coffee with a unique blend. If I am not mistaken, it contained a shot—or two—of whiskey."

Richard confirmed the obvious with a chuckle and then inquired about Darcy's experience at the card table.

"I think I acquitted myself quite well considering that some of the cards were dealt from the bottom of the deck. Because such dealings were accompanied by winks and nods, I imagine I was involved in some type of initiation process. I had a similar experience during my first year at

Cambridge."

"But, Fitzwilliam, isn't dealing from the bottom of the deck against the rules?" Georgiana asked.

"It is only against the rules if you are playing with fellow Americans. No such rules apply when playing against an Englishman."

"But only the first time, Darcy," Richard said, laughing. "The locals are merely trying to take your measure. If you are a good sport, you will be welcomed back. However, if the victim makes too much of a fuss, he will find himself playing cards exclusively with the neighborhood dowagers."

With all the talk of food, dancing, and cards, Darcy was not questioned about the local beauties, for which he was grateful. If pressed, he would have had to mention a dark-haired, dark-eyed young lady with an infectious laugh, and as the carriage pulled up to the Bingley home, he regretted that he had not sought an introduction.

Chapter 4

Mr. Bennet did not speak Dutch, and after years of sitting in the Old Dutch Church listening to sermons in a language he did not understand, Tom Bennet had walked down the road to the Episcopal Church and had joined its fellowship. The congregants were meeting in an old stone building that had once served as a mission church for the purpose of converting the local Indians. During the war, it had been ransacked by the British, but with polish, paint, and prayer, the parishioners had succeeded in bringing it up to its pre-Revolutionary War blandness.

But Mrs. Bennet *did* speak Dutch and had an emotional attachment to the church where she and her five daughters had been baptized. So when the new minister, Rev. Thomas Smith, announced to his congregation that the entire service would be conducted in English, Mrs. Bennet expected her husband to return to the fold, and he did, but for all the wrong reasons.

Mrs. Bennet was well aware that she was married to a man who delighted in pointing out the absurdities of life: the ancient widow Sullivan wearing a red petticoat under her black dress, Mrs. Maastricht conversing in Dutch when she was fluent in English, Mr. Dumont pretending to be of French Huguenot descent when he was born in County Cork to Catholic parents, and Mr. Hofstra, who buried bones on his property so that his dogs would have something to dig up. One of Mr. Bennet's favorite quotes encompassed his philosophy: "For what do we live but to make sport for our neighbors and to laugh at them in our turn."

Thus, it was the eccentricities of Mrs. Jemima Smith that had lured Mr. Bennet back into the family pew at the Old Dutch Church. Being well versed in Scripture, the pastor's wife felt it was her right to stop her husband during the service whenever she believed he had erred. More irritating was her habit of locking her husband in the house on Sunday, leaving his waiting flock to wonder why their shepherd did not appear. But it was the sight and sound of Mrs. Smith driving the minister's horse up and down the post road to distract the congregants that delighted Mr. Bennet the most, but which caused Mrs. Bennet to walk down the road to the Episcopal Church and to join its fellowship.

However, there were difficulties, the major one being a shortage of Episcopal priests in the United States, and the growing congregation realized it would be necessary to look to England, the birthplace of their denomination, to solve their problem. And that was how Mr. William Collins, formerly of Kent, England, came to be the pastor of St. Matthew's Episcopal Church of Tarrytown, New York.

* * *

Georgiana looked at her brother, William looked at Charles Bingley, and the three stared at the preacher climbing the steps of the elevated pulpit. How on earth did Lady Catherine de Bourgh's curate come to be the pastor of a congregation in New York?

"He must have followed us here," Georgiana whispered to her brother, and the very thought startled Darcy until he realized his sister was in jest.

The mystery was soon solved. Mr. Collins, seeing the nephew and niece of his former benefactress, introduced them to the congregation and explained the series of events that had led to his being offered a parish in Westchester County.

"My former patroness, Lady Catherine de Bourgh, the daughter of an earl, the wife of the late Sir Lewis de Bourgh, and a friend to members of the aristocracy as well as the Archbishop of Canterbury, was so good as to invite me to dine at Rosings Park, the estate of Her Ladyship, while our noted visitors, Mr. Darcy, Miss Darcy, and Mr. Charles Bingley, were visiting. Whilst seated in the *main* dining room, under a chandelier of cut glass imported from Dresden, Mr. Bingley mentioned a recent letter from his uncle, Mr. Richard Bingley, a member of our congregation, stating that in New York there was a congregation in need of a pastor, and so I wrote to..."

Mr. Collins droned on for another ten minutes sharing with his parishioners an exchange of correspondence that could not possibly have been of interest to anyone other than the parson and Lady Catherine. In brief, after a trial period, Mr. Collins had been offered a permanent position as the congregants found him to be a kind man who recognized the seriousness of his position and the needs of his parish. An added benefit was that he was unattached. Because it was expected that the pastor would marry in order to set the example for his parish, it was assumed he would choose a local girl for a wife, possibly Charlotte Lucas, a neighborhood favorite. All in all, Mr. Collins was considered by the elders to be an excellent find.

After service, Charles Bingley and Miss Darcy were surrounded by members of the congregation, but there was something about Mr. Darcy that caused people to hesitate. As a result, he stood apart, silent and austere, scanning the crowd while looking at no one in particular, thus confirming Lizzy's opinion that the man was above his company.

Lizzy stood alongside Jane, Charlotte, and a pouting Joshua Lucas, who was unhappy because he had been unable to get near the lovely Miss Darcy, now standing in the midst of a throng of admirers.

"If they get any closer to her, she is at risk of being suffocated," the young Lucas complained.

"Joshua, you should use your military training and force your way through the crowd and rescue her," Lizzy teased.

"Promise me you will not resort to swordplay," Charlotte said, laughing at her brother's expense.

"Since when did Tad Van Tassel start attending St. Matthew's?" Joshua asked. "He should be in his family's pew at the Old Dutch Church. The only reason he is here is because of Miss Darcy."

"I believe we can date Tad's interest in our church from, let me see, last night," Lizzy answered while laughing. "If Miss Darcy stays with us for any length of time, we may end up having the largest congregation in the Hudson Valley—or at least the church with the most bachelors. I actually think Miss Darcy could give Caroline Bingley some competition."

The mention of Caroline's name brought Lucas back to earth. It was true that whenever Caroline was in the neighborhood she captured most of the attention of the bachelors and did so at the expense of the other young ladies who, unlike the golden-haired beauty, actually enjoyed the attention.

"What a fool I am," Joshua said, slapping his forehead with the palm of his hand. "Here I stand with three of the prettiest girls between the city and the capital, and I speak of another lady. Forgive my poor manners. Ladies, please," he said, extending his arm to Lizzy and Jane, while Charlotte locked arms with her friend, and the four departed leaving behind the English visitors and their new-found friend, Mr. Collins.

* * *

Lydia and Kitty, who had remained at St. Matthew's, came running into the house giggling. It was such a common event that those gathered in the rear parlor paid no attention to their hilarious entrance. But as usual, there would be no peace in the Bennet household until the cause of their laughter had been shared.

"Mr. Bingley went to church this morning at St. Matthew's," Lydia said, fairly bursting with laughter.

"Yes, I know, dear. We were all there," their mother said, not looking up from her knitting. "Why do you find Mr. Bingley's presence in church to be so amusing?"

"Oh, Mama, did you not notice how Mr. Bingley could not take his eyes off Jane," Lydia said, dropping to her knees next to her mother so that she might rake her fingers through her daughter's long blonde tresses. With the exception of Lizzy, the Bennet daughters had inherited their father's light hair and blue eyes. It was only Elizabeth who favored her mother with her black eyes and dark curly tresses. "He is already so in love with her that he was willing to sit through one of Mr. Collins's boring sermons just to see her."

Mary, who liked Mr. Collins very much and was sympathetic to his status as a newcomer to a community that had been together since the founding of the colony of New York, entered the fray. With her shy demeanor and clubfoot, she knew what it was like to be different, and so she had made every effort to befriend her pastor.

"How would you know if Mr. Collins's sermons are boring?" Mary asked Lydia. "You never listen to what he has to say. You fidget and fuss because you want the young men to look at you."

"Just like you stare at Mr. Collins hoping he will pay attention to you," Lydia snapped back. "But he hasn't, has he?"

Mary gathered up her needlepoint and stormed out of

the room. After giving her daughter a look of disapproval, Mrs. Bennet said, "Lydia, please open the Bible to Matthew, Chapter 7, and read it out loud."

"Mama, I didn't mean anything by it. I was only teasing Mary. Why does she have to be so sensitive?"

"Begin with Matthew, Chapter 7, and Kitty you will also remain." Kitty glared at her sister for ensnaring her in her punishment.

Lydia brought the King James Bible from her father's study. Because she had been required to recite this passage on so many occasions, she had committed it to memory:

Judge not, that ye be not judged. For with what judgement ye judge, ye shall be judged: and with what measure ye mete, it shall be measured to you again. And why beholdest thou the mote that is in thy brother's eye, but considerest not the beam that is in thine own eye?

After Lydia had stopped reading, her mother told her to continue. "I shall let you know when you may stop," she said, with a smile in her voice and a nod of approval from Mr. Bennet.

* * *

"Why are Lydia and Kitty so hateful to me?" Mary asked Jane and Elizabeth, who had followed her upstairs. With her tears steaming up her spectacles, she declared that she did not love Mr. Collins. "I mean I do not love him romantically. I only care about him as a friend and fellow Christian as commanded by Scripture."

"You should not let the silliness of your younger sisters bother you," Jane said. "They only say these things because they know you will respond. As Lizzy and I have told you on so many, many occasions, ignore them. That is the best revenge."

"They think I want to marry Mr. Collins, but I do not," the nineteen-year old girl said, continuing her protests. "I do not want to marry *anyone*."

In this Mary was sincere. The demands of marriage were more than someone who was so physically and emotionally delicate could possibly handle, and she had come to the decision that she would live the single life, a choice fully supported by her parents.

"Why cannot people just take me at my word when I say I do not wish to marry?"

"Perhaps the time you spent in Mr. Collins's company at the festival was misinterpreted," Lizzy suggested. "Besides, whether something is true does not matter to those who thrive on gossip, and such a scene does get tongues wagging."

"I was talking to Mr. Collins about Charlotte. Because Charlotte is so busy running Lucas Mercantile, she has little time for anything else," Mary explained. "Ever since her father was elected to the assembly, Charlotte, Maria, and Jacob are left to run the store. It is not fair to any of them, but most especially to Charlotte. She is twenty-seven years old, and her prospects are diminishing. Unlike me, she *does* want to get married."

Everything Mary said about Charlotte was true. Mr. Lucas's election had definitely gone to his head, and in order to widen his access to the most prominent families in the state, Mr. Lucas had leased a townhouse in Albany while the legislature was in session. But with Joshua at West Point and older brother John attending Yale College, the only ones at home who were old enough to take their parents' places in the store were Charlotte, Maria, and Jacob.

But there were hints that Mary's behind-the-scene maneuverings were succeeding. Mr. Collins had written to Charlotte to ask if he might call upon her as soon as her parents returned from Albany. Charlotte's response was immediate. With five Lucases at home and neighbors willing to act as chaperones, there really was no reason to wait for her parents to return.

* * *

"Mr. Darcy, I was not aware that you knew Mr. Collins," Richard Bingley said as he and his guests sat at the table for their afternoon meal. "I hope your aunt is not unhappy with me for luring her curate to a former rebellious colony."

Lady Catherine is frequently unhappy," Darcy answered. "If it were not Mr. Collins's departure, she would have found another reason to be vexed. I know that whenever any of her cottagers are quarrelsome, discontented, or too poor, she sallies forth into the village to settle their differences, silence their complaints, and scold them into harmony and plenty."

Georgiana and Charles nodded in agreement at this description of the great lady.

"Is Mr. Collins well received by his parishioners?" Georgiana asked.

"Mr. Collins would benefit by making fewer references to his former patroness. But, yes, he has been warmly received, especially by the members of the congregation who are in their twenties and thirties, many of whom spent their childhood years in the Old Dutch Church listening to a service entirely in Dutch. There are still a few families, such as the Bennets, who brought up their children so that they would know the language of their ancestors, but they are the exception, at least in the lower Hudson Valley.

"So Mrs. Bennet is Dutch?" Georgiana asked.

"Yes, the lady is the former Anetje Schuyler Gardiner," Richard stated. "The Schuylers are a very old Dutch family from a time when New York was New Amsterdam. Despite his English surname, Mr. Bennet is a mix of English,

French Huguenot, and Scots-Irish. However, Longbourn, the Bennet estate, was named after the family's ancestral home in Hertfordshire."

"Longbourn Manor in Hertfordshire!" Darcy said, echoing Richard's words. "I am familiar with it. It is but five miles from the estate Charles is currently leasing and is a very pretty property. Here we have another coincidence. First Mr. Collins and now a link to Hertfordshire. This certainly leads credence to the assertion that, despite our differences, Americans remain our cousins."

"I agree with that statement, Darcy," Richard said. "Even though Mr. Bennet lost three toes on his right foot from frostbite during the war, he seems to harbor no resentment against those of English birth."

Although Darcy found the subject to be of interest, not so Charles. *His* interest was in the eldest Bennet daughter, and he had been sorely disappointed that he was unable to talk to Jane after church.

"Because today is Sunday, I imagine there is little socializing because of the Sabbath?" Charles inquired in the hopes he was wrong and that he would somehow get to see Miss Bennet.

"It depends upon the family. There are those who choose to sit quietly in their homes reading the Bible, as much to avoid those who would criticize Sabbath breakers than anything else. However, on Sunday evenings, families, such as the Bennets, find no harm in listening to music. Mary, the middle daughter, the one with the spectacles, plays the lap harp well and the pianoforte a little. Jane also plays a little, but her talents rest in the visual arts. She is a fine painter."

"Miss Elizabeth does not play?" Darcy asked and then realized that his question had aroused the curiosity of the others. "In my experience, the younger daughters are trained in the same manner as the eldest. That is all I meant."

"A logical conclusion," Richard replied. "However, Elizabeth is very much a tomboy. The first time I encountered her, she was climbing down out of a tree with a bag full of walnuts tied to her waist. Lizzy's talents are with the pen as she is a writer of stories."

Even though Darcy had been in the company of Elizabeth Bennet on only one occasion, the idea of her being a tomboy did not surprise. Instead of gliding and taking small steps, she strode with the confidence of a man. But it was her laugh that truly set her apart. No demure chuckle from behind a fan for this lady. She laughed heartily and with a laugh so contagious that one would join in her merriment without knowing the reason.

"Jane sketched the pictures on the wall behind us," Richard said, and Charles immediately jumped up and examined them as if he were admiring one of the Old Masters. The first was a pen and ink of yachtsmen racing their ice boats on a frozen Hudson, complimented by a second sketch of families ice skating on a frozen pond with a lovely Georgian-style house in the background.

"Jane also did a sketch of Caroline which is in my bedroom. The likeness is quite good. And speaking of Caroline," Richard continued, "She has decided to leave Saratoga Springs early so that she might spend time with her cousin. This is quite a gesture on my daughter's part as she usually remains in Saratoga Springs for most of the fall. Then she is off to the city for the winter season. As a result, I doubt she is in Tarrytown above two months in the whole of the year, and when she is here, she prefers to stay with the Storms whose mansion overlooks the Hudson. I expect her in about ten to fourteen days."

Darcy's thoughts now turned to the first time he had met the daughter of his host. The introduction had taken place a year earlier at the wedding of her sister to Edward Hurst of Sussex. Although it was Louisa's wedding day, Caroline, with so little effort, had managed to steal the show. With sapphire-blue eyes, hair the color of spun gold, a perfectly oval face, and swan neck, all eyes were upon her.

When Bingley invited Darcy to visit Netherfield Park, Caroline had been there to act as hostess. During the next few weeks, they had walked in the park or driven about the estate in a phaeton. Their mornings had been spent on horseback, and Caroline proved to be an accomplished equestrian. And there was so much more to admire. She was well read, fluent in French, sung like an angel, played the pianoforte beautifully, and danced as if stepping on a cloud. He was greatly taken in by her charms, and she knew it.

"Darcy, old boy, we seem to have lost you," Charles said. "My uncle was asking if you would like to play cards."

"Yes, of course," Darcy answered, and because he did not want to think about Caroline Bingley, any diversion would be welcome.

Chapter 5

With all lingering effects of his seasickness finally gone, Darcy was now feeling hale and hearty. Having been denied exercise since leaving England, he felt the need to use his body and decided to act on Richard's suggestion to board a ferry so that he might cross the Hudson to Fort Lee and enjoy the scenery on the opposite shore.

"During the Revolution," Richard explained, "5,000 British troops under the command of General Cornwallis traveled up the Hudson River in barges and negotiated the steep incline of the palisades, forcing Washington's retreat across New Jersey to Pennsylvania. But I should warn you that the loss of Fort Lee is not a popular topic of discussion among the locals," Richard cautioned his visitors before entering a nearby tavern. "Despite the defeat, to Americans, Fort Lee is hallowed ground as George Washington encamped here and that is enough for any patriot."

While Darcy saw the excursion as time well spent, Bingley and his sister respectfully disagreed. They could observe Nature to their heart's content at home in England, but there was only a limited time to enjoy the company of Americans. Finally, an exasperated Bingley said he could hardly believe there would be a time when he would eagerly look forward to going to church. "At least, I will see *people* there and not just rocks and mountains." Darcy responded by taking another deep breath.

On Sunday, Charles was not taking any chances. As

soon as church services had ended, he made a dash for Jane Bennet. Mrs. Bennet soon joined them and invited Charles and the others to come to Longbourn that evening for dessert and some music.

"Mr. Bingley, this is not my first attempt to invite you to Longbourn," Mrs. Bennet said. "I sent a messenger to Richard's house on two occasions, but was told you were across the river enjoying the scenery."

"Darcy is a great admirer of landscapes," Charles explained, while making a face indicating that he was not, "so we have made several excursions to the western shore of the river and have visited Bear Mountain and the bastion at Fort Lee."

Knowing of his interest in Jane, Mrs. Bennet sympathized with the young man, and she was in a position to put an end to his suffering. "Shall we say 6:00?"

* * *

"Mr. Richard is coming," Lydia announced as she bounded up the four steps leading to the veranda facing the Hudson. Situated on a rise, the manor house had a glorious view of the river and the sloops and ships moving their goods to their destinations.

"And his guests as well," Kitty said, who was so close behind her sister that she was practically walking in Lydia's shoes.

"Maybe Richard and I can have a game of chess," Mr. Bennet said. "It has been three weeks since we last played."

"On the Sabbath, Tom? We will make a poor impression on Richard's company," his wife scolded.

"Nonsense. We are not performing manual labor or riding in a conveyance or any of those other prohibitions your Dutch relations cling to as if they were lifeboats to heaven. Chess is merely an intellectual exchange performed on a wooden board. And, my dear, may I point out that they are coming to us; we are not calling on them."

The approach to Longbourn was an avenue of elm, spruce, and towering Lombardy poplars. The house, an example of the Federal style manor houses that were replacing the gambrel-roofed structures favored by the Dutch of an earlier era, was a handsome house of two stories and an attic, with five windows up and four down, and enclosed by a veranda on three sides. Painted in a beautiful yellow gold, it had a neoclassical swag hanging over the entrance and Doric columns framing the front door. The residence was surrounded by a wrought-iron fence that the visitors soon learned was to keep out the pigs that roamed freely and the dogs that chased them.

"And here are our visitors," Mrs. Bennet said, putting away her knitting. "Richard, welcome. Your timing is impeccable as my husband is in need of a chess partner."

"Mrs. Bennet! I am shocked you would even think of such a thing—and on the Sabbath?" her husband replied in all astonishment. "But now that you mention it..."

After viewing the manor house with its extraordinary view of the Hudson, Darcy decided that the Bennets were prospering. However, despite owning a house in the latest style and Mrs. Bennet wearing a flattering frock, Mr. Bennet appeared more comfortable with the fashions of an earlier age. In addition to having his hair in a queue and tied with a ribbon, he was wearing hose, reminding Darcy of his own father.

"Mr. Darcy, Miss Darcy, and Mr. Bingley, I shall warn you that you must take everything my husband says with a grain of salt as he is a terrible tease," Mrs. Bennet said by way of greeting. "As for chess, since Richard beat him handily the last time they played, Tom has been eager for a rematch."

"As Richard knows very well, I was not paying

attention that evening as there were too many distractions," Tom Bennet said while wagging his finger at his wife and daughters, and then made a motion with his hand indicating that they talked too much.

But Charles Bingley cared nothing about chess or a pretty house with a fine lawn and flower gardens. His mind was otherwise engaged on the missing eldest daughter. "Miss Bennet is not here?"

"*I* am Miss Bennet, and I am here." Lydia chirped, "and so is Kitty, who is Miss Bennet, and Mary, who is also Miss Bennet. There is no lack of Miss Bennets at our house, Mr. Bingley."

An embarrassed Charles explained that in England the eldest daughter was addressed in such a way to acknowledge her rank in the family.

"How odd," Lydia responded before her mother asked her to see how much of the apple pie was left from Saturday's dinner.

"Oh, there is a whole other pie, Mama. Plenty enough for our guests" Lydia answered, retaining her position on the top stair. Her mother, pointing her finger at Lydia and then in the direction of the kitchen, indicated that her youngest daughter should make a more accurate assessment and gestured for Kitty to follow her.

"Mr. Darcy, I noticed at the festival that you did not eat dessert, but perhaps I can entice you to have a slice of my Dutch apple pie. It is an old family recipe and different from others in that my crust is cross hatched and sprinkled with lemon juice and cinnamon crumbles."

The mere description of such a confectionary delight caused Darcy's mouth to water. "I would be most obliged, ma'am, and if it is proper, may I ask that you call me Fitzwilliam or William, whichever is your preference." Darcy had noticed at the festival that young, unattached males and females were addressed by their Christian names.

Georgiana and Charles seconded both requests, and the Bennets agreed to drop the formal addresses. And who could pass up apple pie?

"Please come in and make yourself at home." Mrs. Bennet gestured for her husband to take their visitors inside.

"While my wife sees to dessert and coffee, perhaps I could show you around the house," Mr. Bennet offered.

The tour began in the rear parlor where, instead of a fireplace, there was a cast-iron stove that Mr. Bennet assured his visitors "would heat the room on the coldest day, so that the ladies might wear only a shawl about their shoulders." The visitors soon learned Mr. Bennet was the sole supplier of Pennsylvania stoves in Westchester County and owned a warehouse on the west side of the river where they were assembled after being shipped from Philadelphia. There were also argand oil lamps that burnt only the finest sperm whale oil, a barrel organ that played four dance tunes, a tilt-up tea table, and because Mr. Bennet was the owner of several sloops, various spyglasses that were used to observe the traffic on the river. "I keep an eye on my competitors," Mr. Bennet said with a chuckle.

In the front parlor, Mr. Bennet asked Charles what he thought of the carved fireplace that reminded Darcy of the Adam's fireplaces at Pemberley with their detailed fretwork and neoclassical embellishments. Although Pemberley's mantles were marble, these were excellent reproductions.

"It is finely carved, sir. May I ask what wood was used?"

"You may, Charles, but I will tell you that no wood was used. It is plaster painted to look like wood, and made at a manufactory I own on the west side of the river. It costs a fraction of what is required for marble. Because there is a growing shortage of wood here in the lower valley, finding an alternative was a necessity."

After admiring displays of fine porcelains, the company

returned to the magnificent entry hall, the largest room in the house, with its faux marble wallpaper, triple arch, and grand staircase lit by a rose window on the landing. In addition to serving as a place to welcome visitors, it was used for dancing, musicales, charades, plays, and card games.

"What do you think of my flooring, Charles?" Mr. Bennet asked, as everyone admired the shiny brown marble with its rich dark veins.

"The marble is beautiful, sir," Bingley answered, but wondered why all of Mr. Bennet's questions were directed to him.

"Ah, you are wrong again, sir. It is not marble, but a canvas floor cloth painted to look like marble. The craftsmen painted it using a turkey feather to effect the illusion of veining. But do not worry. It fools everybody, not just you. The canvas was made by a company in Yonkers of which I am part owner."

"I assume your canvas company is on the west of the river," Charles said in an attempt to be clever.

"Charles, Yonkers is just above Manhattan on the *east* side of the river. I thought you would have known that since you passed it on the way to Tarrytown," Mr. Bennet said while winking at Georgiana, but Charles reddened at his error. "Now, if you will follow me to the third floor, I have a lookout in the attic from where I observe the night skies."

"Oh, no you don't, Tom," Mrs. Bennet said, carrying a tray laden with an apple pie, peach cobbler, and cookies. The mistress was followed by two Negro serving girls, also carrying trays with dishes and utensils. "Our visitors will have ample time to admire your instruments and whatnots on another visit."

The party went into the more formal parlor where the pies were sliced and coffee and a mild cider served. Darcy could hardly wait for his first taste of apple pie and was rewarded by the most delicious thing he had ever tasted, and it showed on his face, causing Mrs. Bennet to smile.

"Please try some koekjes or cookies as my husband calls them or biscuits as our English friends call them," Mrs. Bennet said, and gestured for Phillis, the older girl, to pass the plate containing the molasses cookies. Georgiana put a napkin to her face because she was afraid she might drool, which she had very nearly done when she had eaten a piece of the peach cobbler.

"More cider, dear?" Mrs. Bennet asked her.

"Oh, yes, please. Thank you, Mrs. Bennet. Everything is so, so very…"

"…delicious," her brother said finishing her sentence, and everyone started to laugh. When they stopped, they found they had been joined by the two eldest Bennet daughters.

"You were all laughing so hard that you did not hear us come in," Jane said, while glancing at Charles. "What was so amusing?"

"Our guests were enjoying the desserts so much, I suspect that if we looked the other way, they would have absconded with the cookies and cobbler," Mr. Bennet answered.

"Oh, no need for thievery," Lizzy said. "There is a lot more where they came from. Phillis and Lottie's mother, Mrs. Wesley, does most of our baking, and none finer in the county, with the possible exception of when my mother makes her famous Dutch apple pie."

"We have just come from Charlotte Lucas's house," Jane said, explaining their absence. "Her terrier, Job, has an upset stomach so we gave him some quassia to help settle his complaint."

"Quassia is very good," Darcy commented, "but to that I would add a mixture of wormwood, gentian, fennel, fleawort, and garlic mixed in with the dog's food. I would advise Miss Lucas to do that twice a day for about two weeks." When Darcy saw the look of surprise of everyone's faces, he added, "When I was a boy, my father kept a pack of hounds, and I learned quite a lot from the master of the hounds."

A know-it-all, Lizzy thought.

"Well, Darcy, I must say I am impressed," Charles told his friend. "Upon my return to England, it is my intention to keep a pack at Netherfield Park. Are you interested in the position of master of hounds?" Everyone laughed. But Darcy, not wishing to supply Charles with additional ammunition, merely smiled.

He cannot take a joke, Lizzy mused.

"Georgiana, do you play the pianoforte?" Mary asked. "We have a very fine instrument."

"Yes, I noticed it earlier. It is as fine an instrument as I have ever seen, but I would prefer to hear one of you play."

"Oh, but no one plays well," Kitty said in a matter-of-fact voice.

"Surely, you are being overly modest."

But all the Bennets shook their heads, indicating it was not an attempt at false modesty. "There are so few piano masters in the valley that we are largely self taught," Mary offered by way of explanation. "My father bought the pianoforte because he likes instruments, musical or otherwise."

"The pianoforte is to let people know we are effluent," Lydia added, "at least that is what Mrs. Vandeveer said when she saw it coming off the ship."

"Affluent, Lydia, not effluent," Lizzy said, correcting her, and everyone dissolved into laughter.

"I am afraid there will be no time to exhibit tonight," Richard said. "I hate to be the spoil sport, but we must start back before our buzzing friends arrive."

Although the visitors had only been in America for a short time, they already knew what that meant. When evening arrived, everyone moved inside, and windows and doors were closed to prevent an invasion of stinging insects. Although the Bennets had erected wood frames covered with millinet for the lower sashes of the windows to keep out the mosquitoes and had done the same for their tenant, if they did not start walking home, they risked being carried off by an armada of pests. Darcy, Charles, and Georgiana had suffered numerous bites at the festival, and no one wanted a repeat of that experience.

"Lizzy and I shall walk with you as far as the road," Jane quickly offered, ignoring her sister's frown, and the two ladies, followed by their youngest sisters, departed.

How long will Mr. Darcy be visiting Richard Bingley? Lizzy wondered as she trudged along the road swatting at insects. *He will return to his London friends with all sorts of stories about Americans and how we use pianofortes for decoration.* It would be a repeat of the events in Bath three years earlier. After Elizabeth had dined with the family of Edward Chamberlain, his parents had decided that their son must be rescued from the clutches of an uncouth American and had sent him into exile.

Lizzy's slow pace did not go unnoticed by Darcy, but he attributed it to her wanting to give her sister an opportunity to engage Bingley in conversation. His friend's fascination with the pretty Miss Bennet came as no surprise to Darcy as his friend was often in love. And why should he not enjoy his brief time in America? When he returned to England, he would entertain his friends with tales of the fair ladies of the Hudson River Valley before returning to London society for the purpose of finding a bride.

Unwilling to risk another lost opportunity with Jane, Charles immediately asked if he might call on her the next day.

"I would be most happy to receive you, Mr. Bingley, but I am afraid that my sisters and I are to go to the farm of the Widow Vreeland to harvest her apples. She is quite elderly and relies on her neighbors for assistance. This exercise represents the beginning of the apple-picking season in this part of the valley and must be done before the start of the rye harvest."

This announcement caused Bingley to go silent, but Darcy immediately volunteered his services. "For myself, I am certainly willing to roll up my sleeves to pick some apples."

"Oh, Mr. Darcy, if you are to take up room in the wagon, you must agree to pick more than just *some* apples," Lydia said, giggling.

"Miss Lydia, I shall commit right now to picking at least two dozen, if not more. Does that answer?"

Lydia started to giggle and turned around and looked at her older sisters. "Mr. Darcy called me *Miss* Lydia. How funny!"

But Lizzy was not thinking about terms of address. Picking apples was a dirty business, and Lizzy could just picture Mr. Darcy in his fine coat and shirt and cream-colored breeches, all made by London's finest clothiers, mingling amongst Mrs. Vreeland's tenants and laborers. The Master of Pemberley picking apples? The whole idea was ridiculous.

"Mr. Darcy, you are a guest here. It is not necessary for you to engage in manual labor and to risk soiling your clothes. The offer is appreciated, but…"

"I have, on occasion, picked apples, Miss Elizabeth, and it would be my pleasure to be of some assistance. All I need to know is where and at what time."

That was generous, Lizzy thought.

After the information was provided, the two groups quickly parted as the hum of mosquitoes and the sweeping motions of the martins that ate them filled the air. It was only when Lizzy was safely back indoors that she had time to digest her brief conversation with Mr. Darcy. After thinking about the gentleman she had overheard at the festival and the one who had come to Longbourn, she wondered which one was the real Mr. Darcy.

Chapter 6

With the Bennet steward and cook, Samuel and Hannah MacTavish, away in Albany attending a party for Hannah's grandmother, who had reached the great age of one hundred years, or thereabouts, as no one was really sure, there were chores to be done, and Lizzy was still rubbing the sleep from her eyes when she went into the kitchen.

"Good morning, Lizzy," her mother said, while stirring a pot of bubbling porridge. "The oatmeal is just about ready. Will you please see to the coffee?"

Lizzy took her apron off one of the pegs on the back of the kitchen door and slipped it on. Unlike Lydia, Kitty, and Jane, who seemed to wake up with smiles on their faces, Lizzy was quiet in the morning, especially if she was late in getting to bed. The previous night, Mary had joined Jane and Lizzy while her sisters had prepared for bed. Recognizing her need for privacy, their parents had given Mary her own bedroom, an L-shaped room over the servants' stairs. Into this small area were squished Mary and the family's two in-house dogs, Goodness and Mercy. So when there was news to be shared, it was shared in the larger bedroom of her older sisters.

"Yesterday, did Charlotte say anything about Mr. Collins?" Mary had asked her sisters.

"Yes, as a matter of fact, she did," Jane answered. "When the pastor visits with Mrs. Creighton on Tuesday, Charlotte will join them for tea."

"I think it will be a good match," Mary said, assuming the courtship and subsequent marriage were already a settled matter.

Mary also mentioned that Georgiana had offered to teach her some tunes on the pianoforte, news that was warmly received by her sisters as Mary was the family's best hope for someone actually mastering the expensive instrument sitting idle in their parlor.

It was nearing midnight when Mary had left Jane and Lizzy to enjoy their nightly discussion. And there was a lot to discuss. Before blowing out the candle, they had talked— again—about the haying festival and their dance partners and the next day's apple-picking excursion before getting around to what Jane really wanted to talk about: Mr. Charles Bingley.

"Mr. Bingley is just what a young man ought to be: sensible, good-humored, lively, and I never saw such happy manners and with such perfect good breeding!"

"He is also handsome," replied Lizzy, "which a young man ought to be if he possibly can."

"I was flattered by his seeking me out after church this morning. I had not expected it."

"Well, I did, and I give you leave to like him. You have liked many a stupider person."

"Miss Darcy is very pretty," Jane said, after laughing at Lizzy's comment. "At first, I thought she might be intended for Mr. Bingley, but I saw no interest from either for such a match."

"I imagine Miss Darcy will marry someone higher in society: the son of an earl or a duke as she is the granddaughter of an earl."

"Tad Van Tassel seemed very interested in her."

"Yes, but Miss Darcy was much more interested in Joshua Lucas. She could not take her eyes off of him while he danced the hornpipe."

"It is a harmless flirtation, I am sure."

"Most definitely!" Lizzy exclaimed. "With a brother as proud as Mr. Darcy, he would never sanction a courtship between his sister and a rustic colonial boy."

"Are you still upset with Mr. Darcy for not asking you to dance at the festival?"

"I was *not* upset," Lizzy said emphatically. "My only comment was that many ladies were sitting down for want of a partner."

Although Mr. Darcy had been pleasant enough during his visit to Longbourn, Lizzy was not quite ready to abandon her first impression of the Englishman.

"Perhaps he is not comfortable recommending himself to strangers."

"A man of sense and education, who has lived in the world, is ill qualified to recommend himself to strangers! I believe it is more a matter that he will not give himself the trouble or that he is above his company. Did you not see how he stood apart after church?"

"I did notice it, but that was a week ago Sunday. He was much more agreeable today. Did you not see him patting Mrs. Happel's son on his head all the while little Billy was clinging to his leg? It was too funny for words. And Lizzy, if it is Mr. Darcy's intention to set himself apart and to speak to no one who is not of his station, then why would he have come to a country where everyone is a stranger and no one is his equal in rank—at least by English standards?"

"Maybe he wishes to publish a journal like Mr. Lewis and Mr. Clark about the fauna found on our continent. *The Bennets of New York* would be immediately in front of *The Birds of North America* on the bookshelf."

"Will you please be serious? I think this might not be about Mr. Darcy, but about Mr. Chamberlain."

"Oh, no! Not you too," Lizzy said, protesting. "Please allow me to reiterate that I was *never* in love with Edward Chamberlain. Although flattered by his attention, there was something in his character, a lack of depth, that was less than satisfactory. I remember talking to you about it even before the dance in the Upper Rooms in Bath. The reason you do not recall the conversation is because you were in the midst of a flirtation with Mr. Tilney. As for Mr. Darcy, I admit I was slightly hurt when he stated unequivocally that he would not dance, even though I was standing but a few feet away from him."

"Lizzy, I know you are a firm believer in first impressions, but I also know you are fair and kind and that you will be willing to give Mr. Darcy a chance to redeem himself. After all, he has volunteered to pick apples for the Widow Vreeland. Does not such an act merit a re-evaluation of his character?"

"It is true Mr. Darcy *claims* he has picked apples before, but my guess is that he plucked one off a tree, shined it on his beautiful coat, and handed it to some belle who, greatly honored by his attentions, was in danger of swooning." Jane shook her head in disapproval at her sister's stubbornness. "All right. I accede to your demands."

"Why the sudden change of heart?"

"Well, if Mr. Darcy is willing to climb up on a ladder to pick fruit, then I should reconsider my dislike as he has very fine legs!

* * *

A sleepy Mary and a smiling Jane were now in the kitchen, but before Mary could take up the task of slicing the bread for sandwiches, she was sent to hurry Lydia and Kitty along.

"Your father has already told Ezekiel to hitch up the wagon. Tell your sisters if they are not down here in ten minutes, they will go to Mrs. Vreeland's without breakfast and by shank's pony," Mrs. Bennet announced, indicating they would walk.

While their mother removed the kettle from the hearth and ladled out exact portions of porridge into wooden bowls, Jane sliced a loaf of rye bread and Lizzy retrieved ham and butter from the larder.

"I did not have an opportunity to speak with Charlotte after church. How is she managing at the store with her parents in Albany?" Mrs. Bennet asked.

Because Lucas Mercantile stocked basic necessities, such as sugar, molasses, flour, and spices, as well as soap, kettles, candles, and cloth, the store was the busiest shop in the village on any given day. With many of the ladies already coming into town to order fabric, lace, and ribbon for their Thanksgiving dresses and hats, there was a non-stop stream of customers. Even with the addition of a full-time clerk, Charlotte, Maria, and Jacob Lucas were working at a fevered pace.

"While I was there, I noticed the new fashion plates had arrived from Paris," Jane said enthusiastically.

"Yes, and according to the new plates, I am out of fashion once again," Lizzy added with a laugh. "Nothing new there."

"Yes, the new designs show copious trimmings and fuller skirts with lots of frills."

"Which will do nothing for those with big bosoms and wide bottoms," Lizzy said, chuckling. "Katrina Van Wart may be in trouble."

After breakfast, Mrs. Bennet asked Lizzy to walk with her to the chicken coops. This was no idle request. Whenever Mama asked Lydia and Kitty to walk with her, the youngsters were in trouble. With Mary, it often meant her middle daughter needed to be reassured about some matter. But with Jane or Lizzy, it usually was an imparting of some old-fashioned common sense or nugget of wisdom.

"Having had an opportunity to visit with Miss Darcy, I found her to be a charming young lady with a generous spirit," Mrs. Bennet began.

"I have only had two brief conversations with her, and although I find her to be a little shy, she was most pleasant. I liked her very much."

"Our local boys were quite taken with her at the festival and after church, but I attribute that to hers being a fresh face."

"Mama, surely you do not think I am jealous of Miss Darcy?" Lizzy asked with a look of astonishment. "Is that the purpose of this conversation?"

"Of course not, dear. But with Mr. Bingley mooning over Jane and Miss Darcy's appearance, I am afraid you took more offense at the words of a certain gentleman than you might have had on any other occasion."

"I haven't shared two sentences with the man. Besides, Mr. Darcy wasn't just rude to me. He slighted every woman who was in need of a partner."

"I would agree with your appraisal if I had not had the opportunity to visit with him yesterday afternoon."

Mrs. Bennet was all praise for the gentleman, especially remarking on his kindness to his sister, affection for his friend, and the interest he had shown in Mr. Bennet's "innovations."

"Your father agrees with my opinion of our English visitor, especially since the two men share an interest in anything mechanical. You will be in his company today, so I would suggest you keep an open mind. Because I think if you are determined to dislike Mr. Darcy, you may have to find other reasons than one unkind comment at a dance."

Chapter 7

When the wagon carrying the five Bennet girls arrived at the Widow Vreeland's farm, Darcy and Bingley were already at work carrying the burlap sacks, bushel baskets, and ladders out to the orchards.

Although nearing her eightieth birthday, Mrs. Vreeland was out in the orchard supervising the workers, speaking in Dutch, and pointing her cane in every direction of the compass. Most of her workers did not understand the language, but since they had performed this chore year after year and could have done it in their sleep, they merely nodded at everything she said, and Lizzy whispered to Georgiana that she should do the same.

Mr. Darcy had said that he had picked an apple or two in his time, and it was soon apparent that the gentleman had done more than that. He had a fluid movement of grab and twist and right into the burlap sack hanging from his shoulder. It was Mr. Bingley who was in need of a primer, which was delivered by Mrs. Vreeland.

"*U bent linkshandig. Zet de zak op je andere schouder,*" the widow shouted at a confused Mr. Bingley.

"You are left-handed. Put the bag on your other shoulder," Lizzy said, interpreting for Charles.

"*Niet op die manier. Draai je pols.*"

"Don't yank, Mr. Bingley. Twist your wrist and pull, and it is fine to leave the stem on."

"*Hij is niet erg slim, he? Zeg hem dat hij op die andere moet letten*," the literal translation being, "He's not very smart, is he? Tell him to watch the other one," Mrs. Vreeland said, pointing her cane at Darcy, but Lizzy elected to tell the rattled Charles Bingley that the elderly lady, dressed from head to toe in black bombazine, was complimenting him on how quickly he had developed the necessary apple-picking skills. With such praise, Bingley readily picked up the fluid motions of his friend.

During the course of the day, while performing the task of sorting apples, Georgiana had been able to share snatches of conversation with Lizzy and Jane. She feared she had made a major *faux pas* when she had declared that in England any woman who had not married by the time she was two and twenty probably would not wed and would thus live out her life as a spinster. During the dinner break, she had apologized for her remark. Even though Lizzy was twenty-one and Jane nearly twenty-three, neither was offended.

"I would think the average age for a young lady to be married in our neighborhood would be about twenty," Jane explained. "We are very fortunate in that we do not have any pressure from our parents to marry early."

"Or at all," Lizzy added, thinking of Mary.

"It is my understanding that couples on the frontier tend to marry much younger than those who live nearer to more populated areas," Jane continued. "And as is the custom in England, there are arranged marriages among the social elite. If you look at my mother's family, you will see that Schuylers married Van Rensselaers, who married Beekmans, who married Livingstons, and so on."

"Some of the best family stories are from my mother's side, especially the ones about Philip Schuyler's five daughters. Four of them eloped!" Lizzy said in a voice indicating she admired the ladies' rebellious spirits. "The only one who did not run away was Elizabeth, who wed Alexander Hamilton. He was President Washington's Secretary of the Treasury, but he was killed in a duel. My favorite amongst the rebels is Cornelia, who climbed down a rope ladder from the second story of her home in Albany so that she might wed Washington Morton. I think it would be fun for your lover to come for you in such a way."

Georgiana went wide-eyed. She could not imagine doing such a thing at Pemberley, but agreed it was a very romantic gesture nonetheless.

"The eldest, Angelica, eloped with John Church, who became a member of the British Parliament," Jane added. "It is my understanding that Mrs. Church was enormously popular in London and that she knew the Prince of Wales, Prime Minister Fox, and the playwright, Robert Sheridan. The Churches now live in a grand townhouse in New York City, and Mrs. Church hosts soirees." Jane pronounced "soirees" as if it was the most exotic thing in the world.

"You speak so casually of elopement," Georgiana said. "In England, such an occurrence would very likely create a scandal. At the very least, it would injure those whom we love best."

"That is true, but in the end, our cousin Philip forgave his four daughters, and they seem to be happy in their marriages, or most of them," Jane said, giving her sister a knowing look. There had been rumors that Angelica had had an affair with her sister Elizabeth's husband, Alexander Hamilton.

"Besides, people are meant to fall in love, and I ask, who amongst us has not fancied themselves to be in love? It is a natural inclination," Lizzy said, trying to lighten the tone. She had noticed a change in Georgiana's demeanor when the topic of elopement had been mentioned. "Jane received some verses from a boy when she was sixteen and fancied herself to be in love with Tapping Brockholst. But it passed quickly enough. Jane, do tell us. Was it Tapping himself or his verses that put out the fire?"

"You may tease, Lizzy, but you too received verses from a certain young man," Jane said, reminding her sister of her flirtation with Dirck Storm.

"In that particular case, it was definitely the verses that extinguished the flame. I wonder who first discovered the efficacy of poetry in driving away love!"

Georgiana was surprised by Elizabeth's remark. She had considered poetry to be the food of love.

"Of a fine, stout, healthy love it may be, but if it is only a slight, thin sort of inclination, I am convinced one good sonnet will starve it entirely away."

Elizabeth's statement only seemed to add to the young lady's confusion, but her thoughts were interrupted when Jane asked, "Georgiana, what happens to those, like our sister, Mary, who choose not to marry?"

"Someone like Mary would be in a very difficult position," Georgiana acknowledged. "She would be entirely dependent upon her male relations, most likely her brothers, and the kindness of their wives. If the wife did not wish for her sister-in-law to live with them, she would have to find other accommodations. She might very well live out the remainder of her life in poverty, relying on the parish for support. It is actually worse for the children who, very often, end up living in orphanages and are hired out as farm workers."

Both sisters shuddered at this information. After the death of his father, their own dear Papa had been raised by his grandfather with the love and attention he deserved.

"I imagine with your beauty, accomplishments, and social standing you will not have any concerns on that account. Unless, of course, you have already set your cap at a certain person," Lizzy said, and then quickly apologized for making such an impertinent remark.

"Oh, no, I am not offended, and I can assure you I have not set my cap at anyone. In fact, I know I am not ready for marriage as there is still so much more to learn about people and their motives."

Georgiana went quiet for several minutes before deciding to reveal her most closely guarded secret. "Last year, while visiting a seaside resort with my companion, without my brother's knowledge, I was visited by a man who had grown up with Fitzwilliam at Pemberley. We were properly supervised at all times, of course," she quickly added. "This person succeeded in convincing me he was all goodness, when he was anything but good. His intention was to convince me that he loved me so ardently that we should elope. But, in truth, he was not interested in me at all. It was my fortune he sought. I am afraid my actions greatly disappointed Fitzwilliam."

"And your brother has not forgiven you?" a surprised Lizzy asked. From what she had observed of the two siblings, both were very fond of each other.

"To the contrary. He has forgiven me over and over again. It is just that I… I have not forgiven myself for causing Fitzwilliam so much unhappiness."

"Oh, how sad for your brother," Lizzy said. "What I mean is that your brother has given you the gift of forgiveness, and you have refused it."

"I never thought of it in that way, but you are right. It *is* a gift." Georgiana let out a sigh of relief. It was as if her sin had finally been purged, and the brother who had absolved her was walking their way.

After asking if he might join the ladies, Darcy set his plate and a tankard of ale on the table and took a seat on the bench so that he was sitting directly opposite to Lizzy. Because there was no way for her to ignore him, Lizzy decided to look directly at him and not shy away, and what she saw was most impressive. He had black hair and green eyes with flecks of brown in them, a less than perfect nose, and she suspected that at some time it had been broken. His brow was high, giving him an intelligent look. His mouth was perfect, but hid less than perfect teeth. But rather than detracting from his handsome appearance, the imperfection seemed to add to it.

Lizzy continued her appraisal. His physique was ideal for a man: six foot, broad in the shoulders with a tapered waist, and long legs, and best yet, he was wearing a loose white shirt opened at the neck, and because of all of his hard work, the sweaty garment was clinging to him, revealing a well-muscled chest. And his smile! My goodness!

But as for conversation, Lizzy had little to say, so Jane thanked Mr. Darcy for his assistance on behalf of Mrs. Vreeland and all of the others who would make good use of the surplus apples the widow could not use. "Later in the week we shall make applesauce, apple butter, and apple jelly."

"Surely, your mother will wish to make another apple pie," Darcy said.

"Not just one, Mr. Darcy, I can assure you of that," Jane answered, laughing.

The conversation was pleasant, but for some reason, Lizzy found it difficult to participate, and when Joshua Lucas asked if Georgiana wished to see a view of the river, Jane agreed to go with them, leaving the pair sitting across from each other with little to say. Finally, Lizzy broke the impasse.

"You bring good weather with you, Mr. Darcy. July was hot and humid, but these first weeks of August have been quite pleasant."

"Yes, it has been most agreeable, and I am willing to accept credit for sunshine and pleasant temperatures."

"Speaking of temperatures, how is your sister faring at Mr. Bingley's? She tells me she is comfortable, but because I lived in that house for the first ten years of my life, I know her room can be very warm in summer, and at night, you hear the owls in the attic."

"Owls! Is that what I have been hearing? Of course," Darcy said, shaking his head. "That is what the holes in the north gable are for. I should have guessed."

"At one time, it was quite common for all Dutch houses to have owl holes to control rodents. Of course, none of the old Dutch families would have had a cat on the farm because of *black magic*," Lizzy said, whispering the last two words. "Obviously, if a cat is nearby, then one can assume a witch is in the neighborhood, and although I am laughing, it was a strongly held belief until fairly recently by many of our neighbors, including Mrs. Vreeland. I wish we had owl holes at Longbourn. I think of them as guardians of the night, and I do so love the sound of their hooting. But to return to your sister, is she content with her accommodations?"

"She has not complained about that or anything else. In fact, she loves the outdoor staircase, and it has fed her imagination. Georgiana is a true romantic, and in her mind, she has drawn a picture of a young lady standing on the landing while her lover serenades her from below. I think she got the idea from Mozart's *Don Giovanni*."

"When we were girls, Jane imagined a similar scene as she is very romantic as well. I, on the other hand, conjured up visions of some vicious intruder creeping up those stairs for the purpose of doing us harm. But I was prepared as I had a weapon nearby: a rolling pin I kept under my bed. So you see, Mr. Darcy, it is not just your sister who has a vivid imagination."

"Miss Elizabeth, you were not at Longbourn when it was agreed that we should adopt the American custom of using one's Christian name. So if it is agreeable, I would ask that you call me Fitzwilliam or William, or as some of my friends do, you may call me Will."

"Not Billy?"

"Good Lord, no! I developed an aversion to the use of Bill or Billy during my days at Cambridge when I noticed that many of the less desirable characters in the songs being sung in the public houses were named Billy, probably because it rhymes with filly."

"Very well," Lizzy agreed. "But Fitzwilliam sounds too aristocratic to my democratic ears, and Will is perhaps too familiar, at least for the present. So I shall call you William."

"Then William it is. But I gather from your statement you do not approve of the aristocracy."

"No, I do not," Lizzy said without hesitation. "I do not believe in the inherent superiority of any group of people. Because one is born to a king or prince or duke does not mean that he is better than I am. *There is a natural aristocracy among men. The grounds of this are virtue and talents.* That is a quote from Thomas Jefferson. Are you familiar with his writings?"

"Yes, I am. I have read the *Declaration of Independence* as well as John Locke."

"But you do not agree with its tenets or the inspiration for the *Declaration*?"

"Elizabeth, if I may call you Elizabeth, I am an Englishman. As such, I am duty bound to honor my king, whom Mr. Jefferson labeled a tyrant. Whether I like His Majesty or not, whether I agree with him or not, I am his subject."

Lizzy looked embarrassed. "I have just broken one of my mother's cardinal rules. She has told me time and again that I should not discuss religion or politics outside of our home because such discussions lead to arguments, arguments lead to fights, and fights lead to war, and she has seen too much of that."

"I wholeheartedly agree with your mother, and I would be wary of getting into an argument with you with or without a rolling pin. Because we are being quite honest with each other, may I say that last night I noticed a reluctance on your part to converse with me. The only conclusion I can draw is that I have given offense, and if I have done so, I can assure you it was unintentional. Have I offended?"

Lizzy was surprised by his frankness, but Americans were famous, or infamous, for their bluntness, and she did not want to disappoint. And he *did* ask.

"At the haying festival, you said quite emphatically that you would not dance with anyone. The impression you left was that the local ladies were beneath your notice."

"I do not recall saying any such thing," Darcy answered defensively.

If Mr. Darcy had forgotten his words, Lizzy had not. "Bingley, I certainly shall not dance. Surely, the ladies of the neighborhood do not rely on visitors from England to supply their dance partners. I cannot be tempted to dance. Go back to the ladies and their smiles. You are wasting your time with me," Lizzy said, quoting him in an impeccable English accent.

"That does sound bad," Darcy agreed.

"I see I have refreshed your memory."

"You have, but you have also misinterpreted the scene. My refusal had nothing to do with you or any other lady at the festival. Before we left Richard's house, I made it clear to Charles and Georgiana that it was not my intention to dance because of the lingering effects of my seasickness, lest I fall victim to the sharp wit of someone, such as your father, by turning green in front of him. However, Bingley was so enamored by your... by his company that he quite forgot our agreement. And here is my sister who will testify to my suffering. Georgiana, I was just explaining to Elizabeth how ill I was on the voyage to America."

"Oh, yes, poor Fitzwilliam. He became seasick while we were still in sight of the English coast. The truth is that he was only able to come on deck four times during the whole voyage. The rest of the time he was..."

"Thank you, Georgiana. I think Miss Elizabeth can imagine the rest. Suffice it to say that I was sick even whilst sailing up the North River and during the carriage ride to Richard's house. I only went to the dance that night because Georgiana would not go without me."

"Oh, Mr. Darcy, I mean William, I feel perfectly awful," Lizzy said, appalled at her behavior. "It is I who should apologize."

"No need. You were unaware of my malady, and if I had overhead such a speech, I, too, would have taken umbrage. We shall have to blame Charles for this misunderstanding."

"Because it was Charles who encouraged you to make the voyage in the first place?"

"No, despite my misery, I have no regrets on that account. The countryside is beautiful and the inhabitants generous and welcoming. I shall blame Charles because he failed to adhere to our plan. Besides, it suits me to blame Charles."

His remarks brought a smile to Lizzy's face, but it also served as a reminder that neither had seen Charles since the dinner bell had rung. However, Jane soon appeared to provide an explanation for his absence.

"Apparently, Mrs. Vreeland has taken a liking to Charles, and he is in the springhouse with her sorting the apples," Jane said, her voice revealing her disappointment. But then a second bell rang out, signaling that the workers should return to their work.

As Lizzy and Darcy walked back to the orchard, Lizzy again apologized to William for what surely must appear to be a willingness to misunderstand him.

"In the future, sir, I would suggest forthrightness. Even though it is true you would have been teased about your lack of fitness as a sailor, it would have been preferable to having everyone think you were above your company."

"Is that what people think?" Darcy asked with a look of genuine concern.

"No, sir. You were fortunate in that Charlotte and I alone heard your remarks, and Charlotte is a true Christian and not a gossip. As for me, I did not have an opportunity to circulate such a report amongst the ladies of the neighborhood," she said with an impish smile. "As for the men, no one will criticize someone who can lose so much money at cards and so graciously."

"I see you are your father's daughter. In the future, I will be cautious around either of you."

"You are a wise man, sir, that is, for an Englishman."

* * *

With the most physically demanding work done, it was time for the girls to take over. Since they were smaller, it was easier for them to reach the fruit clinging to the interior branches. These apples would be segregated from the others and put into storage for use during the coming winter.

Georgiana would have liked to have done more than sort apples and carry water, but even in her plainest dress, her clothes were too fine for any other task. Instead, she stood on the bottom rung of the ladder, taking a full bag of apples from Lizzy and handing her an empty one to replace it.

While everyone was hard at work, Ezekiel had brought the Bennet's share of the crop to Longbourn where Mrs. Bennet was already sorting through them looking for the best apples for her Dutch apple pie. Ezekiel lifted up the few remaining bushel baskets into the wagon, one of which contained badly bruised apples that would be fed to the livestock. Lizzy sifted through the basket until she found one that was more mash that meat, and with a deadeye, hit Joshua Lucas dead center in his back.

Although Joshua gave out a cry of surprise, he really wasn't. Throwing rotten apples was the traditional finale of the apple picking outing, and Lizzy's volley was a signal to let the games begin. The missiles were the discarded apples that lay scattered about the yard. All of the girls fled to the perimeter so they might watch the exhibition, and Mary Bennet took a stunned Georgiana by the hand to get her out of harm's way.

The growing din outside allowed Bingley to break free of Mrs. Vreeland, and he emerged from the springhouse just in time to take a flying piece of mash squarely in the chest. The newly liberated Charles let fly a steady stream of apples in every direction. But it quickly became apparent that the local boys wanted to leave an impression on their English visitors, and Charles and William became their principal targets. With the clang of a bell, the frenzied throwing came to an end. As the Bennet sisters climbed into the wagon, the closing scene before them was of the two men jumping up and down trying to shed the pulp clinging to their clothes and the pigs rooting through the mash at their feet.

* * *

By the time the wagon pulled into the barn, Lydia and Kitty were asleep, and Mary was very close to joining them. However, Lizzy was wide awake. She always enjoyed this annual ritual, but today there was the added interest of European visitors. More importantly, the misunderstanding between William and her had been cleared up. A chastened Lizzy was surprised at how willing she had been to think ill of William, and she wondered why she had acted in such a way. Did she harbor a resentment for all English men because of the way she had been treated by Edward Chamberlain's family?

Jane, on the other hand, was definitely not happy. She felt the Widow Vreeland had been particularly rude to Mr. Bingley.

"Granted, Mrs. Vreeland's comments were offensive," Lizzy said. "However, if Charles cannot withstand insults from a little old lady speaking Dutch, then what is he to do when he finds himself sitting across from Papa and his rapier wit?"

Jane merely shook her head in dismay. "I cannot wait until I am in my eighties so that I may be rude to others without consequence."

"You wish to be in your eighties? Well, you may be in a hurry to be a withered, toothless old lady, clothed in widow's weeds, discussing aching joints and the other unpleasant complaints of old age, but for my part, I will live my life to the fullest, one day at a time."

But Jane refused to be diverted. Because Charles would only be in New York for another three months, she wanted to make the most of their time together, but that was not how the day had progressed. When they had walked to the river with Georgiana and Joshua Lucas, Lydia and Kitty had joined them and had monopolized the conversation. After that, Mrs. Vreeland had got hold of Mr. Bingley, and then the rotten apple fight had taken up the last ten minutes of their time together.

"Jane, do not look so downhearted. From his looks, I can tell you that Charles shares in your frustration. Trust me. He will find an excuse to visit Longbourn."

But Jane was not mollified. "You spent more time

talking to Mr. Darcy, whom you do not like, than I did talking to Charles, who I do like—very much."

"It is true Mr. Darcy and I had a lengthy conversation, but it is no longer true that I do not like him. The gentleman definitely improves upon acquaintance."

Chapter 8

Behind Longbourn's barn, bushel baskets filled to overflowing with yesterday's apple harvest were lined up waiting to be turned into apple butter and applesauce. At first light, farm laborers had dragged large iron kettles out of storage and had stacked piles of kindling next to them to keep the fires going. This was a task that would usually have been supervised by Hannah and Samuel MacTavish, Longbourn's cook and steward, but Mrs. Bennet had decided it would be a nice surprise for the MacTavishes if this hot and arduous chore was completed before their return from Albany.

"Have I peeled and sliced and cored enough apples, Mama?" Lydia asked in an exhausted voice.

"Is your basket empty?" Lydia shook her head. "Then you are not done. However, if you prefer, you may take over stirring the kettle from Lizzy, Jane, or Mary."

"But why must we do this nasty chore at all? That is why we have help."

"My dear, first of all, *you* do not have help. Your father and I have help," Mrs. Bennet said, while smiling at Lottie and Phillis, who were paring apples without complaint. "Secondly, it is important for all of my girls to know how to take care of themselves."

Mrs. Kraft, an elderly lady who had arrived at Longbourn four years earlier from Philadelphia accompanying a shipment of cast-iron stoves, nodded her head in approval at Mrs. Bennet's correction of her daughter.

"Mama, I know you did all these things during the war, but that was a hundred years ago, and we are no longer at war."

"You never know what the future may hold. If the wooden heads in Washington have their way, we may yet have another war. Or you may marry a man who cannot afford help, and you must do these things by yourself."

Lydia's mouth dropped open. "Marry a man who cannot afford help! I think not. And when I keep my own house, I will never make apple butter or apple sauce. All I will do is eat it."

"At the moment, you do not have a husband or help, so you will learn to make apple butter as your older sisters have done. Mary, please instruct Lydia on how best to stir the kettle."

"But this morning you said I was too young to stir the pot," Lydia protested.

"That was this morning. You are older now."

After wiping her hands on her apron, Mrs. Bennet indicated she was returning to the house. When Lydia started to say something, she was warned there was kindling to be chopped for the fire, and the youngster said no more. But that was not the case with Mrs. Kraft. The stern lady reproached Lydia for speaking back to her mother. "Thou should not speak in such a way to thy mother. Scripture commands us to honor thy father and mother." She then followed her mistress back to the house.

Lydia rolled her eyes, her usual response to Mrs. Kraft's admonitions. "When is she going to learn to speak English properly?"

"When are you going to remember all Quakers speak like that," an impatient Mary answered.

"Thou sayeth that every time," Lydia said, spitting out her words. "I don't think she likes me very much."

"I can't imagine why," Mary said and handed her sister the wooden paddle.

* * *

"Oh, no! Charles is coming," Jane said, looking down the path that circled around the barn and then at her sweat-stained frock.

"Oh, Lord! William is coming," Lizzy mumbled, checking to see if her curls were in place.

"Lizzy, I look a wreck, a sweaty, smelly wreck."

"Well, I don't exactly look like a George Romney portrait either."

"But it does not matter what you look like. Charles won't be looking at you."

Charles and William were joined by Georgiana who had a bounce in her step. She reminded Lizzy of a wide-eyed child on her birthday, and her visit to America was her gift. In fact, she was so happy to see the Bennet sisters that she quickened her pace and would have hugged them if she had not been stopped.

"Georgiana, we are absolutely filthy," Jane said to the young lady while looking at Charles. "But what a pleasant surprise you have come," Jane said, not meaning a word of it.

"We walked to the village today as Fitzwilliam needed to post letters to some businessmen in Albany, and I bought material for six new frocks—very simple cotton dresses I can wear everyday and not have to worry about stains or tears. Mrs. Dumont is to make them for me."

"So you have had a visit with Charlotte Lucas," Lizzy said, wondering about William's correspondence with businessmen in Albany. Her father would be interested to hear that.

"Yes, and Mr. Collins as well. He was in the store purchasing… Fitzwilliam, what was Mr. Collins buying at the mercantile?"

"Time, I believe," and everyone laughed. "My guess is that his purpose was to visit with Miss Lucas, not to purchase provisions."

This report produced a broad smile from Mary, who could see the stars aligning for the two lovers.

"You find us hard at work today," Jane said. "We do not usually perform this task, but our cook is away. But as you can see, we have a lot of help," Jane said, pointing to the farm laborers, who had taken over the job of stirring the kettles. "You have already met Lottie and Phillis who are the daughters of Mr. Wesley who runs the farm for my father."

"My grandmother got Mr. and Mrs. Wesley as a wedding present," Lydia said. The thirteen-year-old did not like it when she was left out of any discussion, but instead of encouraging conversation, her comment produced confused looks from their visitors.

At that moment, Jane could have strangled Lydia, but instead she tried to explain her remark. "My Grandfather Schuyler owned slaves, as was common amongst the old Dutch families. However, when Grandpa died, our grandmother remarried Mr. Gardiner, and they freed the Wesleys. And they have been as free as you or me for a great many years."

But the silence continued with Charles and William exchanging uncomfortable glances. Fortunately, Mrs. Bennet, followed by Mrs. Kraft, came bearing fruit, apple cider, and sandwiches for the visitors and laborers.

"With Mr. Bennet in the city," Mrs. Bennet said to her guests, "I must be the one to tell you that this apple cider was pressed at our own cider mill across the river. According to my husband, it is the best cider in the lower Hudson Valley, and I cannot disagree with that statement."

Jane gave a sigh of relief. Once again, her mother had come to the rescue. Mr. Bennet frequently stated his wife had a sixth sense, and none of her children would have challenged that supposition.

"It is fortunate you all stopped by today as you have saved me the trouble of sending a messenger to Richard's house," Mrs. Bennet said. "Mr. Bennet will return from New York tomorrow, so I was going to invite everyone to supper on Friday. Is that agreeable?" All three nodded, none more enthusiastically than Georgiana.

"Excellent. We look forward to it." Turning her attention to Georgiana, she asked, "Did you sleep well last night? I am sure you must have been exhausted after picking apples all day under a hot sun."

"Oh, yes. I was very tired, so tired, in fact, that for the first time since my arrival, I did not hear the owls." Realizing her remark sounded like a complaint, she quickly added, "not that they bother me. It is just I do hear them."

"When we lived in the house, we plugged up those holes as owls take their kill back to their roost, and you can hear them going about their business throughout the night. But Richard likes them, and he asked if he could open up the holes again. But what a racket they can make! You really should mention it to him," Mrs. Bennet said, looking at William and Charles, "or, better yet, I think Georgiana should come to stay with us. She can stay in Mary's room. After all, why should a young girl be confined to a house where you have owls in the attic, only men for company, and no musical instrument to pass the time?"

Georgiana looked at her brother, and with her eyes, she implored him to say "yes."

"If it is not an inconvenience, Mrs. Bennet, I have no

objection," Darcy answered, "I am sure Georgiana's preference would be to stay at Longbourn." Upon hearing such news, Georgiana jumped up and down, and Mary joined her new friend in celebration.

"Thank you, Fitzwilliam," Georgiana said. "Oh, but what will Mr. Richard say? I do not wish to appear ungrateful and possibly hurt his feelings."

"Oh, don't worry about that," Jane quickly interjected. "Caroline was always hurting his feelings, so he is quite used to it." Jane then looked at Charles, Caroline's cousin, and said, "Sorry."

Charles started laughing. "You need not apologize, Jane. You are not telling me anything I did not already know."

"So it is agreed. Friday at 6:00," Mrs. Bennet said. "And when you come, please bring Georgiana's things, and we will get her moved in with Mary." Everyone smiled in agreement, including Fitzwilliam Darcy, who was very pleased by the turn of events as it would provide him with additional opportunities to be in the company of Elizabeth Bennet.

Chapter 9

"Well, today was a disaster," Jane said as she and Lizzy prepared for bed. "If it wasn't bad enough that I reeked of apple mash, I was sweating like a laborer, and my hair was plastered to my head as if I had been caught in a rainstorm, Lydia mentions that our family has owned slaves."

"In the first place, few people are attractive when they sweat, but you are one of them. As for slavery, although the British have abolished the slave trade, they have not done away with slavery. There are very few who have clean hands in that matter. Besides, I think Mama's timing with the cider and sandwiches was perfect and that awful subject was quickly forgotten."

"But there is another thing I have wondered about. Why does Papa talk so differently to Charles than he does to Mr. Darcy? Charles is only a few years Mr. Darcy's junior, but Papa talks to him as if he were a boy."

"I think you have your answer in your question. Why is it that we are so comfortable in calling Mr. Bingley, Charles, or Miss Darcy, Georgiana, but stumble over calling Mr. Darcy, William? There is something about Mr. Darcy that bars intimacy. Besides, there is more of the boy left in Charles, and I think that is part of his charm. Papa obviously sees something of a son in Charles, but does not in Mr. Darcy. But my question to you is, just how serious are you about Charles? Everyone has teased you quite a bit about your interest in that gentleman, but what are *your* feelings?"

"I do not know. How could I? Since the first night when we danced at the Van Tassels', I have not had an opportunity to have a private conversation with him. If it is not Kitty badgering him with questions about England or Lydia telling him how adorable his accent is, it is Mrs. Vreeland taking up all of his time and Papa talking about the constellations, which I think is a subject of little interest to Charles, but he is too polite to mention it. So if you are asking if I am in love with Charles Bingley, I cannot answer that question with any certainty. All I can say is that I think about him at all hours of the day, and I believe him to be a man I could fall in love with if given half the chance."

Jane went quiet for a few minutes before continuing. "I remember well when all our friends and neighbors were so critical of me when I refused Pieter Schuyler's proposal. I was mocked because I wanted to marry for love, but you came to my defense. You said that marriage should not be viewed as an alliance between families but a coming together of hearts and minds and that you would have done the same thing in a similar situation. Whenever I have experienced doubts about my refusal, I have clung to those words, and now I feel as if I have met someone where there is an agreement of hearts and minds, but little opportunity to explore it. But let us not speak of it because I have no way of knowing what Charles feels, if anything, and I do not want to have my heart broken."

For a long time, the two sisters lay in bed holding hands with a veil of silence between them, but then Jane turned and faced Lizzy. "If Charles and I do get married, I shall have to move to England, and England is so very far away."

So much for not speaking about it, Lizzy thought as she blew out the candle.

* * *

"Darcy, I am not sure it was a good idea to just drop in on the Bennets. We should have sent a note or something—not sure how they do it here. Jane looked very uncomfortable the whole time we were there."

"Well, wouldn't you be uncomfortable if you were wearing your simplest frock while doing a dirty job and the man you are interested in comes by dressed to impress her?"

"Did you notice how her flock clung to her, and even with her soiled dress, she looked beautiful."

But Darcy had not been thinking about Jane and her clinging frock, but of Elizabeth and *her* clinging frock, through which the outline of her light and pleasing form had been visible.

"I agree," Darcy said, shaking the lovely Elizabeth from his thoughts. "I think it is impossible for Jane Bennet not to look beautiful. But, Bingley, I have to ask. Just how serious are your feelings for the lady?"

"I hardly know since we have had so little time together. But I can tell you that I am finding it difficult to think about anything else. At night, my dreams of her... Well, it is rather embarrassing to talk about."

"I understand," Darcy said, stopping Bingley before he could elaborate. "But you must take into consideration that she is an American."

"Oh, I do not mind that at all."

Darcy laughed. "I mention her nationality because if you intend to marry the lady, then you will either have to live here in America or she will have to move to England."

"Oh, I could not live here. I am an Englishman to my very core."

"You may find the lady feels as strongly about America as you feel about England. After all, you will be taking her from her home and transporting her to a land 3,000 miles from Longbourn."

"But isn't it the duty of a wife to follow her husband?"

"Haven't you noticed Americans are rather an independent lot? Nonetheless, I do think Jane would agree to move to England as she is of a compliant nature— certainly more so than her sister Elizabeth."

"Yes, Elizabeth is fearless. I saw her hit Joshua Lucas squarely in the back with a rotten apple, and when he took aim at her in return, it was only her quick footwork that prevented Lucas from hitting his target."

"It is not her aim with an apple I fear, but her aim with pointed comments. I have never met anyone like her."

"I think she favors her father in temperament. Speaking of Mr. Bennet, why is it that he seems to direct all of his comments to me and, rarely, you?"

"Bingley, Mr. Bennet is a lawyer and loves to argue. Because you refuse to engage, he pokes and prods in an attempt to have you take up the challenge. He is merely testing your mettle. Trust me on this. He wants you to push back."

"But, Darcy, I am not a great tall fellow like you are. I do not intimidate people merely with a look or a sarcastic remark."

"You think I intimidate people?"

Bingley started to laugh. "If it were possible to patent a look, I would recommend taking one out on the look you wore when talking to Mr. Collins; that quizzical furrowed brow of yours had him shaking in his little black shoes."

"I must confess I find the man to be annoying. At Rosings Park, his obsequious behavior was repellant. However, when I saw him talking to Miss Lucas at the mercantile, my opinion softened. His intention was to make a good impression on the lady. I liked that because I like the lady."

"But, Darcy, you must know you have a reputation for

intimidating people, and because of that, it is all the more remarkable that Elizabeth Bennet is not afraid of you. If you were to marry her, she would challenge you."

"Bingley, what are you talking about? Marry Elizabeth Bennet! Have you taken leave of your senses? Yes, she is an attractive lady with many fine qualities, but she would not suit me at all as we would be arguing all the time. Besides, I am not looking for a wife, and certainly not an American."

"As you say." But Bingley was beginning to think Elizabeth Bennet would not only suit his friend, but that she would be a perfect fit.

Chapter 10

Upon their arrival at Longbourn, Mr. Bennet had his three English visitors climbing the narrow stairway to the tower he had built for the purpose of celestial observation. The observatory contained an impressive array of instruments that would have been the envy of a college, but not that of a seventeen-year-old girl. After five minutes and a good deal of ribbing, Georgiana was excused so that she might join the ladies in the parlor. Charles looked longingly in the direction of the doorway and freedom, but it was necessary for him to suffer through an additional fifteen minutes of a discussion of the heavens before he was finally granted his release.

"William, now that it is just the pair of us, I thought we might talk business. It is my understanding that you are in correspondence with certain parties regarding the building of a canal between the Hudson and Lake Erie. Oh, I can see you are surprised, so please allow me to explain. My source is Stephen Van Rensselaer, a cousin by marriage. It is his opinion that the canal will be built but with private, not public, money, and he approached me a few months ago about joining a group of investors, which includes Governor DeWitt Clinton, to raise the necessary capital required for such an enormous undertaking. I confess to being intrigued.

"As am I, Mr. Bennet, and as soon as Mr. Van Rensselaer and I have had our meeting, I will seek your counsel regarding this great canal. In the meantime, I see that you have a copy of Cicero's orations on your shelf."

* * *

When Georgiana went into the parlor, she found the ladies were not alone. Splendidly attired in his West Point cadet's uniform was Joshua Lucas, and the young miss burst into a smile as soon as their eyes met.

"Mrs. Bennet was generous enough to invite me to supper so I might take my leave of you," Joshua said, rising. "I must return to the military academy on Thursday."

"Oh" is all that Georgiana could manage.

"However, if you are still in New York on October 26, there is a ball being held at the academy, and I would ask that you accompany me. I know this request will require the permission of your brother, and it will necessitate a journey by sloop as West Point is thirty-five miles north of Tarrytown. But if Mr. Darcy has no objections, all these details can be worked out."

"I shall speak to Fitzwilliam." Georgiana immediately went in search of her brother.

"From that I take it Miss Darcy would be agreeable to attending the ball as your guest, Joshua," Mrs. Bennet said as she watched Georgiana climbing the stairs, and everyone started to laugh.

But Georgiana would not have her answer tonight as her brother had too many questions to ask of the young man before granting his permission.

"Georgiana, I am not saying you cannot go. I am merely saying that I require more information. After I speak to Joshua, I will give you my answer. Is that agreeable?" It wasn't, but Georgiana had no choice but to adhere to her brother's wishes.

While waiting for dinner to be served, the Bennets asked many questions of their guests. Georgiana spoke of all the preparations necessary for her debut in London society when the season began in earnest in the spring. Charles mentioned the source of the Bingley wealth, a sprawling empire of mercantile concerns spanning three-quarters of the globe. He also spoke about his cousin, Louisa Hurst, who was expecting her first child. This was news to everyone, except Richard, who had agreed to Charles "letting the cat out of the bag."

While Georgiana and Charles were happily conversing, Darcy's mind was also agreeably engaged. He had been thinking about Elizabeth and the great pleasure a pair of fine eyes in the face of a pretty woman could bestow. His mind then drifted from her eyes to her lips, and he wondered if they would taste as delicious as they looked. He imagined kissing her deeply and repeatedly, and he then crossed his legs and thought no more of her fine eyes and lips or surely he would embarrass himself.

In the dining room, Darcy noted the fine furnishings and service, including a lovely set of Serves porcelain china, with each plate and bowl individually painted with a different scene of the French countryside. There were cut glass candelabra and a fireplace with plasterwork on the mantle depicting a Roman chariot race that he admired. All in all, it was an impressive room with a view of the Hudson that even a Darcy could envy.

At table, there were the seven Bennets, Joshua Lucas, Georgiana, William, Charles, and Mrs. Kraft. Although Mrs. Kraft was introduced to the visitors by name, there was no explanation as to her relationship to the family. She was not a sister or cousin or friend; she was simply Mrs. Kraft. So Lydia leaned over and whispered to Darcy, "Mrs. Kraft came with the stoves," which only added to the mystery.

"Do you mean that when you opened the crate containing the stove, Mrs. Kraft was inside?" Darcy asked.

Now Lydia looked puzzled, but Lizzy found herself

giggling. "Don't be silly, William. She had her *own* crate." After they had stopped laughing, Lizzy explained. "When my father was in the Continental Army during the war, he was taken ill and nursed back to health by a German family in New Jersey. The family heated their home with a cast-iron stove, and it was the first time in my father's life that he had been warm in the winter. Years later, he went to Philadelphia and bought a dozen stoves from Mrs. Kraft's family, only to find that people here in the Hudson Valley thought the stove made the house *too* warm and feared the heat would prove injurious to their health. So Papa asked Mrs. Kraft to remain in Tarrytown. Since she was in her late sixties, people would see that despite having lived a good part of her life in houses with cast iron stoves, she was in excellent health. Sales picked up considerably after that, and she never returned to Philadelphia."

"Very clever promotional tool," Darcy said, nodding his head in approval.

But Lydia shook her head, indicating that the disadvantages of Mrs. Kraft's prolonged visit—she refused to admit the situation was permanent—far outweighed any benefits derived from increased trade. "Thou dost not know her or thou would not sayeth that," Lydia said in an attempt to imitate the speech of her tormentor, and Lizzy gave her a stern look.

During supper, Georgiana was all praise for the room, the food, and the hospitality, and it was clear she had developed an attachment to Mrs. Bennet. Having lost her own mother when she was only seven, it was only natural for her to respond to the mother of five daughters.

"Were you born in Westchester County, Mrs. Bennet?" Georgiana asked.

"No, I was born in Albany. But when I was about ten years old, my mother remarried, and we moved to my step-father's home a few miles north of Tarrytown. However, it no longer exists as it was burnt to the ground."

"Oh, I am sorry. Did the fire start in the kitchen? That is the usual cause of house fires, at least in England."

"It didn't *catch* fire; it was *set* on fire—by the British during the war."

Georgiana went pale at hearing such news. "I am so sorry."

"Well, you did not do it, dear, and it was a long time ago. But it is a rather interesting story. So if you will oblige me, I shall tell it.

"After the British defeat at Saratoga, British General John Vaughan went on a rampage and was burning the houses of Patriots in the Hudson Valley. Because my stepfather, Mr. Gardiner, was a colonel in the Continental army, his home was targeted. So my mother and I fled up the river to *Clermont*, the Livingston estate, where my mother's cousin, Margaret Beekman Livingston, lived. But when we got there, we found the British had burnt her house down to its foundation.

"We then went to the home of my mother's cousin, Philip Schuyler, who was a general in the Continental army, in Albany. When we arrived, his wife was in the fields burning the wheat crop so the British would not have it. Aunt Catherine sent us back down the Hudson to New Paltz where we stayed with a French Huguenot family.

The winter of 1777-78 was bitterly cold, and my poor mother suffered terribly. You see, if you wanted to eat, you had to earn your keep. I was young and quite capable of performing manual labor. However, my dear Mama, who had been raised with personal servants, knew only those accomplishments expected of a lady. However, one day, a soldier came to the house with yards and yards of linen and told us that we must sew shirts for the Continentals, and my mother was able to do that. She also learned to spin, and she wore homespun, just as Martha Washington did, for the duration of the war."

Georgiana wondered if she would have been able to adapt to the changes forced upon a population during a time of war. Looking down at her pretty blue silk dress, she tried to picture it as a coarse homespun fabric. She could not.

"But this story had a happy ending. While I was living in New Paltz, a young man came from the Ulster County militia to ask for provisions for the Continental army wintering at Valley Forge. The whole time the transaction was being negotiated between the officer and the DuBois family, this same young man had been flirting with me. Of course, it was Mr. Bennet."

"Oh," Georgiana sighed, "and you fell in love and got married."

"Yes, we fell in love, but 'no' we did not get married. I did not see Tom for more than three years. He was with General Greene's army in Virginia when General Cornwallis surrendered the British forces at Yorktown in '81, and he walked home from there. My father was with Greene's army as well and asked that Tom go to the farm in Ulster County where we were living and bring his wife and daughter back to Tarrytown, which he did."

"And then you got married."

"No, not then. My stepfather was a lawyer, and Tom served as his clerk. Tom was quite insistent that we not marry until he was licensed to practice. That took another four years. But, finally, in 1785, we tied the knot in the parlor of what is now Richard Bingley's house, and he has been a thorn in my side ever since," a statement that brought smiles to everyone's faces.

"Gentlemen, I shall advise you never to marry a Dutch woman as they are natural scolds," Mr. Bennet said.

"And I shall warn the ladies never to marry a man who is of French and Scots descent as the sensible nature of the

Celt is overwhelmed by the impulsive nature of the Gaul," his wife countered.

"Please make note my wife neglected to mention that I am also of English descent, but *I* shall not deny it. *I* am not bitter."

"But so many terrible things *did* happen to you, Mrs. Bennet," Georgiana said. "Do *you* not harbor any bitterness?"

"About Mr. Bennet?" Everyone burst out laughing, and a red-faced Georgiana asked, "No, about the war?"

"There was no time for bitterness, my dear. We had a farm to run and a country to build."

"As long as no one in your family is a Redcoat serving in the British Army, Miss Darcy, then why should we be bitter?" Mr. Bennet asked, peering over his glasses at her.

A picture of her cousin, Colonel Fitzwilliam, resplendent in his regimentals, appeared before Georgiana, and she looked to her brother. But Fitzwilliam gave her a smile, and taking her cue from him, she said, "Our cousin, Richard Fitzwilliam, is a colonel in an artillery regiment now serving in the Peninsula, but I suspect that that does not bother you at all. I think you are teasing me again, Mr. Bennet."

"Georgiana, my father only teases those he likes," Mary said, sticking up for her friend.

"Well, then he must like me a great deal," she quickly answered, and everyone again burst out laughing.

The main meal was followed by coffee and dessert served in such variety that the visitors mentioned it equaled anything served in the finest houses in England. After sampling a little bit of everything, the party went into the rear parlor where Mary performed a pleasant piece on her lap harp, and after she had finished, Georgiana was asked to perform on the pianoforte. The young lady, who was growing more comfortable with her company, asked if she should play a dance tune, and cries of "yes" went up.

The remainder of the evening was divided between dancing to tunes played by Miss Darcy and the four favorites that could be played on the barrel organ. Mr. and Mrs. Bennet joined the young dancers, and at the end of the evening, Mary was coaxed on to the dance floor by Georgiana.

Lizzy was engaged by William for three dances, and she found her partner to be an excellent dancer. That night, after rehashing every last detail of the evening with Jane, Lizzy fell asleep thinking of her time with William Darcy.

Darcy's thoughts were less chaste than those of Elizabeth as his dreams were filled with passionate kisses and heated embraces. But he realized that these delightful fantasies must stop as his time in America would be of short duration. He would be better served if he kept his distance from the lady during the day so he might keep her out of his dreams at night.

Chapter 11

From the veranda of Longbourn, Lizzy looked out on a sloop hugging the shore as it made its way to Tarrytown harbor. Most of her family had boarded a similar vessel that morning to take them to the city for a few days of shopping. Only Mary, Mrs. Kraft, and she had remained behind. Unlike Jane, Lydia, and Kitty, Lizzy had little interest in making the rounds of stores and warehouses, especially since her mother had agreed to pick up the few items Lizzy had requested: some lace to trim a dress and pins for her hair. Because of her thick curls, she was always in need of pins, but this time, she had asked Mama to select something a little fancier and wondered why she had asked for such "baubles," as Mary called them. Ruffles and flounces, ribbons and bows, and pretty hairpins belonged to Jane's world, not Lizzy's.

Lizzy turned her attention to the paper on her portable writing desk. She was in the midst of writing a story inspired by her parents' experiences during the Revolution. She had already written a non-fiction account of the capture of Major John André, who had been seized by three Patriots in Tarrytown while carrying documents revealing Benedict Arnold's treasonous plans to deliver West Point to the British.

She was so engrossed in her tale that she had not heard an approaching wagon until it was nearly to the front porch of Longbourn. Most surprising of all was the driver:

William Darcy. She had assumed he had gone into the city with his sister, but knowing of his extreme distress during the transatlantic voyage to America, she should have guessed he might forego any excursion that required negotiating the temperamental waters of the Hudson south of the Tappan Zee.

Because the Bennets were not the only ones to have issued invitations to their English visitors, other than church on Sunday, Lizzy had seen little of the gentleman..

"Good afternoon, Elizabeth," Darcy said as he climbed out of the wagon. "I have just come from taking Mrs. Haas to church for Wednesday worship. She hinted that if I came to Longbourn I might be invited to supper, and so here I am."

"How kind of you to take Mrs. Haas, but I am surprised Mr. Mercer did not do it."

Although Mercer had offered to drive the cook into the village, Darcy had told his manservant that his coats needed brushing and his boots required the application of linseed oil. He had no idea if that was true, but because it was his intention to stop at Longbourn on his way back from the village, *he* must drive Mrs. Haas. He understood he was acting contrary to his own advice, that is, to stay away from Elizabeth Bennet, but it was a difficult thing to do when she was the first thing he thought about in the morning and the last thing at night.

Poor Mercer. I have probably hurt his feelings because everything is always exactly as it should be. I will give him a day off. Darcy nodded, satisfied with his generous gesture.

"You are most welcome to dine here this evening, but it will be a simple repast, possibly a cheese sandwich, as our cook is away and Mrs. Kraft has gone into the village."

"If your cook is away, who was responsible for that delicious dinner we had the other night?"

"My mother and Mrs. Kraft made the desserts. Jane, Mary, and I prepared the fruits and vegetables, Phillis and Lottie stood watch while the hams spun in the roasters, and Ezekiel grilled the trout in the summer kitchen. I can see you are surprised to learn the Bennet daughters perform tasks usually left to the help, so please allow me to explain.

"At my mother's insistence, everyone in this house must learn how to cook. But our efforts go beyond the kitchen and the parlor. We mend our own clothes, sew quilts, knit shawls, and tat lace. We gather eggs, milk cows, and groom our own animals. Of course, on many farms, this is not at all uncommon, but for those of us whose families have gained greater wealth, it is rare indeed. But there is a downside. Because I have less time than others, I do not net purses or paint tables. However, I can cook porridge and make a pumpkin pie, and my family will never go hungry."

"And you write," Darcy quickly added.

"Yes, I write." Lizzy briefly summarized the story she was working on. "Most of my stories are historical fiction about events that happened here in Westchester County during the war, but I also write non-fiction."

"I am currently reading a work of non-fiction that I found on Richard's bookshelf about Major André. I am sure you are familiar with him as he was captured right here in Tarrytown."

Lizzy chose not to share that she was the author of the André book. She would prefer to remain anonymous and hear his opinion on her efforts.

"Yes, I know a little something about the subject," Lizzy answered.

"Are you aware there was a great deal of resentment in England because the major was hung instead of being shot by a firing squad as was his due as an officer in the British Army?"

"Yes, I was aware of British resentment, but please allow me to disagree with your premise of what was *owed* to Major André. The major was *not* in uniform when he was captured and was using an assumed name, and spies, such as our own Nathan Hale, who had been hung in New York City a few years earlier, are usually not given the option of deciding how they are to be executed."

"Yes, but Alexander Hamilton, an aide to General Washington, argued on André's behalf, stating that he had planned to meet Arnold on neutral territory here in Westchester County and was lured behind enemy lines."

"You are correct in stating that Westchester County was *declared* to be neutral territory, but there were bitter battles fought here throughout the war between Loyalists and Patriots. Houses and churches were ransacked and goods stolen. The only reason Richard's house still stands is because it was used by the British to store grain," Lizzy said, her eyes ablaze. But then she paused. "This has the making of a quarrel, so we should change the subject."

"So the Bennets are a Renaissance family. Jane is a painter, Mary is a musician, and you are a writer," Darcy said, steering the conversation away from the topic of war.

"Yes, but in England, a lady would be expected to know all those things as well as learning to speak the modern languages. For a while, we did have a French tutor and spoke passable French, but Monsieur Alain resigned his position because of Lydia and Kitty. The problem was that he did not know how to maintain discipline in a classroom, and what child, knowing of such a weakness in a tutor, will not take advantage of the situation?"

"I must plead guilty as well, except the lesson being taught was German. I liked neither the subject nor the tutor, and I was very nearly sent home from Winchester College because of it. I was quite stubborn when I was young, and you do not look in the least bit surprised."

"Was stubbornness the reason for your broken nose?"

"Ah, you noticed my imperfection. It was not broken, but it did move a bit to the left," he said, reaching up to touch it. "No, I was defending a lady's reputation. Nonetheless, it was an unfortunate display of temper on my part, and it will not happen again." In order to change the subject, Darcy added, "I believe you mentioned something about a cheese sandwich."

"If you are not absolutely famished, I first need to check on my pony, Timber. He has not been feeling well of late, and nothing I do seems to help. I puree his food, and because he does not seem to shed, I brush him every day and work his muscles." The list of her ministrations went on and on.

"How old is he?"

"He is only twenty-six."

"*Only* twenty-six? Would you like me to have a look? I know my way around a stable."

As soon as Darcy saw Timber, he knew why Elizabeth's efforts were not working. The pony was in the advanced stages of old age, and because she loved the animal so much, she was blind to this natural progression.

Darcy ran his hand up and down Timber's muzzle before checking every inch of the equine as if he were a veterinarian. After he had finished, he put his head against Timber's forehead and rubbed him behind the ears. "You have had a good life, haven't you, boy?" Darcy said in a soft voice. "You have been given much love and care. You have no complaints."

When Darcy looked at Elizabeth, he saw tears welling up in her eyes. "Are you saying that he is dying?" she asked.

"I am saying that he is old. His teeth are worn down from nearly three decades of grinding his food. His eyesight is impaired, and he has lost muscle. As you said, he is not shedding. These are all signs of old age, and they cannot be reversed, no matter how much you would wish that it be otherwise. All that can be done is to keep him comfortable, and you are already doing that."

"But ponies can live to be more than thirty years old, and he was only a work horse for a dozen years and has been with us ever since." And Lizzy looked at Timber, and the tears flowed. After resting her head against her equine friend, she looked at Darcy and asked, "Do you not hug in England?"

"Of course we do," and Darcy took Lizzy into his arms. "I know exactly how you feel," he whispered. "I had to say goodbye to my favorite horse when he was only six. Caesar had broken his leg, and there was no help for it. And even though I knew I was doing the right thing by putting him down, it was of no comfort to me."

Lizzy stepped away from him and accepted his offered handkerchief. "Are you saying Timber will die soon?"

"Oh, I really can't say. He may live six months." Although he doubted it very much, he added, "possibly a year."

Mary, who loved Timber nearly as much as Lizzy, had come into the barn, followed by the spaniels, Goodness and Mercy, to find her sister and William standing only a foot apart and noticed that Lizzy had been crying. Having no idea what had precipitated such a scene, she tried to retrace her steps, but Lizzy called her over to the stall.

"I had come to check on Timber, and Mr. Darcy came with me. He tells me Timber will live at least another year, if not longer."

"Elizabeth…," Darcy said, trying to caution her against irrational optimism.

"Oh, that is very good news. Thank you for checking on

him, William." Seeing Lizzy's tear-stained cheeks, Mary offered to remain with the pony. "Why don't the two of you go for a walk and leave Timber to me. I shall feed him his supper and brush him."

"Thank you, Mary, but I think we shall go to the kitchen and have something to eat. With Mrs. Haas gone for the evening, Mr. Darcy is worried about his next meal."

"I am not embarrassed to admit I am hungry."

"Then let us go." And Lizzy led the way.

Chapter 12

As the two made their way back to the house, Darcy asked Elizabeth why she continued to call him Mr. Darcy. "Am I such an intimidating figure that you cannot bring yourself to use the more informal term of address?"

"I shall try to do better, *William*. But I must confess there is something in your countenance and in the way you stand apart that causes people to be a little bit afraid of you."

"But *you* are not afraid of me." Lizzy merely smiled.

The entry to the kitchen was by way of rear-entry steps that went to the cellar of the house. The beams of the wall housing the hearth were painted a bright blue which, Lizzy explained, was because the Dutch believed flies and other insects did not like that color. "I have no opinion on the matter," Lizzy responded to Darcy's quizzical expression, "but my father does believe the argument has some merit."

After hearing Elizabeth and Darcy's voices, Phillis and Lottie quickly came into the room from their quarters adjacent to the kitchen. But after fetching some buttermilk from the springhouse, they were dismissed for the evening, and Lizzy got to work. After putting on her apron, she stoked the fire in the huge hearth framed by Delft tiles depicting seascapes and scenes of rural Holland. When she was satisfied with the heat being generated, she sliced pieces of bread and cheese and placed them in a toaster. While the cheese grilled, she sliced apples and cucumbers, poured the buttermilk, and placed the plates and napkins on the table.

After unfolding her napkin, Lizzy held it up for Darcy to see. "This is my handiwork, and because you are a gentleman, you must admire it. But I shall tell you that Mary and Jane's handiwork is used in the dining room upstairs, while mine remains below stairs. That will give you an idea of my talent in that area. Now, eat up!"

Darcy bit into the sandwich, causing the melted cheese to ooze out it sides, and with his host's permission, he shed his coat and finished the sandwich.

"Excellent!" Darcy proclaimed. "It reminds me of my childhood at Pemberley. Of course, the cheese for our sandwiches was Stilton or Cheddar, and although they were quite good, this is even better. When I was a lad, the son of our steward and I would sneak down into the kitchen and pester the cook until she agreed to make us something to tide us over until supper. It was all a game. She would pretend to be annoyed, and we would swear an oath not to do it again."

"It seems you had a happy childhood."

"Yes, I did. I do not think I was denied anything until I was eight years old when I was sent to Winchester, where I was denied everything. When I was ten, Georgiana was born. That event occurred while I was at school, and I remember being very surprised as I did not know my mother was increasing. I believe she meant to tell me when I came home after the Michaelmas term, but Georgiana arrived early." But then Darcy stopped. "I apologize. I don't know what made me say that. Considering your country was founded by Puritans, I may have offended."

"I think you are confusing Puritans with Pilgrims. The Pilgrims came to the New World to start a new church, and a grim lot they were. On the other hand, the Puritans wished to purify the Church of England from within, and although they too frowned on people having too much fun, they were more lenient than you might expect. For example, have you heard of the practice of bundling? No? Well, allow me to explain.

"Puritans believed strongly in matrimony, and in order to ensure its success, a suitor would be allowed to sleep in the same bed as the girl he was wooing. However, they were bundled individually in a garment that was sewn shut, and a bundling board or pillow was placed between them. In that way, the couple could get to know each other before they wed, greatly increasing the chance of success for the marriage."

"They were put together in the same bed so that they might get to know each other!" a wide-eyed Darcy said. "I am sure they did."

"I will not say this arrangement was foolproof, but any bundle of joy resulting from the experiment would be welcomed into the family because, by that time, the couple would most definitely have married. Obviously, they got on."

Darcy burst out laughing. "Obviously. And here I thought Cromwell, the Protector, and his followers had no fun at all."

"I think you are correct in assuming that the ruler of your Commonwealth and his adherents were disciples of the 'all work and no play' philosophy, and there are many here in America who, to this day, think laughing on the Sabbath is a sin. But during the Colonial Era, bundling was widely practiced in New England, and the Dutch had a similar custom called "queesting, which means "searching after a wife," and was carried out in the same manner as bundling. But both customs have died out."

Although Darcy offered no opinion on the subject, he certainly had one.

When Darcy arrived at Richard's house, he was greeted by Joshua Lucas. He knew the reason for the young man's visit. He would shortly be leaving for West Point, and he wanted to know if Darcy would grant permission for Georgiana to attend the first ball of the season. Although Darcy liked the young Lucas, he was reluctant to encourage anything resembling a romance between an American and his seventeen-year-old sister.

"If a possible objection is the lack of a chaperone," Joshua began, "I will tell you that Jane and Elizabeth Bennet will also be attending as they go every year. Georgiana would stay with them at a hotel that has been reserved exclusively for this occasion for female guests of the academy. Because Jane and Elizabeth will be going, we shall travel on Mr. Bennet's sloop. The journey usually takes between eight to ten hours, but the accommodations aboard ship are quite good."

"Joshua, it is not that I object to my sister going to the ball or the length of the journey," Darcy explained, "but you must understand my position. In addition to being Georgiana's brother, I am also her guardian, so I often find myself acting in a role usually reserved for a parent. If I could come as well, I would readily agree to her going as it is something that should not be missed if at all possible. Of course, I would not attend the dance, but I must be nearby throughout the journey and during her time at West Point."

Joshua smiled. Even with restrictions, at least now he knew Miss Darcy would be allowed to attend the ball.

"I am presently serving as captain of the guards, and rank does have its privileges. I would be able to secure lodgings for you and, let us assume, Mr. Bingley. However, they will be primitive, something akin to spending the night in a hunting lodge."

"Which both Charles and I have done on many

occasions, including a particularly daunting experience while grouse hunting in Scotland. When a torrential rainstorm roared down the valley and caught us out in the open, we found refuge in a hearthless stone hut at the invitation of a shepherd who had never had a bath in his life. It occurred three years ago, and Charles and I still speak of it frequently—with much embellishment, of course." After hesitating for another few minutes, Darcy rendered his verdict. "Because you have addressed all of my concerns, I shall say 'yes,' as I am quite certain my sister is purchasing material for a ball gown as we speak."

After inviting Richard to join them, the three men settled down to an evening of cards with a large glass of hardy ale for each of the players.

"Joshua's father is currently serving in the assembly," Richard said, with his clay pipe clamped firmly between his teeth, "which is no small feat since the Lucas family has only been in Westchester County for two generations, and thus Mr. Lucas is regarded as a newcomer to the area. Also, he is not Scots or French or Dutch, but English, which can be a considerable handicap, especially when one is out canvassing for votes."

"That is true, but when you consider there is hardly a family in the lower Hudson Valley who has not enjoyed credit at Lucas Mercantile, you will understand my father's chances of being elected were quite good," Joshua said. "Of course, once he received the endorsement of Mr. Bennet and the tacit support of Mrs. Bennet, his election was assured. They are what pass for royalty in this part of the world, Mr. Darcy."

"I agree with that statement," Richard said. "Although Mr. Bennet's ancestors married into the DeLancey and Jay families, both prominent New York families, as far as I am concerned, it was Tom Bennet who plucked the finest fruit from the tree. Mrs. Bennet was the sole heir to a large fortune and thousands of acres near Albany. Although Tom came into a good deal of money when a lawsuit was settled in his favor that was not the case when Annie first met him.

"And the man is a genius. I am sure you know about his cast iron stoves," Richard said, pointing with his pipe in the direction of the one in front of his fireplace and then again to the rooms above. "But he also sells leather reclining Campeachy chairs that are used by those suffering from ailments of the lungs. I have one in my bedroom, and the darn thing is so comfortable I often fall asleep in it at night.

"As much as Tom enjoys a reputation as a man of business," Richard continued, "one of the most telling things about the gentleman is how he treats his daughters. And since Charles is away, I may tell you that Jane had an offer of marriage from a wealthy Schuyler cousin in Albany, but refused him, and Elizabeth discouraged Dirck Storm who lives at Storm Hall. I can assure you that both would have been excellent matches, but the parents accepted their daughters' decisions without protest."

"Because we are speaking of marriage," Joshua said, "I shall tell you that you are shortly to hear news that Charlotte is to be married to the Reverend Collins. I am happy for her because she is a kind and generous lady who deserves a home of her own, and Mr. Collins is a man who will greatly benefit from an association with so sensible a person."

Joshua rose to take his leave, and while shaking Darcy's hand, he thanked him for allowing his sister to join him at the academy ball. "I know that once my fellow cadets see the beautiful Miss Darcy I will be lucky if I am able to secure a second dance with her, but, oh, how I will crow after the ball."

Darcy assured the young man he was looking forward to the excursion as well and wondered if he had made his decision to allow Georgiana to attend the ball when he had learned that Elizabeth Bennet would be going as well.

Chapter 13

The day after Georgiana's return from her shopping expedition to the city, she called on Fitzwilliam. While she had been in New York, she had seen so much and was eager to share it with her brother. But the main reason she was walking to Mr. Richard's house at 8:00 in the morning was to find out if Fitzwilliam had spoken to Joshua Lucas about her going to West Point. As she approached the house, smells of cinnamon, apples, and pumpkin filled the air, and she found Mercer, Charles, Richard, and Fitzwilliam eating apple fritters and pumpkin cornmeal cakes.

Darcy knew why his sister had come. Tom Bennet's sloops made daily excursions to New York for the purpose of commerce, but they also carried the mail. In the short time Georgiana had been away, she had managed to dash off a letter to her brother asking if she might go to the ball at the military academy. It included a list of all the reasons why she should go, and only one reason why she should not: her brother's opposition.

After teasing her about her letter, Darcy told Georgiana that he knew why she had come. "Before leaving, you charged me with finding a place where we could ride, and I have done so. Dirck Storm has offered the use of his family's stables during our visit, and he said we should feel free to ride about the property. There is a bridle path that provides excellent views of the river. I reconnoitered just such a trail only yesterday."

What Darcy did not share with his sister was that the reason he had approached Dirck Storm had nothing to do with trails or river views. He wanted to get a good look at the man who thought he merited the attention of Elizabeth Bennet. Dirck was not tall nor did he have a broad chest. His smile was unexceptional, and his teeth merely passable. Although he had a firm handshake, Darcy's overall opinion was that, except for his wealth, there was nothing special to recommend him.

"But, Georgiana, you do not seem pleased," Darcy said, again teasing his sister. "Did I not do as you asked?"

Georgiana was most definitely not pleased, and her face showed it. There was a ball to be held at West Point, and Fitzwilliam spoke of riding and bridle paths!

"Excuse me, gentleman," Darcy said to Charles and Richard. "I think my sister has something on her mind," and the two of them climbed the stairs to the second floor.

"Oh, how you delight in vexing me," Georgiana said as she paced back and forth. Since the length of the room could be traversed in four strides, she resembled a colt unhappily confined to her stall. "You know exactly why I have come. William, will you not put an end to my misery and tell me of your decision?"

"So now it is 'William' and not 'Fitzwilliam?' I can see you are adapting to American ways. Shall I hear you refer to autumn as fall and biscuits as cookies? Or will you 'take the bull by the horns' and 'strike while the iron is hot'?"

But Georgiana's silence signaled that she was in no mood to discuss the differences in American and British English. After remembering just how young his sister was, Darcy thought he had teased her long enough. "I spoke to Joshua two days ago, and I have consented to your going to West Point as long as I go with you. Is that agreeable?"

"Oh, William, thank you. I thought you would say 'no.' But it is even better now that you are coming."

"But, Georgiana, I do have concerns. In our short time here in New York, I have watched you blossom, and it is just as I had hoped it would be. But you do understand that we must return to England. There will be no 'foreign entanglements' to use the late President Washington's words."

"Oh, now I understand your concerns. You are afraid I shall fall in love with Joshua Lucas and not want to go back home. But I can assure you that that is not the case at all. In the first place, Joshua plans to make the military his career, and he wishes to be posted to the frontier, the farther west the better. He believes there will come a time when the United States will span the width of the continent, and it is his hope that he will be posted to a fort on the Pacific coast. Can you picture me trudging across plains, crossing mountains, negotiating wild rivers, and God only knows what else? No, Joshua is a dear man, and once I return to England, it is my intention to correspond with him. However, I have no romantic feelings for him."

"And in the second place?" Darcy said, doubting the truth of her last statement.

"William, I am a selfish being," she said in a confessional tone. "Do not shake your head. In the short time I have been living with the Bennet family, I see how pampered and spoiled I am. The Bennet women are *never* idle. When they are not filling baskets for the poor of the parish, they are grating nutmeg, ginger, and cinnamon or shelling walnuts, and it is they who make the ginger beer. And when they are not in the kitchen, there is mending to be done, yarn to be rolled, or quilts to be made. While performing these tasks gives me a greater appreciation for what our servants do for us at Pemberley, I do not want to do them. I want my sugar to come in fine granules in a pretty sugar bowl, not in a cone to be nipped away at with nippers. And although I love America, and I *do* want to stay here as long as possible, I am an Englishwoman. So you can rest assured that I shall return to England without complaint, but with wonderful memories."

Darcy's relief was audible. Remembering his own first flirtation, he had been concerned his sister would take this first blush of love too seriously. From watching Joshua, he knew that the young man was besotted with his sister, but she had reassured him.

"Now that we have settled the matter of the military ball, tell me about your visit to New York."

Georgiana was all praise for everything she had seen, except for the pigs. "They are everywhere, mingling with the best society on an equal footing, and you must give way as nothing deters their progress, except for the dogs, who also roam wild." But other than the aggressive scavengers and excessive spitting, she compared New York, with its bustling streets and shops filled with goods of the finest quality, to London at its best. She spoke of visiting the milliner, the draper, the bookseller, and the jeweler, as well as going to warehouses near the docks that were filled to bursting with merchandise from every corner of the globe. "New Yorkers talk very loud, very fast, and all at the same time. It is quite comical to try to decipher what they are saying."

Georgiana continued to relate the wonders of New York. "First, we went to the Park Theater where we saw *The Tripolitan Prize* in which the American Navy fights North African pirates near Tripoli. To be honest, it was not very good. But the theater itself and the sets were gorgeous, and the ladies in the audience were dressed so beautifully and in the latest fashions from Paris. After the play had ended, we went next door to Dyde's Hotel to dine and were introduced to Mr. John Jacob Astor, a part owner of the theater and someone who many believe to be the richest man in America, but who has the most appalling table manners. It quite took my appetite away.

"And while visiting with Mr. Astor, we also met the author, Mr. Washington Irving, who refers to New York as Gotham, which he told me means 'goat's town' in Anglo-Saxon, and everyone is using the name as they find it to be quite amusing. He has written a book called *A History of New York from the Beginning of the World to the End of the Dutch Dynasty by Diedrich Knickerbocker*. But it is entirely made up, including Mr. Knickerbocker. Mrs. Bennet said these stories do nothing but ridicule her Dutch ancestors, turning them into buffoons instead of hard-working pioneers, and because of that, she *would not* speak to the author. But Mr. Bennet said for that very reason he *would* speak to the man because he had got it right. He is a terrible tease," Georgiana said, smiling.

"Mr. Bennet told me that in the city there is still some resentment against the British because there was a great fire during the occupation that razed much of the town. Because of the scale of the destruction, the British ousted people from their homes to quarter their officers, and those churches that were not Church of England were converted into prisons, barracks, or stables. However, most of the complaints of the native New Yorkers are now directed at Washington City because the War Hawks in Congress are determined to 'finish the Revolution.'"

"And where did you stay?" Darcy asked, ignoring all references to past or future wars.

"In an elegant townhouse, beautifully furnished. During the Revolution, the house was the scene of many grand parties attended by British General William Howe and his mistress, Mrs. Loring of Boston. Mrs. Sutton told me that there are some who believe the British lost the war because the general did not attack the rebels at Valley Forge as he was otherwise engaged with his mistress in Philadelphia. Can you imagine such a thing changing the course of history?"

"Georgiana, please! That is not a suitable subject for a young lady."

"Oh, William, do you really think I do not know about such things? Even though I am not out in society, I have friends whose older sisters are, and they share gossip with us. But, William, there is so much talk of war between England and America, it is impossible to avoid the subject. Mr. Bennet says I should have no fear that hostilities will commence any time soon as armies do not clash in winter, but he said that once spring arrives, anything can happen. I think I should become ill if we were to return to England only to learn the British are fighting against our friends in America."

"It saddens me as well, but these decisions will be made in Whitehall and Washington. So let us speak of other things. How did you spend all those coins I gave you?"

With the ball at West Point forefront in her mind, Georgiana had quickly parted with her money in buying fabric for a ball gown as well as ribbons and lace. She also purchased painted fans made in Spain, kid gloves, and two pairs of dance slippers. But she had not thought only of herself. "I bought something for you in a bookstore that will greatly surprise you, and I shall give it to you when you come to visit me at Longbourn. But I have something else as well." After reaching into her pocket, she pulled out a carved ivory hair clip. "It is for Elizabeth. Although she needs little decoration because she is so beautiful, I thought it would look pretty in her dark hair."

"That was very kind of you, Georgiana. But do you really think Elizabeth is beautiful? What I mean is that whenever someone speaks of a beautiful Bennet daughter, they are almost always referring to Jane Bennet."

"I agree that Jane is very pretty, but in a more common way. I know this sounds contradictory, but because her face lacks symmetry, it adds interest. And her eyes! They are luminous and reflect what she is feeling. Mrs. Bennet said of her daughter, 'Poor Elizabeth. She could never get away with anything when she was a child because her eyes always betrayed her, and when and if she marries, her husband will never have to guess at what she is thinking.'"

Darcy thought of Elizabeth's dark eyes that drew you in like a black hole in a night sky. *When the lady marries, her husband will be the luckiest of men.* But he chose to keep that comment to himself.

Chapter 14

Everyone in the house knew when Mr. and Mrs. MacTavish had returned to Longbourn because Goodness and Mercy were scratching at the front door demanding to be let out. From their perch in Mary's window, the dogs had seen a wagon carrying Hannah and Samuel and their four sons coming down the road. Because Hannah saved kitchen scraps for them, Mrs. MacTavish was second only to Mary in the spaniels' affections, and with the canine claxon sounding, the house soon emptied of all Bennets who had come outside to welcome their friends home.

Unlike Samuel, who was part Mohawk, Scots-Irish, and French, his wife, Hannah Monpuy, was a full-blooded Mohican. While Samuel looked and dressed like all the farmers of the lower Hudson Valley, the copper-skinned Hannah wore her long black hair in two braids that cascaded over her ample bosom. She was also more traditionally dressed, with her bright red skirt, beaded blouse, hoop earrings, and an ample waist encircled by a belt of stamped silver links and oyster shells.

News from the state capital was eagerly anticipated, and they were not disappointed. The building of a canal between Albany and Lake Erie was the hot topic. Those in favor of the enterprise saw dollar signs everywhere, but for the skeptics, it was referred to as "the big ditch." Tom Bennet belonged to the former group. He understood that if the engineering issues could be solved, it would be a boon to every town between New York City and the western terminus of the canal. Additionally, it would open the newly-settled lands of the American interior to commerce, and new towns would sprout up along its route like newly planted corn. Of course, residents living in the cold climes of New York State and the Midwest would need to heat their houses, and shipments of Tom Bennet's cast iron stoves would naturally follow.

After sharing their news, the MacTavishes were informed of the arrival of three visitors from England. Despite Jane's efforts to speak of Charles as if he were no different than any other young man of her acquaintance, Hannah was soon on to her, and Jane abandoned any pretense that she did not have feelings for Charles Bingley.

"I do like him very much," Jane admitted. "During our time together in the city, we fell into such easy conversation, and while we were walking along the Battery, his looks seemed to imply an interest that went beyond friendship."

Georgiana Darcy was also discussed, and all agreed that she was a sweet girl, delightful company, and a considerate guest. That left Mr. Darcy, and although Mrs. Bennet spoke very highly of him, she admitted he was a bit of a cipher.

"I think William suffers in comparison with his friend's openness. However, the longer I know him, the more I like him as he has a wry sense of humor that reminds me of Mr. Bennet's, although he talks a good deal less than Tom. But doesn't everyone?" Mrs. Bennet put her finger to her lips. "I hear Kitty and Lydia. I assume that means they have been successful in having Georgiana join us."

Since her arrival in Tarrytown, Georgiana had heard stories about Hannah and Samuel MacTavish and their children. The MacTavishes were responsible for the upkeep of Longbourn Manor, its demesne and outbuildings, as well as the gardens. But in all that time, no one had thought to mention that Hannah was an Indian with skin the color of a copper coin and eyes so exotic as to make one think of far-off Cathay. After introductions were made, Georgiana apologized for staring. "I have never met a red man, or I should say, a red woman before. Oh, that is probably wrong, too."

"You need not apologize," Hannah said, and she took Georgiana's hand in hers. "Although I am red on the outside, on the inside, there is no difference at all," she said, pointing to her heart. "I am glad to meet you, and I am especially glad to be back at Longbourn. For a month, I have been forced to live a life of idleness, and I am ready to get back to work. And Samuel is eager to get out into the gardens." This remark caused everyone to look around for Mr. MacTavish, but they found that both Mr. Bennet and he had slipped away. They could be seen in the distance walking toward Longbourn's vegetable gardens.

* * *

With the MacTavishes's return, everyone had more time for leisure, and the most desirable activity for Lizzy and the visitors from England was to go for long rides on horseback. Although Jane was a competent rider, she took little pleasure in such outings, preferring to spend her free time at her easel, but with Charles going, she was not about to be left behind.

The party arrived at the Storm residence in a wagon driven by Lizzy who had refused all offers by Charles and William to take the reins.

"Gentlemen, when you are all safely aboard a ship bound for Liverpool, I will be driving about the farm without assistance from any man."

With Darcy sitting beside her in the front seat, she snapped the reins and eased the wagon onto the road.

As soon as Dirck saw that Lizzy was amongst the party,

he decided he would join them, and Darcy's pursed lips signaled his thoughts on the addition to their group.

Although it was a cloudy day, the temperature was perfect for a ride along a bridle path paralleling the Hudson. Little was said because the riders were busy watching the traffic on the river, including the *North River* steamboat on its way to Albany, and they were treated to the sound of its whistle as it passed Tarrytown harbor.

"In a short time, we shall all be on a sloop going to West Point," Lizzy said. "I can hardly wait as there are so many delightful sights to be seen along the river."

Darcy, too, was eager for the trip to the military academy. It was the part about being on a ship for hours at a time that was a cause for concern. Hopefully, negotiating a river would be easier on his stomach than a vast ocean with its waves and swells and dipping and heaving. *I just hope I don't embarrass myself again*, Darcy thought.

"I was recently on Breakneck Ridge climbing Anthony's Nose," Dirck said to Lizzy.

Lizzy explained to William that Pierre Van Cortlandt, who owned the mountain, named the promontory for Sea Captain Anthony Hogan, who had a nose to rival that of Cyrano de Bergerac's. "Captain Hogan must have required the use of a long spoon or a short oar whenever he ate his soup."

"I shall look for Antony's Nose during *our* journey to West Point," Darcy answered Elizabeth while actually directing his remark to Dirck. Although he certainly appreciated the use of his family's stables, Darcy would have preferred if Dirck had remained behind at Storm Hall. His attention to Elizabeth was proving to be an annoyance.

The party stopped for a light lunch prepared by Mrs. MacTavish, and after they had finished, all agreed a walk along the river would be most agreeable. Because of the narrowness of the path, it was possible for only two to walk in tandem, and Dirck agreed to accompany Miss Darcy. After Lizzy assured Darcy that Dirck was a perfect gentleman, her brother agreed to the arrangement, and Lizzy and Darcy made their way through a narrow path until they came to a clearing with a glorious view of the Hudson. Darcy had already developed a deep fondness for the river. One of his greatest pleasures was watching the storms that frequently arose in the afternoon on the far side of the Hudson with lightning striking distant mountaintops and the roar of thunder cascading down the valleys.

At Lizzy's request, Darcy spoke at length about London, and it was only after he had finished waxing eloquent about the largest city in Christendom that Lizzy revealed she had visited England three years earlier and had spent three weeks in London.

"Why did you not say? You have twice allowed me to go on and on about a place you have visited."

"But it was from the point of view of a native, and you spoke so eloquently of a place you love."

"But I do not care to talk about what *I* have seen. My interest is in what *you* have seen."

Lizzy mentioned watching a balloon launch, witnessing spectacular fireworks, and viewing tightrope walkers at Vauxhall Gardens. "We also attended a production of *A School for Scandal* at Drury Lane and visited the British Museum, where a colossal bust of Ramses II was on display, quite the biggest man-made thing I have ever seen."

"Kitty and Lydia, who were only ten years old at the time, greatly enjoyed the Exeter Exchange as we saw all types of exotic animals, including lions, tigers, and camels, and when we went into the street, we had some excitement. The lion, after giving a great roar, had frightened a horse pulling a hackney, and it took off down the street. We learned that no one was injured. Nonetheless, we decided to walk a fair distance before hailing a cab.

"We also went to the Bond Street Bazaar, and I purchased a Chinese porcelain tea set for my hope chest. Jane requested we visit the exhibitions of Mr. Romney and Mr. Lawrence. From the many portraits on display, it was obvious Mr. Romney was quite taken with Mrs. Emma Hamilton as we saw four different paintings of her, including one in which she posed as a bacchante for her famous attitudes."

Darcy wondered if Elizabeth knew that Mrs. Hamilton had been the mistress of Admiral Horatio Nelson, and although he suspected she did, and despite the fact that she had spoken freely of the custom of bundling, *he* could not bring up the subject.

"For Mary, the highlight of our time in London was attending a concert in Ranelegh Gardens in which we were treated to an eloquent performance by an Italian soprano."

"So Kitty and Lydia liked the animals at the Exeter Exchange, Jane enjoyed the shops and galleries, and Mary savored her time at Ranelegh. But what pleased Elizabeth?"

Without hesitation, Elizabeth answered: "The Tower of London."

"Well, I doubt you were impressed by the menagerie as you had seen the Exeter Exchange, so was it the ravens and beefeaters or were you intrigued by the place where two of Henry VIII's wives spent their final days, along with countless others who had earned the wrath of that ill-tempered king?"

"Neither. I wanted to see Traitors' Gate where Princess Elizabeth professed to her warders: 'I pray you all bear me witness that I come as no traitor but as true a woman to the Queen's Majesty as any as is now living.' She was only one and twenty, exactly my age, when she uttered those words. I greatly admire her courage. She was truly a prince worthy of her people."

Darcy should not have been surprised by her choice.

She quoted Thomas Jefferson from memory, lauded Benjamin Franklin as an inventor and statesman, and from Georgiana, he knew that a print of *The Apotheosis of George Washington* hung over Elizabeth's desk similar to the one over Richard Bingley's fireplace. He could easily understand why one of England's greatest sovereigns would earn her admiration.

"If you promise not to repeat my words, especially to your father, I shall tell you that I consider Elizabeth to be our last great monarch." Because William had admitted such a thing, Lizzy rewarded him with her silence.

"Well, tell me what else you did whilst in England?"

"Most of our time was spent in Hertfordshire at Longbourn with our Bennet cousins. Our Grandpa Bennet, who helped raise my father, said that he wished to see the place of his birth one last time before he died, and Mama was able to convince Papa to take all of us to England. My mother described Grandpa Bennet as a cantankerous, cranky, crusty old curmudgeon; even so, she adored him. As the time for our departure neared, Grandpa informed my parents that he would not be returning to America because he was going to die in England, a statement my father dismissed as utter nonsense. However, Mama suggested that we delay our departure date and visit Bath. One evening, shortly after supper, Grandpa stood up and announced, 'I am tired of all this. I am going to bed.' When a servant went to call him for breakfast, he was dead!"

"My goodness! He had predicted his own death."

"Yes, but my father always said his grandfather would go to great lengths to prove he was right," a comment that elicited a laugh from Darcy. "So back we went to Hertfordshire for the funeral, and after the solemnities had concluded, booked passage to New York."

Elizabeth and Darcy were joined by the others, and the riders soon left the narrow bridle path for the wide open spaces of the Storm estate. Darcy was impressed and pleased by Elizabeth's equestrian skills as she rode with confidence and innate ability to sense the capabilities of her mount. For a brief moment, a vision of Elizabeth riding on one of Pemberley's fillies appeared before him, but he quickly pushed it out of his mind. He was still dealing with the effects of holding her in his arms when they had been together in the barn. Although he had held her like a brother would a sister, that night, and each succeeding night, had been pure torment for him. Whether he was awake or asleep, he imagined the two of them together making love—repeatedly and with great passion. The only thing that could replace such thoughts was the idea of biting into a slice of her mother's apple pie.

Chapter 15

Once the wheat and oats were picked and the orchards stripped of their fruit, social events of every stripe increased. There were teas, quilting parties, dinners, dances, and frolics. At an afternoon lawn party at the Van Tassel estate, Lizzy soon found herself wearing a blindfold and playing a game of blind man's bluff. Because of the wide expanse of the lawn, it had taken Lizzy several minutes to find someone. When she did, the field immediately narrowed to three. Because of the height of the gentleman, it could only be Jamie Martling, Tad Van Tassel, or William Darcy, and she hoped it was the last.

First, Lizzy took one of his hands in hers and declared him to be a gentleman. "This one does not work," she said to everyone's amusement. Then she felt his broad shoulders, "but he might be a boxer as he is strong." Finally, she placed her hands on his cheeks, and feeling a little bristling, declared that it could not be thirteen-year old Thomas Van Wart. Instead, it must be his older brother, Peter, who was sixteen. Everyone gave a roar when she made her declaration. After removing the blindfold from her face, she said, "Oh, it is you, William. You must not know how to play the game as you were so easily found."

Darcy leaned over and whispered that it had been his intention to be found, a statement he immediately regretted as it sounded very much like flirting, which it was, because he *did* want to flirt with Elizabeth. *Why does Elizabeth have to be an American? If this were England, I would be suggesting long walks in a garden so that I might steal a kiss.*

To add to his frustration, Dirck Storm had joined them. Had the man never heard that "two's company; three's a crowd?" and Darcy imagined him stranded and alone on Anthony's Nose.

In addition to the social gatherings, there was at least one betrothal to celebrate. Charlotte Lucas and William Collins had become engaged with a wedding to take place in the spring. Because Charlotte's parents were visiting the newly married James Fenimore Cooper and his bride, Susan DeLancey, in Otsego, with an introduction provided by her cousin, Tom Bennet, they would be unable to attend their daughter's wedding and shared their good wishes by post. With Charlotte's parents absent, it was quickly decided that a celebration of their engagement would be hosted by the Bennet family.

By 5:00, the wagons and carriages were already turning into Longbourn's drive where they were met by Ezekiel Wesley and the four MacTavish sons. Upon entering the house, they were greeted by Mr. and Mrs. Bennet and the engaged couple. As expected, Mr. Collins was effusive in his praise of his future wife, and although Charlotte was frugal with her accolades for the parson, everyone agreed there was real affection between them. But Lizzy needed to be reassured that her friend was not trading the drudgery of the store for the very challenging role of wife of a minister. There were many who speculated that it was the onerous duties of a minister's wife that had caused Mrs. Jemima Smith, the pastor of the Old Dutch Church, to go off her rocker.

Sensing her friend's unease, Charlotte pulled Lizzy into a recess under the stairs. "When you have had time to think it over, I hope you will be satisfied with what I have done. I am not romantic, you know. I never was. I ask only a comfortable home, and considering Mr. Collins's character and situation in life, I am convinced my chance of happiness with him is as fair as most people can boast upon entering the marriage state." Lizzy remained skeptical. "Lizzy, he is a kind man, and I like him very much."

Further assurances were impossible as Mr. Collins had ferreted them out. "Oh, there you are, my dearest Charlotte. Miss Elizabeth, you see before you the happiest of men." Turning his gaze upon his betrothed, he looked at her in such a manner that made Lizzy's stomach lurch. "Is she not the most beautiful of women?" a comment which drew a request from Charlotte that he refrain from making such pronouncements in public, a promise he broke within minutes.

Because of the popularity of the English visitors, Jane had little time with Charles, and Lizzy, but a moment with William. But in that moment, he had managed to ask her for the first dance, if there was to be a dance, and if not, could they at least have dessert together?

"I can assure you there will be dancing as we need much less of an excuse than an engagement to kick up our heels. As for dessert, you really must try something other than apple pie." Darcy shook his head. "My mother also makes the best pumpkin pie in the county, with the possible exception of Mrs. Haas," she whispered, "but please do not tell Mama I said that."

"Pumpkin pie? I am not sure I would like it. On the hand, I am very sure about your mother's apple pie." But that was the last word he uttered before being whisked away by Katrina Van Wart, who insisted that only Mr. Darcy could settle a dispute regarding a certain park in London.

Before the dancing could begin, Mr. Bennet proposed a toast for the happy couple, and knives and forks were tapped against the glasses to get everyone's attention. After the clinking had ceased, the guests anticipated that their host would make the toast. But Mr. Bennet said he must defer to someone who knew Mr. Collins longer than he did, and he asked Mr. Darcy to assume his place on the stairs of the entryway so that everyone might hear his pronouncement.

After scanning the room for a sympathetic face, all Darcy found were smirks and smiles from amongst those gathered, and a look of absolute glee on the faces of Tom Bennet, Charles Bingley, and Elizabeth.

"Thank you, Mr. Bennet, for this honor," Darcy began. "It is true that I was acquainted with Mr. Collins in England, but please allow me to begin this toast by saying something about Miss Lucas. Although our acquaintance may be measured in weeks, it only took one meeting for me to recognize her value. You all know her to be a good and obedient daughter, much loved sister and friend, a devout Christian, and an honest merchant, which is a rare find on either side of the ocean," and because everyone laughed, Darcy was encouraged to continue, "and I would be proud to call her friend.

"Such a lady deserves a good husband, and she has found one. I only know Mr. Collins in his capacity as an ordained minister, but as such, I know that he is admired by his congregation and neighbors and performs acts of charity within the community with a generous spirit. But probably his best trait is his ability to find an excellent wife." Again, his speech was met with laughter and nods of approval.

"But before we join in toasting the happy couple, may I take this opportunity to say something on my own behalf? When I made the decision to come to America, I had no idea what I would find or how seasick I would be." After the roar of laughter had subsided, Darcy continued, "Because we have so much in common, people in England speak of Americans as either 'our cousins' or 'damn Yankees,'" and the crowd broke into cheers, "and that is how I thought of you as well. But now that I have lived in your midst for several weeks, I think of you as my friends. Charles Bingley, my sister, and I have been warmly welcomed into your homes and have been invited to join in your celebrations, and for this, we thank you. However, no one in this room needs to be told that Britain and America have a troubled relationship with thorny problems to be resolved, and I am sorry to say that there are dark clouds on the horizon. I can only hope our leaders will find a peaceful solution to the issues that divide us. But I can say that no matter what is decided in Congress or in Parliament, nothing will affect the deep regard I have for you.

"Now, let us return to the reason why we have gathered here this evening. Please raise a glass in celebration of the union of Miss Charlotte Lucas and Mr. William Collins."

After shaking numerous hands, he finally worked his way back to Elizabeth's side. "Was it all right? Too long? Did I sound foolish?"

"William, it was truly lovely, and I will be happy to eat apple pie with you any time."

* * *

Lizzy enjoyed the fall season more than any other. There were berries to be picked, and orange, yellow, and red leaves to be pressed into books. Cooler temperatures meant long walks and picnics. But in the Bennet family, the arrival of fall commenced on October 3, the day of liberation for the Dutch from Spanish rule and celebrated by Hollanders everywhere. When the liberators of a besieged Leyden had entered the city in 1574, they brought with them herring and white bread to feed the starving population. But there was also a miracle to be found outside the city walls: scores of cooking pots containing stew left behind by the fleeing Spaniards, which was why William, Charles, and Georgiana found themselves eating herring, white bread, and mutton stew brimming with carrots, onions, and potatoes in the Bennet dining room.

Leyden's liberation was quickly followed by a corn-husking frolic. The visitors from England were warned that husking corn was a dirty business and to dress accordingly as most of the evening would be spent sitting in a barn on straw bales.

"A frolic is merely an excuse to have young people come together," Mrs. Bennet explained to Georgiana, William, and Charles. "The price of admission is your willingness to shuck corn, and one lucky young man, who finds a red ear of corn, will be rewarded with a kiss from the lady of his choice."

Although Georgiana would not have minded being kissed by Joshua Lucas, it would be a real challenge to accept even a long-armed handshake from some of the young men in the community who seemed to be strangers to a water pitcher and basin. Mrs. Bennet knew exactly what Georgiana was thinking. "If the girl does not wish to be kissed, then she holds out a withered ear of corn, and the man must accept her decision."

"When I was a lad," Mr. Bennet said, "I carried a red ear of corn in my pocket in case of an emergency. Charles, I would advise you to do the same," and he winked at Jane.

But it wasn't Bingley who found the red ear, but Darcy. Suspecting it was no accident, he pretended to be all nerves at having to choose "from amongst so many beautiful ladies." In her eagerness to be kissed, Katrina Van Wart fell off a hay bale and went ass over tea kettle. But Darcy did not see how he could possibly benefit by singling out any lady and handed the red ear to Bingley and was roundly booed for his trouble. However, good cheer was restored when Charles handed the ear to Jane Bennet, and he was allowed to claim his kiss on the cheek.

Darcy knew that if the crowd had insisted that he choose

a lady, it would have been Elizabeth Bennet, and he wondered if he had erred in passing up such an opportunity as he might never have another. But within the week, everything changed.

Chapter 16

Caroline Bingley studied herself in the mirror and was pleased with what she saw. Esther, Amanda Beekman's maid, was unmatched in her ability to do hair, and this time was no exception. For the evening's gala that was to be held here at Storm Hall, she had decided to wear her blonde tresses up with only a few curls gracing her beautiful neck, and if any admirers had been at risk of missing her sapphire blue eyes, the carefully placed curls around her face would draw them in.

"I still do not understand why you are making such a fuss," Amanda told her friend. "Why have you chosen your best dress and your mother's pearl necklace? Why was it necessary for us to go to the city to buy accoutrements when you have drawers full of shawls and purses and gloves? Except for your cousin Charles, it is the same old crowd—unless there is something you have not told me." Caroline, who was busy admiring her dress in the mirror from every angle, said nothing. "I remember you saying that you had no interest in Charles Bingley or have you changed your mind about him?"

"Charles Bingley?" Caroline tut-tutted. "He is a boy."

"Caroline, I know you are up to something," Amanda said, continuing to probe. "So if you do not answer me, I shall pull out all of your hairpins, and you will have to begin again."

"It is not necessary to be so dramatic, Amanda. If you

calm yourself, I shall tell you," Caroline said, finally giving in to her friend's persistence. "Charles was accompanied by another gentleman, Fitzwilliam Darcy of Pemberley in Derbyshire, a member of the landed gentry and the grandson of an earl."

"A grandson? Who cares about a grandson? You told me that while you were in England the son and *heir* of an earl was interested in you, but you passed him by."

"It is true Lord Corman was interested in me, excessively so, but he was tedious, homely, bore the scars of smallpox, and was constantly inebriated. Mr. Darcy is all that a gentleman should be and more. He is also a member of the Norman aristocracy, and there are few in England who can make such a claim."

"If he is such a catch, then why did you not secure his affections while you were in England?"

Caroline, who had been using her fan to practice different poses, snapped it shut. "Because there was a misunderstanding between us that I intend to clear up, and in doing so, that will clear the way for other things."

"Marriage?"

"Amanda, you know I always play to win, and in this case, the prize is Mr. Darcy. Does that answer your question?"

* * *

Lizzy could hardly believe the fuss she was making about the Storms' ball. Granted, it was the premier event of the season. Everyone always wanted to look their best because the family had the largest ballroom in the lower Hudson Valley, and there would be a crush of couples on the floor dancing jigs and reels until the wee hours of the morning. The house would be decorated with multi-colored gourds and carved pumpkins, and garlands of brightly colored leaves would be draped across the buffet tables. Everyone would step lively to tunes played by the finest musicians from New York City, and the quality and quantity of food would be discussed for weeks.

"Lizzy, I do not think I have ever seen you look lovelier," Jane said after watching her sister fuss and fidget with her curls.

But Lizzy was not satisfied. "Why is it that I am the only one in this family with curly hair?" To demonstrate what she considered to be a defect, she pulled on a corkscrew side curl and watched as it sprung back into place.

"You know how we all envy you your curls."

"But not tonight. With such high humidity, my curls will explode, and I shall look either like Medusa or a mad woman."

"But, Lizzy, this is so unlike you. Is there a *particular* reason why you are spending so much time at your toilette?"

Lizzy was rescued from answering the question by their mother. Despite her age and having given birth to five children, Mrs. Bennet was still an attractive woman, and her daughters commented on how nice she looked in her dark green dress. But she dismissed their compliments, insisting that she was looking at the belles of the ball.

"Has Lydia stopped crying?" Lizzy asked.

"No, and she will not until she reaches her fifteenth birthday and may go to the Storm gala. She does not understand that it is one thing to attend a festival dance and quite another to go to a fancy ball. Besides, the dance floor will be crowded as it is. Her time and Kitty's time will come soon enough, but you cannot tell that to a thirteen-year-old girl."

"And how does Georgiana get on?" Jane asked.

"Well, I think she is realizing the importance of a lady's

maid. Our young friend could use the services of… What is the name of the girl who attends Amanda Beekman?"

"Do you mean Esther, their slave?"

"Yes, that is who I was thinking about."

"But you would never own a slave!" Jane said aghast.

"Of course not. I was not thinking of her in particular, but of someone with her talents." An image of Esther, an intelligent and kind woman, appeared before Mrs. Bennet, and she shook her head in regret at the thought of this child of God being bound to a life of servitude. "Oh how I wish the Storms would free her. They certainly can afford to pay for her services."

Although the New York Legislature had passed an act for the gradual emancipation of its slave population in 1799, slaves who were already in servitude before that year, including Esther, remained slaves for life unless they had the money to purchase their freedom from a consenting master or someone purchased it for them.

"They *should* free her. It reflects poorly on the family," Jane said. "Few people in this part of the valley still own slaves."

Despite Jane's assertion, Mrs. Bennet could think of a dozen families who owned at least a handful of slaves, including the Van Cortlandts and Beekmans.

"Well, he who is without sin…," Mrs. Bennet said with a sigh. Her family had held slaves for generations, and her own nursemaid had been one. "…so let us not cast stones."

The Storm mansion was half again the size of Longbourn and with three times the acreage. At the end of the Revolution, Loyalists had suffered the confiscation of their properties. When the property of the Loyalist, Frederick Philipse III, had been sold off to multiple bidders, the Storms had bought out every farmer who was willing to sell, making the family one of the largest land owners in the lower Hudson Valley.

The interior of the house was as impressive as its classical exterior. The furniture was French and upholstered. Bohemian chandeliers and cut glass candelabras lit the public rooms, their light reflected in six Florentine mirrors. The staircase was grand, and the entryway paved with real Italian marble, not painted canvas.

Mr. Storm was accompanied by his second wife, Sarah Van Rensselaer, a cousin to his dearly departed wife, but who was half her age and only eight years older than Dirck.

Dirck, who had been in love with Elizabeth since they had played hoops together in their youth on the lawn of Storm Hall, was waiting for her at the door. "At last, the beautiful Bennet sisters," Dirck said, and he kissed the hands of Elizabeth, Jane, and Mary, "and their even prettier mother," he said, bowing. "And Miss Darcy, how good it is to see you again. Have you come to break our Colonial hearts?"

Georgiana blushed and shook her head and stepped aside to reveal her brother.

"Your brother does not intimidate me, Miss Darcy. If he chooses to accompany someone as beautiful as you, he must be prepared to hear such compliments. But let me not detain you as there are gentlemen already here who have indicated that they wish to dance with you. In fact, Tad Van Tassel has been pacing since his arrival, and here he comes."

After indicating that William, Charles, and Georgiana should go into the ballroom, Dirck gestured for Jane and Elizabeth to follow him, leaving additional salutations to his father and his wife.

"I have a surprise for you." Both girls smiled in expectation of what Dirck had to share. "But it is not a good surprise. I have been meaning to tell you about it all week, but I did not know how to go about it."

"Well, what it is it?" an impatient Lizzy asked, but the answer, in an exquisite sky-blue gown, was making her way down the stairs to the oohs and aahs of everyone. Caroline Bingley had arrived.

* * *

"Before coming to Storm Hall, Caroline first went to New York to visit the shops," Dirck informed the Bennet sisters. "While she was in town, she spent most of her time having a dress made so that she might make a grand entrance. You must admit she has succeeded."

Dirck had a long history with Caroline—most of it unpleasant. It had all started a decade earlier when Amanda Beekman's parents had been lost at sea during an Atlantic hurricane while returning from the West Indies. The child had become the ward of Dirck's father, but as a widower, with a house full of sons, Mr. Storm did not know how to care for a grieving ten-year-old girl, and so he had asked Richard Bingley if Caroline and Louisa might stay with them for a while. Richard, who spent most of his time during the week in the city seeing to the Bingley business interests, readily agreed. But over time, Louisa and Caroline came to call Storm Hall home.

The relationship that had developed between Caroline and Dirck consisted of Caroline pretending to regard him with sisterly affection while Dirck avoided her whenever possible as he considered her to be the most selfish person he had ever met. He particularly hated the digs she took at Lizzy.

"Do you think she is after Charles?" Jane asked with real concern in her voice.

"No, she is after bigger fish. She wants Mr. Darcy."

"Mr. Darcy!" Lizzy said surprised. "But if she wanted that gentleman, why did she return from England?"

"I wish I could tell you, but I have been sworn to

secrecy by my confidante."

"Oh, balderdash! You know we will not repeat anything you say," Lizzy said, pressing the young man.

"Lizzy, we should not ask. Mama would not approve."

"Then step away, Jane, as I mean to hear what Dirck has to say."

Instead of leaving, Jane drew closer and listened as Dirck revealed that his source was Louisa Bingley Hurst who had told him why Caroline had returned to America.

"Louisa, you say? Yes, I know, sisters. Two peas in a pod and all that," Dirck began. "But being new to London society is difficult enough without having your golden-haired sister hogging all the attention of the young men. And you know how women are. If the men like you, the ladies do not, and they were punishing Louisa because of Caroline. After Caroline's return, Louisa wrote to me to complain that while she was in London, her sister had been flirting with every unmarried man of wealth or rank and that these chaps were following her around like trained puppies."

"Surely, not Mr. Darcy. A trained puppy? I do not see that at all," Lizzy said.

"No, he was the exception, and that is why she wanted him. For a time, it seemed as if she would have him as they most definitely had a romance. So whatever came between Darcy and Caroline must have been serious or she would not have come back to New York where none but us yokels live."

"But why *did* she come back?" Jane asked.

"Apparently, Louisa's letter to her father did the trick, and Richard sent for her. Even so, Caroline pleaded with Louisa that she be allowed to live with her. But it was clearly stated in the letter that Richard could not continue to support two daughters living abroad, and that is the truth.

The embargo nearly wiped Richard out, and his finances are just now recovering."

"But why is Richard supporting Louisa and her husband in the first place?" Jane asked. "I thought she had married a man of wealth and one who owned lots of property."

"Mr. Hurst does have a lot of property, but no hard cash. It is a disease of the British upper class. Now, you will have to forgive me as I must see to the guests as my father has sent for his Campeachy chair. But before I leave, I insist upon a dance with both of you, and, Jane, I do not care what Charles Bingley thinks about that."

After Dirck left, Jane turned to Lizzy, "Mr. Darcy and Caroline. Surely not?"

"What can I say, Jane? Who would know better than Louisa? After all, she was there."

* * *

Instead of joining the dancers in the ballroom, Lizzy went into the dining room where the older and heftier guests were gathered around the buffet tables and their bounty. Even though she would have preferred to dance, she did not want to see every eligible bachelor in the county paying court to Queen Caroline Bingley. But she was to pay a penalty for trying to avoid such a scene. She now had to dance with Mr. Collins who had encountered her in the dining room.

Lizzy did not understand why a man who danced so poorly would choose to exhibit in front of his neighbors, many of whom were members of his congregation. It seemed as if Mr. Collins was incapable of being embarrassed, and Lizzy wished she possessed the same immunity. The only saving grace was that because the attention of so many of the guests was fixed upon Caroline, there were few to witness the spectacle.

Despite the admiring throng, like Moses parting the Red Sea, Miss Bingley made way for one particular gentleman:

Fitzwilliam Darcy. After accepting her extended hand, he led her to the dance floor, and as Lizzy watched them dance, there was no doubt in her mind that there was more than one reason why Mr. Darcy had come to America.

Chapter 17

As soon as the dance had ended, Lizzy made good her escape and went outside, only to find the portico and drive crowded with smoke-enshrouded politicos engaged in vigorous debate about a possible war with Britain. The men had gathered around the former mayor of New York City, who had recently returned from the nation's capital. Jacob Radcliff spoke with authority of an "imminent and inevitable war" with Great Britain. But Lizzy had no stomach for such talk. As she turned to go back inside, she found her way blocked by William Darcy.

"Ah, there you are, Elizabeth. I have been looking for you. Have you forgotten that you promised me the third dance?"

"Excuse me?" an unsettled Lizzy asked.

"The third dance," Darcy repeated. "On Sunday, after services, you promised me the third dance. Or are you committed to dancing with Mr. Storm?"

"Mr. Storm?" Lizzy was so unnerved by the sight of William and Caroline dancing that the only one she could think of was the elder Mr. Storm. "Mr. Storm no longer dances. He suffers from an old war wound."

"You misunderstand me. Are you engaged for the next set with *Dirck* Storm? It is obvious that he admires you greatly as he practically dragged you away as soon as you came in the door."

"No, Dirck and I are engaged for the last set as he has

responsibilities as the son of the host."

"Was that what you were discussing earlier under the stairwell? His responsibilities as host?"

So William had noticed my conversation with Dirck. Now, that's interesting.

"Elizabeth, why do you not answer? Are you feeling unwell? If you are not, we may forego the next dance, and instead we can go into the dining room and have a slice of apple pie."

Lizzy burst out laughing in that infectious laugh Darcy loved. "Sir, you are the first person to suggest pie as a remedy. A glass of wine is usually offered. But it is not necessary as I am fine. It was very crowded in there, and I needed a breath of fresh air." Lizzy started to laugh once again. "A slice of pie, William! In England, is it the custom to eat dessert before you have your main meal?"

"In England, I rarely have what we call 'the pudding,' as it causes my breeches to shrink, but while I am in America, I eat apple pie at every opportunity. I fear I shall return to England a few pounds heavier than when I came. I can most definitely say that Mercer, my man, will have put on weight. He cannot stay out of Mrs. Haas's kitchen."

"I noticed Mrs. Haas brought a plate of *olykoeks* with her. Would you like a few of those to tide you over until dessert?"

"Oh, yes, please. I love her doughnuts. I am seriously thinking of making Mrs. Haas an offer to become the pastry chef at Pemberley. Our current chef has indicated a wish to retire, and if I could convince the lady…"

"Stop right there, sir. Mrs. Haas is a culinary treasure, and one who belongs to the people of Tarrytown. If you tried such a thing, you would find yourself running to the ship in fear of your life. You would never make it back to England."

But all levity came to an end when Caroline put in an appearance, and in her usual dramatic fashion, took over the conversation and pretended an interest in Lizzy.

"Oh, Elizabeth, how good it is to see you again, and you look so lovely. I remember admiring that dress last year at Mrs. Van Cortlandt's birthday celebration, but you have added some lace, I believe. My goodness, it has been months and months since I had the pleasure of your company as I have spent most of the summer in Saratoga Springs."

"How was Saratoga Springs?" Lizzy asked.

"Delightful. Although Mr. Darcy would find it rather dull, Saratoga Springs has become quite a popular holiday retreat. Another hotel is being built near General Putnam's, but, of course, I stay with the Beekmans who have a residence there. I anticipate the Springs will become the premier resort in the Northeast. No one goes to Ballston Spa anymore," Caroline said of a holiday retreat favored by the Bennets. "Mr. Darcy, some of the gentlemen in Saratoga Springs choose to amuse themselves by racing their horses or carriages. Do you still race curricles?"

"I do, but it is usually spontaneous, and very often the result of a challenge from your cousin, Charles."

At that moment, Jonah Bogart appeared at Caroline's side and requested the next dance. Caroline looked at Mr. Darcy in hopes that he would claim the dance for himself, but when he said nothing, an uncomfortable silence followed. It was only when Darcy informed Miss Bingley that he was already engaged for the next dance that she agreed to Jonah's request. To cover up her embarrassment, Caroline requested some punch, and Darcy offered to get both ladies a glass.

"I knew Mr. Darcy in England," Caroline explained, and there was such sadness in her statement that Lizzy realized she was in love with Fitzwilliam Darcy, and for the only time in her life, Lizzy found Caroline Bingley to be a sympathetic character. "When I learned from Papa that he was here, I came right away. We got on so well together and were in each other's company for weeks at a time at Charles's estate in Hertfordshire and again at Mr. Darcy's estate in Derbyshire. Pemberley Manor is exquisite. I remember telling Charles that when he built his own house it should be in the manner of Pemberley. Ah, but I shall say no more as here is Mr. Darcy."

After taking a sip of punch, Caroline asked him what he had been doing during his time in America.

"I have been quite busy. The Storms have given Charles, Georgiana, and I full access to their stables, which I take advantage of every morning when the weather is fine, and there seems to be a dinner or dance every other day. We have also ventured across the river so that we might climb the palisades—or at least I climb the palisades. Charles and Georgiana walked along the shore collecting oyster shells. I was also privileged to have attended an engagement party."

"Perhaps, you have not heard, Caroline. Charlotte and Mr. Collins, the pastor at St. Matthew's, are to be married in the spring," Lizzy explained.

"Charlotte Lucas is engaged! I am all amazement. I never thought she would marry. Well, I am very happy for her. She is good sort of person and will make a fine wife for a pastor. But how else have *you* occupied your time, Mr. Darcy?"

It seemed to Lizzy that Caroline would not be happy until she had learned how William had spent every waking minute of his time in America, and there were several activities mentioned that drew grimaces from Caroline, especially his time spent picking apples for the Widow Vreeland and driving a pony cart to transport Mrs. Haas to the village.

"Be careful, Mr. Darcy, or you will find yourself at a

corn frolic holding a red ear of corn, and in front of an audience, you will be forced to kiss a female." Caroline said it in such a way that she left no doubt there was no one in the county who would be worthy of a kiss from Mr. Darcy of Pemberley.

"Well, I *have* been to a corn frolic, and I *did* find a red ear of corn," he said, smiling. "But because I am a coward, I passed the ear off to Bingley."

"A very wise decision on your part," Caroline said, tapping his arm with her fan." I can tell that you have been spared nothing, so I shall warn you that if you do not learn to say 'no,' there are some who will have you sitting on the front porch carving faces into pumpkins and seeing how far you can spit their seeds," her distain for such things obvious in her tone. "You will not find such happenings in England."

"But I came to America to observe the differences in our cultures. If one does not do that, then one might as well stay in England."

"Yes, of course, but spending an evening in a barn, sitting on bales of hay, can hardly be called entertainment on either side of the Atlantic."

The conversation came to an end when Jonah Bogart returned to claim his dance, but before leaving, Caroline had succeeded in exacting a commitment from Mr. Darcy for another dance.

While dancing, Darcy revealed to Elizabeth that Caroline and he had first met at her sister's wedding. Afterwards, he had spent a good deal of time with her in the country while visiting Charles's manor house in Hertfordshire and again during her two-week visit to Pemberley. "But once we reached town, I saw a good deal less of her as she was drawn into the whirlwind that is London society during the season, and she was quite popular. Shortly thereafter, she returned to America."

Not only were their stories the same, Lizzy thought, but the tale was told in the same sobering tone of voice.

"I can just imagine Caroline being the talk of the town. At least that is the way it is when she is here. She always has admirers following her around, and it is the same wherever she goes. Two years ago, Jane and I were on our way to the very unfashionable Ballston Spa, and we broke our journey in Saratoga Springs. When we attended a public ball, it was as if young gentlemen had traveled from all over the Northeast just to see Caroline. She bore it all with equanimity. On the other hand, I would have found it to be rather burdensome as she did not have a minute to herself."

"I doubt very much that Miss Bingley would see such attention as burdensome. In fact, I think she thrives on it. But why are we speaking of Miss Bingley? Let us change the subject."

"To what, William? Apple pie?"

"You cannot go wrong there, Elizabeth."

Chapter 18

The morning after the ball, Caroline paid a visit to Richard Bingley's home. If it were not for Mr. Darcy's presence, she would never have darkened the door of her father's too humble abode. She hated everything about it: the outdated design, the lack of privacy, and its stark interior, but the thing she hated the most was that it had only one eating area, serving both master and servant.

To make matters worse, there was Mrs. Haas, who disliked Caroline because she considered her to be an inattentive daughter, oblivious to the health concerns of her father. Caroline was aware of Richard's declining health, and she laid a good deal of blame at the door of Mrs. Haas. Her requests that her father not be served a breakfast consisting of stacks of pancakes smothered in maple syrup and accompanied by cups of coffee that were more sugar than brew went unheeded. As a result, the man suffered from gout and had an ever-expanding girth. She had repeatedly cautioned her father about his excessive smoking. From sunrise to sunset, he had a clay pipe in his mouth with a plume of smoke coming out of it, but again Mrs. Haas undermined her efforts as she kept the long-stemmed tobacco-filled pipes lined up on the mantle.

When those habits were coupled with his lack of attention to his attire, Richard Bingley reminded his daughter of sketches she had seen of Dutch patroons in Mr. Irving's novel, and he was an embarrassment to her. But despite everything, Caroline loved him, and as soon as she entered, she immediately went to him and kissed his bald pate and was pleased that he had finally, and forever, abandoned wearing a wig.

After greeting all the men seated at breakfast, she asked where Miss Darcy was. "I had little opportunity to speak with her last night as she was engaged for every dance. However, I have come to rescue her from a household consisting entirely of men," Caroline said, directing her statement to Georgiana's brother.

"But Georgiana has not been with us since a few days after her arrival," her father said. "She is staying with the Bennet family and shares Mary Bennet's room."

"Well, then I shall go to the Bennet house and invite Miss Darcy to stay with Amanda and me at Storm Hall. I have been in Mary's bedroom, and there is barely room enough for one no less two people."

"Georgiana makes no complaint, and after all this time, I doubt she will want to change."

"But it is not just a matter of accommodations, but the company, to say nothing of the lack of a personal servant."

Darcy, who had remained silent up to this point, wanted to hear Caroline's objections.

"Well, let us take Mr. Bennet. Do you really want your sister to hear stories about how he lost three toes to frostbite at Morristown?"

"Caroline, that is unfair," her father quickly said. "Tom Bennet never speaks of it. It is others who mention it, not he."

"But then there is the banter between Mr. and Mrs. Bennet. They are constantly teasing each other in a way that I consider to be disrespectful of the institution of marriage. Although they find it amusing, I find it tiresome. And I disagree with how Mrs. Bennet runs her household. Very often, she can be found in the kitchen cooking at the hearth like a slave, and I do not think it proper that Lydia and Kitty are being educated along with the servants. With their confused roles, not one of the Bennet daughters will be properly trained to run a household."

"Surely, a four-month stay with the Bennets will not do any harm," Darcy said, "or at least none that cannot be corrected once we return to England. Besides, Georgiana has agreed to teach Mary to play the pianoforte."

"So you believe in miracles, Mr. Darcy," Caroline said in an amused voice.

"Mary's goals are quite modest," Richard quickly added. "She does not expect to become a proficient. She merely wishes to improve her fingering. As for Mrs. Bennet cooking at the hearth, her children are well aware that she was deeply affected by events that took place during the war. It was a time of great hardship, and she did what she had to do in order to survive. She wants to make sure that if her daughters should ever find themselves in similar straits, they will be able fend for themselves. I find it admirable."

"As do I," Darcy said, seconding Richard's comments.

"Well, of course, Mr. Darcy, you know what is best for your sister. Excuse my interference. It was kindly meant."

Darcy nodded his head, but chose not to respond. However, her father refused to remain silent.

"Caroline, I have something to say to you," an agitated Richard said as he walked his daughter to her carriage. "Your words about Mr. Bennet were both unkind and unfair and could not have come at a worst time. As a result of the embargo, I have lost a great deal of money. Because of Tom Bennet's generosity, I am not paying rent on the house, and I have free use of his garden. But most importantly, he has found a position for me in his company. If your comments should reach Tom's ears, he would think I was unappreciative of all that he has done for me." Richard shook his head in disappointment and mumbled, "Badly done, Caroline."

"Papa, I knew nothing of this," a chastened Caroline said.

"But even if you did not know about this particular act of kindness, you do know that it is only because of Tom Bennet's willingness to rent this house to me that we live here at all. Without Mr. Bennet, you would not know the Beekmans, the Storms, and the Van Cortlandts, all the names that drop so easily from your tongue."

"But, Papa, you must admit Mr. Bennet can be ridiculous. Men stopped wearing their hair in queues when President Washington died a dozen years ago, and as recently as last year, he was wearing ornate buckles on his shoes to church."

"He is whimsical man, and you are concentrating on his outward appearance. I am thinking of the generous heart that beats inside that man. But you were not content merely to ridicule Mr. Bennet; you also criticized his wife. Have you forgotten the hours you spent in the Bennet home when you were a little girl or the introductions Mrs. Bennet arranged on your behalf? It was Annie Bennet who suggested to Mr. Storm that Louisa and you go to stay with Amanda at Storm Hall in the first place."

"I am sorry, Papa. I shall not say another word about the Bennets."

"But there is more. Your interest in Mr. Darcy…"

"What do you mean?" Caroline asked, her voice elevated.

"Caroline, I may be a simple man, but I am not a simpleton. I knew of your interest in Mr. Darcy as soon as you wrote to say you were coming. When it was just Charles, you showed no interest in visiting Tarrytown, but when I revealed your cousin was in the company of

Fitzwilliam Darcy, you could not get here fast enough. So let me give you a word of advice. If you have set your cap at Mr. Darcy..."

"Please, Papa. That is such a vulgar phrase."

"Very well. If your intention is to secure Mr. Darcy, I suggest using honey instead of vinegar. The man does not like gossip, and you gave him a plateful."

"I understand, and I promise to hold my tongue."

Richard could only hope Caroline was as good as her word, but knowing his daughter, he did not think it likely.

* * *

Despite Caroline's arrival in Tarrytown, Darcy's routine altered little. Every morning of fine weather, Charles, Georgiana, and William climbed into Richard Bingley's pony cart to travel to the Storm estate so they might ride its excellent mounts. Even the conversation did not vary. Charles spoke almost exclusively of Jane Bennet while Georgiana continued to wax eloquent on the wonders of America, working in the occasional aside about Joshua Lucas. Savoring the excitement of her first formal dance, she loved to hear Charles and William's comments that her debut had caused quite a stir amongst the young bachelors and that she had them eating out of her hand.

But once the equestrians arrived at the Storm estate, there *was* a difference. Each morning, Caroline Bingley was waiting at the stables to ride with them. However, she had taken her father's advice to heart and decided the best way to please Mr. Darcy was to befriend his sister. Miss Bingley talked about those subjects that would be of interest to a young lady who was shortly to come out into society: fashion, accessories, dances, breakfasts, and balls, and Caroline spoke of her own debut in New York four years earlier.

"Although New York is nothing to London, we are not

as provincial as you might think, Miss Darcy. We have concerts and plays and fine restaurants. The shopping is quite good, and all of the milliners and dressmakers have the latest fashion plates from Paris. We even have our own, albeit smaller, version of Vauxhall Gardens. Except for the extensive art collections, everything that is available in London is here in New York."

"Oh, I agree, Miss Bingley. I find New York to be absolutely fascinating, and although I love being in the city, when I am here in country, I am quite content to have it so."

"If you love the countryside, I urge you to visit Saratoga Springs, and you must stay with Amanda Beekman and me. After all, it isn't fair that only the gentlemen of Tarrytown have the privilege of your company. We must think of the men of Upstate New York and New England as well."

"That sounds wonderful, but I do not think it is possible as my brother and I are to leave for England during the first week in December. There is another difficulty. William and I are to go to West Point on October 23rd to attend a military ball."

This was news to Caroline, and she asked as many questions as was necessary for her to ferret out every last detail.

"I attended a ball two years ago as the guest of Nathaniel Van Cortlandt, and it was quite enjoyable. You know, I think I shall go with you as there can never be too many ladies at these military balls as there are always too many men, and we shall bring Esther who is brilliant at doing hair. It will be so much fun. Are you open to such a plan, William?"

So it was William now, Darcy thought. Caroline had heard Elizabeth address him by his Christian name, and she would not be outdone.

"I will not be attending the ball, Miss Bingley. As you said, there are too many men, and I might risk being thrown out on my ear if I attempted to gain admittance. But I have been invited by Joshua Lucas to tour the military academy, and it will be an opportunity for me to view the beauties of the Hudson Highlands from the deck of a sloop."

"Excellent" was Caroline's only comment.

Chapter 19

"I was eagerly looking forward to our excursion to West Point," Charles stated while slouching in his chair, "until I saw how the men acted around Jane at the Storms' ball. They were like scavengers on carrion."

"You might want to think about that analogy," Darcy said to his unhappy friend, "especially since it appears that Jane is the carrion."

"Oh, you know what I mean. It will be much worse at a military ball."

"I imagine it will. Those young men can go for months without seeing a pretty face, and Jane is very pretty."

"My preference would be for us to go together and that she be introduced as my betrothed."

"Excuse me, Bingley, but you seem to have missed a few steps here. You must first ask the lady to marry you and then you must secure the permission of her father, and why do you hesitate? It is obvious to everyone that you are in love with Miss Bennet and Miss Bennet is in love with you. Your temperaments are so similar, so compliant, that you may look forward to your servants taking advantage of the pair of you every day of your lives. You will get along famously."

"You may joke, Darcy, but to me it is not in the least bit funny. I would marry Jane tomorrow, but as you say, I must ask Mr. Bennet for her hand in marriage. As far as Mr. Bennet is concerned, 'Fee, fi, fo, fum! I smell the blood of an Englishman.'"

"Bingley, I do not understand you. Why have you made Mr. Bennet into a giant who must be slain? The man is harmless."

"Harmless? You would not say that if you were with us in New York. At the Battery in lower Manhattan, there is a nice promenade with a spectacular view of the harbor. A circular fort is being built on a small island in preparation for a possible war with the British. Mr. Bennet described the need for its construction and the layout of the fort, spoon feeding me little bites of information as if I were a child. And it was not on that subject alone that I needed to be educated. I learned that the lower Hudson River is actually an estuary with strong tides, which I did not know, making the harbor difficult to navigate, which I did, as I had only recently sailed through the Narrows. On any other occasion, it may have been of some interest to me, but not at that moment. All I wanted to do was to walk with Jane and possibly speak of a future together, but her father would not forego his lesson on tidal estuaries. To my mind, he did it deliberately to keep us apart. It was only when Mrs. Bennet took her husband by the arm and led him away that I was able to talk to Jane."

"I will tell you again, Bingley. Mr. Bennet wants you to come back at him," Darcy said in response to his friend's litany of woes. "Look at it from his point of view. You will be taking his daughter to a far-off land, and he needs assurances that you can take care of her."

"What does he want by way of demonstration? Shall I roll up my sleeves and pummel him? Pull on his queue? Kick him in the shins and dirty his hose? Please tell me what is expected."

"Nothing physical is required," Darcy said, trying to suppress a laugh. "However, when you ask for his daughter's hand, be assertive and stand up straight.

Whenever you are nervous, you always slouch. Let him see you are firmly in control."

* * *

"Jane, please come into my study," her father said. "I have a note here from Charles Bingley asking me to grant him an interview. Do you know what this is about?"

"Papa, you may tease Charles, but it will not work with me," Jane answered, scolding her father. "You know very well why he wants to see you."

"Do you love him, Jane?"

"Very much, Papa. He is the kindest man I know, and I am confident he will be good to me."

"You know England is very far away, and travel can be difficult. Please do not forget that it took forty-one days for us to reach Liverpool. And you are so close to your mother and Lizzy. How will you bear it?"

"In the same way you bore your many separations from Mama during the war. You have said that you loved her from the first time you saw her. When I think of the scene you described—Mama chopping logs—it really is amazing that you found romance in such a setting."

"It was only a little axe as she was chopping wood for kindling."

"Please excuse my inaccurate retelling," Jane said, teasing him. "Of course, I shall miss Mama and my sisters, to say nothing of the MacTavishes and Wesleys, and all our friends and neighbors, but I love Charles. I love him so very dearly. I was beginning to think I should never marry, and now I can think of little else."

"Well, when he comes tomorrow morning with William to retrieve Georgiana, perhaps he should forego the pleasure of riding and instead have the pleasure of visiting with me."

Jane jumped up and kissed her father and implored her

145

father to be nice to Charles. "Please."

* * *

After shaking Charles Bingley's hand, Mr. Bennet gestured for his daughter's suitor to go into his study and asked that he be seated, but at Darcy's suggestion, Bingley remained standing.

"If Mr. Bennet is seated and you are standing, you will be addressing him from a superior position. That will give you an advantage," Darcy had advised.

"Well, if you will not be seated, then I shall remain standing as well." Mr. Bennet had immediately recognized Charles's refusal to sit down as a move to establish dominance, an old trick used by lawyers everywhere.

"As you wish," Bingley said, while taking a seat, but he was soon on his feet again. "Mr. Bennet, I want to marry your daughter, and I have come to ask for her hand in marriage."

"I assume you have not come about the twins as they are much too young, Mary's preference is to remain single, and Lizzy is a handful. Are we speaking of my eldest daughter?"

"Mr. Bennet, I come on serious business. As you well know, it is Jane I love, and I want to marry her. I can promise you that I shall love and honor her all the days of my life."

"Yes, Charles, as you say, this *is* serious business, and I am impressed by your forthright declaration. But you must understand I have real concerns. You wish to take my daughter across a vast ocean to a place where she knows only three people: Georgiana, William, and Louisa Hurst. Knowing what snobs the British are and the importance they place on rank, to say nothing of their dislike of all things American, it could prove to be quite a challenge for her."

"Yes, there will be challenges, and it is true that English society can be difficult for an outsider. So you will be happy to know I care little about such things because I, too, am an outsider. With the exception of Darcy and one or two others, most of my friends and associates are from those families who made their fortune in trade.

"And, sir, this is about Jane and me—not Jane and the whole of England. We get along so well that if there were no one else, I would be quite content. And you mentioned Louisa, who speaks so highly of Jane. In fact, before I left England, noting our similarities in temperament, she specifically mentioned that I should seek Jane out. And Georgiana just adores her, and she will smooth the way for Jane in society.

"As for finances, I can assure you that I can provide for your daughter. I have inherited a great deal of money, most of which sits in Coutts Bank in England, but I can write to them requesting they release all the details of those accounts. Additionally, I will be most generous in Jane's marriage settlement. She will not have to look to her family for any incidentals."

Mr. Bennet understood that Charles was referring to Louisa Hurst. Her requests for money were proving to be a drain on her father's meager reserves.

"Charles, if I needed such proof of your ability to support my daughter, I would never have entertained the thought of Jane marrying you. I believe you to be an honest man, a good man, and worthy of my daughter, so I will give you my consent. All I ask is that you take care of my sweet Jane."

"It will be my pleasure to take care of *our* sweet Jane."

When Mr. Bennet and Charles came into the entryway, they found Mrs. Bennet, her five daughters, Mrs. Kraft, Samuel, and Hannah sitting on the stairs waiting for them. Even the tutor for Kitty and Lydia had joined them, and

Mrs. Bennet warned her husband that if he made one joke about what had just occurred in his study he would have to answer to her.

"Mrs. Bennet! Do you really think I would make light of such a serious business? We are speaking of the institution of marriage, a holy rite, and our future grandchildren. And that reminds me. Charles, will you agree to name your first-born son after me?"

"I shall name all of our children, male or female, after you if that is what is required to gain your consent," and everyone laughed.

Jane came and stood by Charles's side, and after taking her hand in his, the looks exchanged were such that no one doubted they were truly and deeply in love. Charles got down on one knee and asked Jane to be his wife and tears flowed—but not from Jane. It was Lizzy who was crying. Her darling sister and dearest friend was going to leave her.

* * *

When Darcy and Georgiana arrived at Longbourn from their morning ride, they walked into a party in progress as Mr. Bennet had ordered a bottle of wine to be opened, and a messenger was sent to the home of Richard Bingley so that he might join in the celebration.

Georgiana was positively giddy in sharing her congratulations. She had come to think of the Bennet girls as her sisters, and she loved each one of them. "Oh, Jane, I am so very happy that you will be coming to England. We shall be introduced into society at the same time."

"But *when* are Jane and Charles to be married?" Lydia asked, eager for a party, and everyone realized a date for the wedding had not been discussed.

Jane did not know what to say, and Charles was at a loss as well, but Mrs. Bennet was not. "Charles, if you intend for Jane to go to England with you when you depart in

December, then she had best go as your wife or she will not go without *me*."

After everyone had stopped laughing, it was quickly agreed that the wedding would take place before their departure date, and the couple realized they must go immediately to visit Mr. Collins so the banns could be announced.

"The wagon is outside. Go to it," Darcy said, handing Charles his driving gloves, and the couple quickly departed. And so did Lizzy who explained she needed to feed Timber. Mrs. Bennet gave Darcy a knowing look. After all, Lizzy would soon have to say goodbye to her beloved sister.

Darcy found Lizzy in the barn feeding Timber a bucket of mashed oats. "I have come to look after my patient," Darcy explained. "How is he doing?"

"Fine" was all the Lizzy could manage.

"Elizabeth, are you crying?"

"Do you mean, am I shedding tears once again? Yes, I am, as your presence seems to bring on fits of crying."

But when Darcy stepped forward to comfort her, Lizzy stepped away from him.

"You are happy for Jane and Charles, are you not?" Darcy asked.

"Of course, I am, but... but I shall never see her again."

"Oh, it is not as bad as all that. You will come to England to visit her."

Lizzy shook her head. "No, she will start a new life there, and Georgiana and Louisa will become her sisters." Now the tears came in steams, and she looked at him in her anguish. "Do you not hug in England?"

Darcy quickly took her in his arms, and placed his hand on her head and brought it to his chest. But the gesture brought little comfort. Because William would soon be leaving for England, Lizzy knew she must push him away or it would be too obvious she had fallen in love with him.

"Timber is doing a little better," she said as she took Darcy's handkerchief with its beautifully embroidered "F" and "D," and she imagined Georgiana had done the needlework. "His appetite has picked up, and, yesterday, I had him out in the yard. So I thank you for coming by to check on him."

"Elizabeth…"

"But you must go, William, and I shall tell you now I shall not be going to West Point."

"Why ever not? You were so looking forward to it."

"Good day, Mr. Darcy," Lizzy said, sweeping past him.

"Mr. Darcy?" William called after her. "Why am I now Mr. Darcy?" But Lizzy would not stop to answer him.

Chapter 20

At Sunday afternoon tea, Lizzy informed her family that she had decided to join Jane and Charles on their shopping expedition to the city for the purpose of buying Jane's trousseau. As a result, she would not be traveling to West Point. But Jane suspected Lizzy's reasons for not going to the military academy had nothing to do with preparations for her wedding.

"I want to know the *real* reason why you are not going to West Point," Jane said as soon as Lizzy and she were alone. "I know how much you love military dances."

"Yes, I do, but it is not every day my sister gets married. I want to be with you as you pick out the material for your dress and buy your slippers and…"

"Lizzy, stop it. You hate shopping. No one knows that better than I do. I think this has something to do with William. Actually, it is more likely it involves Caroline Bingley, who, I understand from Georgiana has included herself in the excursion to West Point."

"All right. It *is* about William," Lizzy answered defensively. "Why would I want to go to a dance and watch him moon over Caroline Bingley?"

"Are you implying that William is in love with Caroline? Because if you are, you are very wrong."

"Jane, did you not see how he looked at her as she descended the stairs at Storm Hall?"

"Yes, I did. It was meant to be a grand entrance on a par with royalty. The only thing missing was a red carpet and trumpets. The eyes of everyone, including Charles, were riveted on her. It is the same as when a neighbor's house catches fire. You cannot help but look at such a spectacle."

"You heard what Dirck said. William and Caroline had a romance while she was in England."

"Yes, but Dirck also stated that something went wrong and that is why Caroline came home and William remained in England."

"Then why is he here? I believe he came to see if he is still in love with her."

"Well, if that is the case, he certainly took his time in getting here as Caroline has been home for over a year. I will not deny something happened between them, but, obviously, it did not turn out as Caroline had hoped."

"I am still not going."

"Lizzy, that is not brave."

"No, but it is wise. Let them have a few days together to see if they want to begin again." Lizzy then stamped her foot in frustration. "But none of this matters. Charles told me that William moves in the highest circles of London society. Do you really think he would want a country bumpkin as his wife?"

"You are not a country bumpkin, and you know it. And if Charles can see past the supposed shortcomings of Americans to marry me, why should William not marry you?"

"I have no wish to take anything away from Charles, but he is not the grandson of an earl. Even though I do not care about such things, people in England do. Mr. Richard told me that while the men of England do their fighting on the battlefield, their women draw blood in the drawing room."

"You are not painting a very rosy picture of my future."

"Oh Jane, I am so sorry," she said, rushing to her sister. "But Charles has a large family, who will love you on sight, and you have such happy manners that you will endear yourself to all who come to know you."

"I still think you should go to West Point."

"No, I have made my decision."

* * *

Darcy stood on the deck as the sloop *John Jay* made its way through the Tappan Zee, the widest part of the Hudson, where wise sailors shorten sail. Vessels of every size and description crowded the water. Small fishing boats shared the inland sea with schooners and barges carrying poultry, grain, and vegetables for the markets in New York while, nearby, dozens of sloops, with their single masts and retractable keels, negotiated around the shoals in the river.

From his perch, Darcy could just make out the colonnaded home of the Storm family and the golden yellow of Longbourn Manor, and he wondered if Elizabeth was enjoying her visit to the city. As the hours passed, the sloop approached the Hudson Highlands, passing Anthony's Nose and Breakneck Ridge. Farther up the Hudson, vast woodlands appeared with their leaves showing hints of the fall colors that would soon burst into a cornucopia of reds, yellows, and oranges and that would ignite the hills from the Hudson to Appalachia in a blaze of color.

The hours passed agreeably, and Darcy charted each mile in his journal, making note of the flora and sites of geological interest along the way. As the waterway narrowed, he watched as the captain navigated a sharp curve in the river, and shortly thereafter, West Point appeared in the distance.

Upon seeing the location of the fortification, Darcy immediately understood its importance to the British during the War of Rebellion. With its capture, the British would have control of the Hudson, and New England would have been cut off from the rest of the colonies. But Darcy knew his history. In 1780, there were so few British troops in New York that capturing West Point by force of arms was impossible. It required intrigue and betrayal. If the gambit of having Benedict Arnold hand over West Point to the British had succeeded, the rebels would very likely have sued for peace. As he pondered the possibilities of what might have been, an enormous ridge came into view.

"If you are Dutch, the ridge is referred to as Boterberg," Caroline explained as she came and stood beside Darcy, "but if you are English, it is Butter Hill, as it is supposed to look like a lump of butter." Caroline had been watching Darcy as he wrote his notes and made detailed sketches in his journal, and she had been waiting for an opportunity to say something that would be of interest to him. "Butter Hill is one of the wonders of the Hudson Highlands. However, I think it deserves a more dignified name, especially considering its proximity to West Point."

"Yes, I agree. It merits a statelier name, and there are the stars and stripes of the American flag indicating that we have arrived at West Point."

Much to Darcy's relief, Caroline had said little to him during the voyage up the Hudson as she had spent most of her time getting reacquainted with Georgiana.

After disembarking, the passengers were greeted by Joshua Lucas, who had assigned a junior cadet to be on the lookout for the *John Jay*. When he caught sight of Caroline, his eyes widened. What on earth was she doing at West Point? Two years earlier, she had declared that she had attended her last military ball, and, yet, here she was. There could be only one reason: Caroline was on the prowl, and her prey was Fitzwilliam Darcy.

"Caroline, what a pleasure," Joshua said. "It has been two years since you last graced us with your presence."

"How kind of you to remember, Joshua," she said with a hint of flirtation in her greeting.

"And Miss Darcy, how good to see you again. As you can see, we are little more than a parade ground, dormitories, and educational buildings. But change is in the wind here at the Point, and I hope to be a part of it."

"Joshua, please," Caroline said, placing her hand gently on his arm. "Miss Darcy is here at your invitation, and you choose to speak about military matters? I think not. You should be talking about tomorrow's picnic."

"But how did you know I had planned a picnic?"

"Because I know you," and she turned to Georgiana. "Joshua and I have been friends since we were children. It was he who gave me my first kiss. On the cheek of course. But a girl does not forget such things."

Georgiana gave her brother an uncomfortable look. Was Caroline implying that Joshua and she had had a romance? Darcy shook his head. Knowing Caroline, he believed she would never have encouraged someone who intended to make the military his career. However, the exchange served to remind Darcy of just how capable Caroline was in reeling in a catch.

Their guide soon directed them to the hotel where Caroline and Georgiana would be staying, and after making sure the accommodations were to their satisfaction, Joshua walked with Darcy in the direction of his much more rustic lodgings.

"While walking across the parade ground, I noticed some of the cadets are very young," Darcy said to the young officer.

"Yes, at present, those as young as ten and as old as thirty-seven may attend the academy, and a cadet may leave after six months or stay as long as six years. But soon that will no longer be the case as great changes are in the offing with regular terms of service and an established code of conduct that will be strictly enforced. We have a nation to build, and I am proud to say West Point will supply the engineers who will build it. We are also the only institution providing artillery training."

"It sounds similar to the Royal Military Academy at Woolwich, 'the shop,' as it is known, where my cousin, Colonel Fitzwilliam first cut his teeth."

"I do not think that is a coincidence, but if the United States is to take its rightful place among the great nations of the world, we must have a strong military with capable leaders. That is what we hope to achieve at West Point. Because there are wars and rumors of war, we must be prepared. But let us speak of more pleasant things, such as the ladies. I am disappointed Elizabeth did not come as she is a favorite of mine. We are very much like brother and sister. You can say anything to her without fear of offending, and you never have to stand on ceremony with her."

No fear of offending! That is certainly not my experience with Elizabeth. It seems I do nothing but give offense.

"Elizabeth did write to explain why she would not be coming, what with Jane's wedding and all," Joshua continued, "and I am very happy for Jane. She is a wonderful girl and deserves a good husband, and I like Charles Bingley very much."

"Bingley *is* a good man, and they are well suited for each other. Will you be attending the wedding?"

"I certainly hope so. Tom Bennet throws a damn fine party. All the beer and ale served in his home and in all the taverns in Tarrytown are made in a brewery he owns across from Croton Point. The man has his fingers in everything, but this is one of his most successful operations as he makes an excellent ale. Speaking of brews, may I buy you a drink before supper?"

"I wouldn't say no."

* * *

While sitting in the mess with Darcy, Joshua corrected something Caroline had said. "Yes, we shall have a picnic, but not tomorrow. When I learned from Richard Bingley that you are an experienced angler, I made arrangements for you to go with a local guide, Prickly Van Riper, who will direct you to a stream where the fish are so plentiful they practically fight amongst themselves to get into your creel."

"I am grateful for your troubles, but Georgiana does not like to fish. In fact, she hates it."

"I did not expect Miss Darcy to go fishing with you, so I have arranged something for her as well. The riding instructor here at the academy has offered to take her on a trail that leads to the top of Butter Mountain. Captain Fredericksen's wife recently gave birth to a robust baby boy with equally robust lungs, and he is eager to spend some time out of doors away from the wailing of an infant. Of course, I will go along and keep watch over your sister."

"But who will watch you, Joshua?" Darcy asked, only half in jest.

"I imagine Caroline Bingley will join us, and she will keep an eye on me," Joshua said before breaking out into a smile. "I understand your concerns, sir, but I give you my word as a gentleman that nothing untoward will happen with your sister. So what do you say, Mr. Darcy?"

"There will be no living with Georgiana if I do not allow her to go; therefore, I shall say 'yes,' but that is conditioned upon Miss Bingley also going. Agreed?"

"Agreed." Joshua raised his mug in appreciation.

* * *

When Darcy returned to the hotel, he found a letter waiting for him from Stephen Van Rensselaer, stating that he had arranged for a packet of information to be delivered to the home of Superintendent Williams for Darcy's perusal. Because it was now a certainty that there would be no support from the U.S. government for the Erie Canal and that the project would be financed entirely with private money, Van Rensselaer had given Darcy the name of the man in New York City whose job it was to put in place the financial instruments necessary for the building of the canal.

"Excellent," Darcy said out loud. Although an Englishman to his core, Darcy could feel the excitement building within him. It was the same feeling he experienced at the start of the hunt, but this time the prize was the untamed wilderness of America's interior and all of its possibilities for greatness.

Chapter 21

Esther was putting the finishing touches on Georgiana's hair, and she could see the English lady was pleased with the result. Esther's mother had been a slave at the *Clermont* estate of Margaret Beekman Livingston, whose family owned vast tracts of land in the mid Hudson Valley, but was eventually sold to Preston Storm in Tarrytown so that she might serve as a lady's maid to his ward, Amanda Beekman. She had served in that capacity for the last ten years, but was often asked to accompany Caroline whenever she traveled alone.

"Oh, thank you, Esther. It looks lovely," Georgiana said, truly impressed with the woman's skills.

"You're very welcome, miss. It's been a pleasure."

Georgiana pressed several coins into the slave's hand, and Esther thanked her. "I'm saving up to buy my freedom. I'm more than halfway there, and every little bit helps."

Georgiana did not know what to say. From a distance, she found the business of slavery to be appalling, but now that she had actually met a slave, she viewed it for what it was: a festering sore in the midst of civilized societies, including Britain's, and it needed to be cauterized.

When Georgiana went into the sitting room, she found Caroline waiting for her, but it was obvious from her dress that she would not be going to the dance.

"I don't understand," Georgiana said. "I thought the purpose of your coming to West Point was to attend the ball."

"I have already been to several military balls, and tonight is your special night. I plan to have a quiet supper in my room, or if your brother is so inclined, I might join him in the hotel dining room."

"Oh, I am sure William will be most pleased," or at least Georgiana hoped so. Whenever William was around Caroline, she noticed his moods fluctuated. "As far as I know, he has no fixed engagements for this evening."

Caroline had made her decision to forego the ball while still in Tarrytown and had convinced Amanda Beekman to remain behind as she would only have been in the way. The wisdom of her plan had been validated the previous afternoon. During their picnic near the landing, William had raced against an officer and had easily bested him, and the challenge, along with the previous day's superior fishing, had the gentleman in excellent spirits. As a result, Caroline and he had strolled along the river admiring the spectacular views, and as they had done during their time together in the English countryside, conversing easily. The day had been sublime, and she hoped the evening would be as well.

When Caroline appeared in casual dress, William was presented with a *fait accompli*. Obviously, she had never intended to go to the ball. But during the picnic, she had been most pleasant company, and it would be no hardship for him to spend an evening with her.

Caroline and Darcy walked with Georgiana and Joshua across the parade ground to the site of the evening's dance, and Darcy could see from the reaction of the other cadets that Joshua was right about his chances of securing a second dance with Georgiana. The young men looked more like animals on the prowl for a mate than future officers attending a military ball, and the female had just arrived.

Darcy watched his sister as she climbed the steps, and the look on her face would have been no different than if she had been attending a ball at Almack's. She did not see the ballroom as a converted canteen, but as an enchanted place where men in uniform and ladies in their beautiful gowns would dance into the early hours of the morning. Darcy stayed long enough to see Georgiana enjoying her first dance with her handsome escort, and he imagined that what he was feeling was something similar to that of a father watching his child taking her first steps.

Darcy offered Caroline his arm, and they walked in the direction of the hotel. The date for the dance had been chosen because it would be a full moon, and the shadows cast by the surrounding mountains created a purple cast, adding to the romantic atmosphere of the evening.

"I can tell this whole evening has stirred the romantic within you," Caroline said, and she relaxed her arm, enabling her to lean against Darcy.

"I hope you do not regret that you chose not to go," Darcy said, ignoring her statement. "I remember how much you love to dance, and despite all the ladies in attendance, the men still outnumber the ladies by a good margin."

"Yes, I do love to dance, but I am quite content to be with you," Caroline purred.

"Joshua mentioned that my accommodations would be quite rustic, and he was not exaggerating. I shared my room with some of the local wildlife who nibbled their way through the night on what I do not know, but possibly my leather satchel."

Caroline found Darcy's banter amusing, but she had not come to West Point to discuss field mice. After finding a good spot for a kiss, she stopped and placed her hands upon his chest, closed her eyes, and waited. How well she remembered the taste of his lips, and the warm feelings she had experienced when in his arms. Darcy placed his hands on hers, but instead of kissing her, he gently took them down and stepped away from her.

"William, we need to talk," Caroline said, alarmed by his reluctance to kiss her. Darcy stood silent. "…about what happened in London."

"Caroline, please. I have no wish to spoil the evening by revisiting that scene."

"But I do wish to revisit it. And do you not owe me that much after what happened at Pemberley? The way you kissed me. The way you held me in your arms."

"Please allow me to remind you that it was *you* who placed your arms around my neck and kissed *me*."

"As I recall, you kissed me back," Caroline said, with panic creeping into her voice.

"We share many enjoyable memories from your time in England," Darcy said, answering her charge. "Why would we want to ruin them by concentrating on something so ugly?"

"William, you have made certain assumptions about that night in London, and I can assure you they are all wrong. Will you not hear me out?" When Darcy gave her no encouragement, she uttered a desperate "please."

After nodding his consent, she began. "I am sure you will recall how hot it was in the ballroom, and so Mr. Wickham and I went out on to the terrace for some fresh air. We had been out there for just a few minutes when you came upon us. I will swear an oath that nothing happened between us."

"I *know* nothing happened, but…," Darcy started to explain why he had gone out onto the terrace in the first place, but then stopped. That event had precipitated others, and he did not want to think about anything involving George Wickham. "Caroline, I would really rather not. We may end up saying things each of us will regret."

"What do you mean you *knew* nothing happened?" Caroline said, refusing to let go of the subject. "If you knew me to be innocent, then why were you so unhappy with me? And why did you allow me to return to America with hardly a word spoken between us?"

Darcy could see the tears glistening in her eyes, and fearing a scene, he looked for a spot where they would be unobserved. Upon reaching a warehouse, the pair stopped and stood in its shadow. But even in this secluded spot, Darcy hesitated. He was afraid that no matter what he said, he would fall short in finding the right words to explain what had happened a year earlier on an August evening in London.

After Caroline's return to America, Darcy had successfully put her out of his mind, but when she had come down the stairs at Storm Hall, he was flooded by fond memories of their time together in the country. But before she had reached the bottom of the stairs that memory was already beginning to fade to be replaced by another: Elizabeth Bennet in a barn, crying in his arms. On that warm evening, as he felt Elizabeth's hands upon his chest, it had taken every ounce of willpower not to kiss her senseless.

"William, I love you," Caroline said, interrupting his thoughts.

"Caroline, please do not say that. You will come to regret it."

"How can I regret loving you? You are everything to me. Even with the passage of more than a year, my feelings for you remain so strong."

"I am sorry to cause you any distress, but you must understand that I have never loved you."

"I don't believe you, William. Up until the moment when you found me with Mr. Wickham, you were in love with me. I am convinced of that."

"No, Caroline, I was *never* in love with you—not at

Netherfield nor in Derbyshire, and most definitely not in London. At the various venues in town, all the men were flocking to you, and you were enjoying the attention immensely. And why should you not? There was nothing to bind you to me. Even so, I was taken aback by your flirtatious manners, especially when you directed your attention to my cousin, Colonel Fitzwilliam, as well as George Wickham, whom I had just introduced as being a childhood friend. And you seem to be under the impression that I just happened upon you on the terrace. That is not the case, so please allow me to tell you what *did* happen that night.

"With growing anger, I watched as Wickham openly flirted with you to the point where the whispers had begun even before you had left the ballroom, but you seemed unaware of the sensation you were causing. Then much to my disgust, I saw Wickham lure you out onto the terrace. Unsure of the customs of your country, I felt it necessary to warn you because such things are *not* done in England. I followed you out onto the terrace as a way of protecting you from someone who was behaving in a most ungentlemanlike manner."

"I do not understand," Caroline said with real fear in her voice. "I would never have gone out on to the terrace with Mr. Wickham if I did not think that you held him in the highest regard. You are speaking of him as if he is a scoundrel."

"Wickham *is* a scoundrel, but it was the night of the ball that I saw for the first time the real George Wickham. Because of his behavior to you, the next day, I visited him at his lodgings. Up until that time, I did not understand why he did not stay with me at my house in town, but I soon found out. He lived a life so dissolute that he did not want me to know about it. Gaming, blood sports, and carousing were the least of his failings. There are other things as well, but as a gentleman, I cannot speak of them to a lady. But please believe me when I say that the man is a debased cur.

"When I confronted him, I demanded an explanation for his behavior toward you. At the very least, you were my guest, and I soon learned that he thought you were a good deal more. At the ball, anger he had suppressed over the years came to the surface, and he saw an opportunity where he could do some real harm. It was his intention to compromise you. Afterwards, he would spread a rumor that he had successfully seduced you, and your reputation would be in tatters. Of course, he anticipated I would shun you as a result of such exposure, his purpose being to make me miserable. He cared nothing about you."

"No, he could not have damaged me because nothing happened." Caroline said, shaking her head in disbelief. "He never touched me. I would not have allowed it. You must believe me."

"I do believe you. But Wickham did not need for an actual seduction to take place. He only needed to create the illusion of impropriety, and that is why when we went back into the ballroom I stayed by your side. It was important for everyone to see that nothing had happened. But something *had* happened. You are truly beautiful, Caroline. But I could never nurture any feelings for someone who would openly flirt as you did, and I knew that as soon we arrived in London."

"But if you have no feelings for me, then why did you come here?"

"Because of Georgiana. While my sister was visiting a seaside resort, Wickham attempted an elopement with her. Fortunately, she alerted me to the situation, but when she realized Wickham's purpose had been to gain access to her fortune and to hurt me, she was devastated. I had to get her out the country."

"I am very sorry for your sister. I truly am. But why America? There were other places you could have gone:

Scotland or Ireland or Nova Scotia, if you wished to go farther. Why did you choose New York? As soon as I learned you were here, I immediately made plans to come home. You must have known I would do that."

"I imagine I did," Darcy said with real regret. "There was a time when I was infatuated by a charming and beautiful woman, but when I saw you at Storm Hall, I had the final proof that my infatuation with you had ended in England."

Caroline turned away from Darcy. From the moment she had received the letter from her father announcing Darcy's arrival, she believed that destiny had brought them back together. But here he was, the man she loved, telling her that he had *never* loved her.

Caroline drew in a deep breath as she was determined she would not create a scene that could very possibly end in her ultimate humiliation. After a few minutes, she found she had regained her composure. She had recovered from their separation once before and would do so again. After drying her tears, she said, "Before I go in, I need to know if Wickham was successful in spreading rumors about me," and she braced herself for his reply.

"No, he was not successful. I threatened him to within an inch of his life if he so much as mentioned your name, and when I learned of his intentions with Georgiana, I demanded he come to Mr. Jackson's Boxing Academy. He was quite confident he could beat me, and he did land one good punch, but only because he was a coward and had not waited for the signal to begin. However, once the signal was given, I beat him to a pulp. But in order to be completely rid of him, I agreed to purchase a commission for him in the army. His regiment was sent to Spain to fight in the Peninsular campaign. Soon after I arrived here in New York, I received a letter from my cousin, Colonel Fitzwilliam, who is also in Spain. An outbreak of measles killed many of the men sailing on the ship taking Wickham's regiment to the peninsula. Wickham was one of them."

Ten minutes earlier, Caroline would have been sorry to learn of the death of George Wickham, but not now. In order to hurt Fitzwilliam, the man was willing to destroy her.

"Well, this has ended badly for both Wickham and me. But you have done me a good turn by defending my honor, so I will return the favor. You know very well how difficult it is to break into London society, so if you are thinking of making an offer of marriage to Elizabeth Bennet, I would think again. Her manners are unrefined, her accent will be mocked, and she is woefully under educated by European standards. By the time the women of the *ton* have finished with her, her spirits will be in shreds, and she will be begging you to return to America. If you care for Elizabeth, do not do that to her. She does not deserve it."

Darcy extended his arm. "I think I should take you back to the hotel."

* * *

Darcy waited in the lobby for Georgiana to return from the dance. For the time being, he had successfully banished thoughts of his discussion with Caroline. Those were best reserved for a time when he was alone as his face would reveal too much.

As expected, Georgiana was walking on air, which was a good thing, as she had worn through her dance slippers. Although Darcy assured her they would have ample time to discuss the evening on the morrow, his sister would not allow him to return to his lodgings. After showing him her full dance card, she described each partner and every dance. By the time she had finished, Darcy could hardly keep his eyes open.

It had been an important day for him as well. He had finally rid himself of any uncertainty about his relationship with Caroline Bingley. Even though he knew he had never loved her, he had liked her very much, and he preferred to think of a time when they were together in Derbyshire before the illusion of tenderness had died a painful death in London.

Chapter 22

The next morning, when Georgiana awoke, she found Caroline had been awake for hours and looked completely worn out.

"I think I am getting a head cold," Caroline explained. "When I looked in the mirror this morning, I looked a fright."

It was true. The beautiful Miss Bingley had a puffiness around her eyes that made her look as if she had been crying. *But why would she have been crying?* Georgiana wondered.

When the two ladies went downstairs, Darcy was waiting for them. As soon as he saw Caroline, he knew tears had been shed, but a look from the lady begged him to say nothing.

"Good morning, William. I have just returned from a long walk, and you should be glad that you are not going home today as there is a storm coming over the mountains. I am afraid Georgiana and you will be confined to the hotel lobby, at least for the morning."

"Georgiana and I? Do you have other plans?"

"As a matter of fact, I do. I have been invited to stay with Superintendent Williams and his wife for a few days. I will not be returning to Tarrytown as I intend to go to Albany and, from there, on to Saratoga Springs."

Darcy, who was completely caught off guard by

Caroline's change of plans, stated that if she must go to Albany he would go with her.

"No, William, you will not. You are in America now. Ladies are not required to travel with a male relation or friend, and it is important I go to Saratoga Springs as I have business there. Since my return from England, I have been courted by Louis Beekman, the son of a business partner of John Jacob Astor. Perhaps you have heard of Mr. Astor as he is thought to be the richest man in America. Louis has asked me to marry him at least a dozen times, and I have always put him off. But I did promise the dear man I would give him an answer when I returned from visiting with my father, and I have decided to accept his proposal."

Darcy's brow furrowed. Was Caroline marrying in haste as a way of punishing him for the previous evening: Because *he* did not love *her*, she would marry someone *she* did not love?

"Unfurrow your brow, William. Louis is a good man and a cousin to Mrs. Bennet. She is fond of him and will gladly give him a reference."

"What will your father say if I return to Tarrytown without you?" Darcy asked. Even if it were the custom of American ladies to travel without an escort, it was at such variance with his own experience he found it difficult to accept that Caroline would return to Albany alone.

"In brief, he will say, 'It is about time Caroline gave the poor man an answer.' Papa likes Louis, and in this way, I shall no longer be a burden to my father. His finances have suffered in recent years, and when I marry Louis, I shall be able to repay all his kindnesses to me."

"But will you attend the wedding of Charles and Jane Bennet?" Georgiana asked.

"No, I shall not, and I do feel rather bad about that. But I shall write to Jane and Charles and explain that a newly-engaged lady should be with her betrothed. I am sure they will understand."

"Caroline, may I have a word with you?" Darcy asked, and he took a step to the side, indicating she should follow him.

"No, you may not because there is nothing to say. You see, once I have made up my mind, it is a rare thing for me to change it. So we shall say goodbye, and I wish you God speed and a safe return to England. And, Georgiana, please do write as I long to hear about all the wonderful things you will be experiencing during your first season in London. However, a word of warning. There are men who will hover about you, speaking words of love, but when they are no longer in your company, they will choose to devalue the endearments they spoke so earnestly a short while before. In any event, I wish you joy," and Caroline left them.

Darcy was nearly at full boil. Caroline had just implied that he had spoken words of love to her when he had done no such thing. Although the lady had greatly wronged him, he remained silent. But Georgiana could see her brother was upset. "William, did you and Caroline quarrel last night?"

"No," he said emphatically, but he could see the doubt in his sister's eyes. "We did not quarrel, but there were matters that needed to be cleared up. During Caroline's stay in England, there was something between us, but it came to nothing—at least on my part, it came to nothing. These things do not always work out. When courting, you try each other on for size, and sometimes the fit is less than perfect. You move on."

"It is the same with Dirck Storm and Elizabeth Bennet."

"How so?"

"Well, I understand from Mary that they were sweethearts, but then Dirck went to Europe for a year or so. When he returned, Elizabeth was not as interested in him. I guess they no longer fit."

"Can you define the word 'sweethearts'?" Darcy asked, Caroline now being all but forgotten.

Georgiana did not know what to say as she felt the word spoke for itself. "They were sweet on each other. They liked each other."

"Sweetheart is an American term, I believe, as I have never been 'sweet' on anyone in my life," Darcy said with impatience. "I find Americans often choose to speak in idiomatic English that creates a language barrier where none need exist."

Georgiana did not think that sweetheart was an American term, but chose not to argue the point. In light of the fact that there were areas of London where it was difficult to understand what a fellow Englishman was saying, and in the North of England, quite impossible, she found his statement to be odd. Obviously, her brother was in a foul mood. As if in confirmation, a clap of thunder was heard overhead.

"Well, it seems Caroline's forecast has come true. We shall be kept indoors by the weather and left to amuse ourselves," Georgiana said. But not for long as two cadets came into the hotel with water dripping from their great coats, and their eyes scanned the lobby before settling on Georgiana.

"William, may I introduce you to Antony Schuyler and Stewart Livingston? We met at last night's ball." A second clap of thunder was followed by the entrance of Joshua Lucas, causing Georgiana to break into a broad smile. "What fun we shall all have!" she said, looking at her brother, whose countenance did not support her conclusion.

* * *

For Darcy, the return trip to Tarrytown was a series of misadventures. The *Mohican* was late in departing West Point, and four hours into their eight-hour journey, the sloop

172

failed to navigate around a shoal, and they found themselves grounded. The ship could not resume its voyage until the tide was favorable, and Georgiana and Darcy found themselves spending the night aboard ship.

While Darcy found their floundering to be an inconvenience, Georgiana saw it as an adventure, especially since several cadets who had danced with her at the ball were on the sloop, and all were happily engaged in reliving the night of the dance. One particular young man had captured Georgiana's attention, and it was necessary to keep an eye on him as he had that look about him, reminding Darcy of his days at Cambridge and his flirtations with the maids in the public houses.

When the *Mohican* once again took to the river, Darcy found no pleasure in the scenery. Unlike his voyage to West Point, the trees and ridges, houses and sloops, passed unnoticed. His thoughts were of Caroline as he was unhappy with how things had ended between them. It was obvious at the Storm Hall ball that she had maintained an interest in him, and he should have dealt with the matter right then. Instead, he went riding with her and had accepted invitations to dine with the Storms, knowing that Caroline would be there. But, damn it, he had dined with the Storms before Caroline had come to Tarrytown. Why should he refuse a dinner invitation because of a year-old flirtation?

But then Darcy's thoughts turned to another lady. In Elizabeth's mind, it must appear that he had paid her a fair amount of attention until Caroline had arrived, and considering the evidence, who could dispute her conclusion? But did any of this really matter as he would soon sail for England? After talking with Superintendent Williams about a possibility of war between their two countries, he wondered if he should not move up the departure date. While the British and American armies might not engage until the spring, there was nothing to stop combatants from doing battle on the high seas. No, his first responsibility was to Georgiana, and he must get her home.

Georgiana came over to her brother and wrapped her arm around his. "A penny for your thoughts."

"I have been thinking about Jane and Charles," he said, trying to cover up his dark musings. "How do you think Jane will be received by London society?"

Georgiana thought about it for a few minutes before answering. "I think she will do fine. She is unassuming and modest in her manners, speech, and dress. I believe it is women who are assertive or who attract too much attention from the men who are targets of the ladies of the *ton*."

"And how do you think Elizabeth Bennet would fare?"

"Is Elizabeth going to England with her sister? Oh, that would be wonderful."

"I have not heard that she would. I am just imaging different scenarios."

"Well, Elizabeth is much more… Oh, what is the word I am looking for?" But the perfect descriptive eluded her.

"American," Darcy said, answering for her. Yes, Elizabeth was an American: intolerant of nonsense and pretense, forthright in debate, and someone who wore her patriotism on her sleeve. She did not hesitate to point out to her English visitors the superiority of the American political system, and although she had stated that she would not engage in political discourse, she found it difficult to refrain from doing so. When Darcy had spoken of his cousin, Lord Fitzwilliam, Elizabeth had seized on the mere mention of his name as an opening to register her opposition to the House of Lords. When he had stated that the upper house of the U.S. Congress was appointed and not elected, she had a comeback. "But when a U.S. senator dies, his son does not immediately assume the seat, sitting in the well of the Senate until he dies of old age at his desk."

Rather than argue, he had pointed to a sloop making

excellent time going down the river. Elizabeth had teased him that she was not a child and would not be so easily diverted, and he smiled at the memory.

"William, I shall be very sorry to leave New York," Georgiana said, interrupting his thoughts. "I understand that we must go, but things are so much better here. A girl may go to a dance without the expectation that she is looking for a husband. It will be so different when I come out in London. If I have two dances with a gentleman, everyone will expect us to announce our engagement. If that were true here, I would be engaged to Francis Storm, Joshua Lucas, and Tad Van Tassel."

"What about that young man over there?"

"Do you mean Alex Hamilton?"

"Yes. Have you danced two dances with him because he is acting as if he merits some particular attention from you?"

"Oh, so you have been watching me?"

"I am always watching you."

"Yes, it is true that I did dance with him twice as he was very persistent," Georgiana said, smiling. "Mr. Hamilton is from New York City. He came to West Point to visit with his brother, William. Joshua Lucas told me that his father was killed in a duel with a famous person, but I do not remember the name."

"So you are telling me that he is from a family of hotheads?" Darcy pretended to be aghast.

Georgiana tapped the bridge of Darcy's nose. "You still have not told me how you injured your nose?"

"*Touché!* I *am* prying, and so I shall ask no more questions. And you may return to Alex Hamilton, son of Alexander Hamilton, an aide to George Washington during the Revolutionary War and Secretary of the Treasury. His father was killed in a duel by Aaron Burr, a former Vice

President of the United States."

"How do you know that?"

"I have been reading some of Richard's books as I have always had an interest in American history. You may not know that our great uncle, Andrew Fitzwilliam, fought in the French and Indian War with General Wolfe, who died on the Plains of Abraham in Quebec in 1757. If you would like to know the details of that battle, I shall be happy to share them with you."

Georgiana backed away from her brother, and holding up her hands as if to keep him at bay, she said, "No thank you. I shall leave you to your musings." But that was the last thing that Darcy wanted.

Chapter 23

Darcy and Georgiana waited on the Tarrytown landing for a farm wagon to finish loading hogsheads filled with produce destined for New York City so that they might hire the wagon. Usually this task would have fallen to Mercer, but Darcy had allowed his manservant to remain behind so that he might cover up the owl holes in the gable. On the night before their departure, Darcy had lain awake listening to the avian predators tear apart their kill. With the owlets now able to fend for themselves, Darcy had asked his host if it was possible to cover up the entries. Richard had immediately gone into the village to purchase the supplies necessary to block their entry into the attic.

Darcy was eager to get to Longbourn. He wanted to speak to Mrs. Bennet about Caroline Bingley and her sudden engagement. He also wanted to know if it was necessary to get word to Richard, who was in the city with Mr. Bennet, that his daughter intended to marry Louis Beekman or had her father already given his tacit approval to the match as Caroline had claimed?

As Georgiana and Darcy traveled down the drive to Longbourn, he could see Elizabeth sitting on the veranda with Dirck Storm, and Darcy's mood darkened.

Why was the man just sitting there like he owned the place? Worse yet, he was drinking lemonade. Wasn't that a drink served when someone was in the midst of a courtship?

After sending the wagon on to Richard's house, Darcy

and Georgiana joined Elizabeth and Dirck on the veranda. Georgiana fairly exploded with details about her visit to West Point. Everything was to her satisfaction, most especially the ball. Darcy said nothing as his sister related all the stories he had already heard at least twice, if not three times. While Georgiana talked, Lizzy noted that her brother looked exhausted, probably as a result of his having served as chaperone to a seventeen-year-old girl in the midst of a large male population. Or did it have something to do with Caroline Bingley? If that were the case, then things had not gone well, and Lizzy found herself smiling.

"You look tired, Mr. Darcy, or are you vexed about something?" Lizzy asked.

"I can assure you I am not vexed," he said in a voice contradicting his statement. "However, it was a rather long journey as we were forced to sit idle during the night as the sloop became stranded on a shoal. It was necessary to wait for the tide to come in."

"A common enough event on the Hudson as it is an estuary with tides and currents colliding," Dirck said, and Darcy thought, *I knew that, and who asked you?*

"I was on deck when the skies opened up, drenching me to the bone, and then the sun came out," Darcy said, pointing to his wrinkled coat as evidence that his clothes had been washed and dried while he had been wearing them.

"All you need is a bath, William," Lizzy said. "That will set you right."

"I shall see to it when I get to Richard's house," an uncomfortable Darcy answered.

"Does Richard still use that little tin tub?" Dirck asked, and Darcy nodded. "Oh, bother that. There is a full-length tub at Storm Hall."

From his look, Dirck guessed that the idea of talking

about something as mundane as bathing had embarrassed the Englishman—probably because it required taking off one's clothes. In that case, it was a good thing that summer had come and gone as it would have been hard to find boys and young men in the hot weather with their clothes *on* anywhere near a pond or stream in the whole of the county.

"Well, why go all the way to Storm Hall," Lizzy said. "We have a room at the back of the house that has a tub in it. Papa calls it a bath-room."

"I could not possibly accept," Darcy said embarrassed that such a thing would be discussed in mixed company.

"Why ever not? It is not as if I will be in the bath-room with you."

Darcy's face flamed, and Dirck burst out laughing. "That's Lizzy for you. She says what is on her mind."

"Well, if you change your mind, it would be an easy thing to send Ezekiel to Richard's house," Lizzy offered, "and Mercer could bring your things here."

"Another time, perhaps. But weren't you supposed to go into the city with Jane?"

"I did go, but after purchasing the material for my dress, I came home yesterday afternoon. Actually, I was sent home. I was told that I was not at all helpful in the important matter of choosing bridal accoutrements, and because I had already seen the play at the Park Theatre and there was little new in the bookstores, I saw no reason to remain."

"I cannot say that I am surprised," Darcy said, his mood lightening considerably.

"What does that mean?" Lizzy asked with her hands on her hips, feigning outrage.

"Since my arrival here in Tarrytown, I have frequently heard your name and the word 'tomboy' used in the same sentence. I do not think it is a secret that you do not like to visit the shops."

"That's Lizzy for you," Dirck reiterated, and to Darcy, the man sounded like his own echo.

"I had hoped to speak with your mother," Darcy said, ignoring Dirck's comment, "but of course, she is in the city with your sister."

Lizzy could tell that William was worried about something, but with Dirck sitting right there, nothing could be said.

"William, it is Wednesday, and Mrs. Haas will be attending church this evening. Would you like to come to Longbourn for a cheese sandwich?"

"Excellent suggestion," Dirck said, sitting up. "I haven't had one of your cheese sandwiches in ages. The Bennet dairy makes some of the best butter and cheese in the lower Hudson Valley."

"Thank you, but no. I shall leave you now as Mrs. Haas will be in need of a ride to town," Darcy said, forgetting that Mercer was at Richard's house and would be the one to take the cook to church.

After saying goodbye to his sister, Darcy walked off with steam coming out of his ears. Elizabeth had invited *him* for a cheese sandwich, not Dirck Storm. And what kind of name was Dirck Storm? Wasn't a dirk a Scottish knife or something like that? So his name was Knife Storm. Doubly stupid.

As Darcy walked the half mile to Richard Bingley's house, he could see a man on the road ahead of him, and he immediately recognized the figure of Mr. Collins. The man was so duck footed that it was amazing he could walk straight and keep to the road. Darcy gave out a sigh of resignation when he realized where the reverend was headed. *When it rains, it pours.*

Darcy hailed the parson, and when the man turned

around, he removed his hat and signaled to Darcy as if he were a figure on a distant shore.

"Mr. Darcy! I can hardly believe it is you," Mr. Collins cried.

"Why is that, Mr. Collins? You are walking in the direction of Richard Bingley's house where I am presently residing."

"Because you are just the person I was looking for."

"It is Wednesday. Are you not supposed to be in church?"

"The sexton is to lead tonight's prayers."

Damn! There were days when a person should not get out of bed—or off a sloop.

* * *

Darcy hated being dirty, and with his wet clothing stiff from baking in the sun, he felt as if his shirt and breeches were a part of him. He needed a bath badly, but with Mr. Collins walking two steps behind him, he would have to wait. When he walked in the door of Richard Bingley's house, he found Mercer eating a meal with Mrs. Haas.

"Mr. Darcy!" Mercer said, standing at attention as if he were a soldier in the presence of a senior officer.

"As you were, Mercer. Good evening, Mrs. Haas. May I ask that you see to Mr. Collins while I go upstairs for a few minutes? I need to wash my hands and face, so if there is water in the pitcher, I can fend for myself, Mercer."

On the way upstairs, Darcy looked at his pocket watch. It was later than he thought, and he wondered why Mercer had not taken Mrs. Haas into the village as she usually visited with her sister before going to worship service. After having removed his shirt, he was throwing the discarded garment in the corner when Mercer appeared in time to help his master take off his boots.

"Thank you, Mercer, but I am fine. You need to get Mrs. Haas to church or she will be late."

"She's not going this evening, sir."

"She is not ill, is she?" Darcy asked with real concern. He was looking forward to her apple fritters in the morning as the food at the academy had been tough, tasteless, and heavily salted.

"No, sir. She's got other things on her mind."

"I hope nothing serious." Other than Mrs. Haas's having a husband who had died of pneumonia a dozen years earlier and that she had family in the village, he knew little about the cook. As for Mr. Collins, he could not even imagine why he was here to see him. He would know soon enough, and he plunged his hands into the cold water.

"Mercer, do you have something on your mind?" Darcy asked as he accepted the offered towel.

"Well, it's about Mrs. Haas. As I said, she *does* have something on her mind, and it concerns marriage."

"Mrs. Haas is getting married! Well, that is the first piece of good news I have had in five days." Hopefully, she would not leave Richard's employ before he sailed for England.

"I've been meaning to talk to you, sir, but you being so busy and all, there was no chance to do it."

Darcy felt his stomach muscles tensing as it did at Mr. Jackson's Academy in preparation for taking a punch. "About what?"

"You see, Mrs. Haas is going to marry… me."

Darcy's mouth dropped open. "What? How? No! Please, no! Mercer, you know that you are indispensable to me. You cannot be spared. I will double your wages."

"This isn't about money, sir. It's about love."

Darcy immediately rebutted the very notion of love:

Love is as swift as a shadow, short as any dream,
Brief as the lightning in the collied night
That, in a spleen unfolds both heaven and earth,
And ere a man hath power to say 'Behold!'
The jaws of darkness do devour it up;
So quick bright things come to confusion.

"Excuse me, sir?"

"Love is fleeting," Darcy said in summary. "Mercer, you told me that the reason you had never married was because you did not understand women and never would."

"Well, I was wrong, sir. I understand Mrs. Haas just fine, and she understands me."

"Excuse me for being so personal, Mercer, but Mrs. Haas is a deeply religious woman. She goes to church three times a week. I know you go but rarely. That alone should give you pause for thought."

"That's true, sir. But Hilda says…"

Oh, God, he is calling her by her Christian name. Darcy was doomed.

"Hilda says that she goes three times a week because it gets her out of the kitchen, doing something different like, and gives her a chance to visit with her sister and her neighbors. She told me that when we got married, she would only go to church on the Sabbath, and she's very open minded. She said that the Church of England would suit her just fine."

"Church of England? As in a church *in* England?"

"Oh, yes, sir. She would come back to England with me. You don't think I want to quit your service, do you? Because I don't," Mercer quickly added. "It's this way, sir. If you insist on me moving on because I'd be a married man, I'll go, but I would rather stay on."

"Bless you, Mercer," Darcy said. "Of course, you will remain in my service. You are my right-hand man, and we shall discuss the necessary arrangements for Mrs. Haas's coming to Pemberley at another time. If you would just run a wet cloth over my back, I would appreciate it. I can take care of the rest."

"Sir, you don't have to stand over a wash basin. I can have a bath ready for you in two shakes of a lamb's tail."

"Thank you, but I do not have time for a bath right now as Mr. Collins has come to see me."

"Well, in that case, maybe me and Hilda *will* be going to church after all."

Chapter 24

Darcy sat down to a supper of oyster chowder and rye bread, but because the past few days had been nothing short of a disaster, he had little appetite. If the business with Caroline had not been bad enough, he had been forced to listen to the cooing of the cadets and Georgiana until the tide had freed the sloop from the shoal. And now Mr. Collins. But those things were mere annoyances when compared to the sight of Elizabeth drinking lemonade with Dirck Storm and hearing him call her Lizzy.

After Mercer and the future Mrs. Mercer had departed, Darcy encouraged Mr. Collins to explain the reason for his visit. He hoped the parson would get to the point quickly, but Darcy's run of bad luck continued.

"I was a lowly curate in a poor parish in Deal when I was offered the position at Hunsford Lodge by the vicar, Dr. Anselm Anglum. Within months of my arrival, Dr. Anglum took ill with an upset stomach and died. Of course, I am not implying that your aunt did not do everything in her power to facilitate the vicar's recovery."

"Mr. Collins, sometimes people just die."

"Yes, of course. As I was saying, the vicar had gone on to his just reward, but I was not offered the position. Instead, I remained a lowly curate. So when Mr. Bingley wrote to me about this vacancy here at St. Matthew's, I had to act on it."

"Yes, Mr. Collins, I have heard you mention how you

came to be in Westchester County on a number of occasions. But what brings you here tonight? Specifically here and specifically now?"

"It seems that I have been missed."

This is going to take forever. "By whom?"

"Lady Catherine de Bourgh! She has written a letter asking that I return to Kent. In brief, I am being offered a vicarage."

Darcy understood that in recognition of such an honor, actually more on the order of a miracle—Lady Catherine was as tight-fisted as they came—that he must make a fuss over his appointment. And so he stood up, patted Mr. Collins on the back as if he were a good old boy, and congratulated him.

"But because I am now an engaged man, there are complications."

For a few minutes, Darcy had forgotten that he was betrothed. It really was difficult to think of someone—anyone—actually being bound to Mr. Collins.

"And what did Miss Lucas say?"

"My dearest Charlotte said that I should feel free to return to England immediately, but it would be impossible for her to do the same as there is no one to take care of the store. She said her father and mother had placed a terrible burden on her when they left for Albany and that she would not do the same to Maria and Jacob. And Mr. Darcy, I cannot go without her. She is as much a part of me as my right arm," and he thrust it forward in Darcy's direction.

"How does Miss Lucas feel about moving to England?" Darcy asked, dodging the upraised arm.

"Actually, she is quite excited about it," Mr. Collins answered, drying his tears with Darcy's embroidered handkerchief. Between Caroline and Elizabeth and now Mr. Collins, he was running short of handkerchiefs. He would have to go to Lucas Mercantile and purchase a new supply, but he was pretty sure a visit to that store was in his near future.

"Even though she has no problem with eventually going to England, Charlotte said she could not possibly travel until spring, and there lies the rub."

Darcy waited and waited. *Spit it out man!* Of course, he could not spit it out because the parson was afraid he would say something about his patroness that might offend the nephew of said patroness.

"I suspect Lady Catherine is insisting you return immediately or forfeit the position. Is that correct?" Darcy could see that he was right, but it had been an easy guess.

"Her Ladyship has said I must make my decision as soon as possible and return to England post haste. She mentioned Twelfth Night, but…"

"It is an arbitrary date," Darcy said, interrupting. "My aunt knows nothing about sailing ships and how long it takes one to cross an ocean. So the question remains, other than the responsibility Miss Lucas feels for Lucas Mercantile, does she have any other objections to going to England with you?"

Darcy could think of at least ten without even trying.

"No, sir, and your grasp of the problem is quite amazing to me."

"And you wish for me to speak to Miss Lucas?"

"That would be appreciated." With his mission accomplished, the parson pointed to Darcy's unfinished soup. "I wouldn't say 'no' to another bowl of Mrs. Haas's chowder." Darcy pushed the half-eaten bowl across the table.

* * *

While Mr. Collins looked on in all amazement, the master of Pemberley hooked Old Fred up to the pony trap. He might be the grandson of an earl, but he knew his way around a stable.

Mr. Collins climbed in next to Darcy, and he rode with his hand on his broad-brimmed hat as if tacking sail all the way to Mrs. Philips's house where he was boarding. Before leaving Richard's house, Darcy insisted that he speak to Charlotte alone. If Mr. Collins was there, he would be constantly interrupted or, worse, the man would be in tears, and he absolutely hated when a grown man cried. Other than the death of a loved one, he could not imagine a situation where he would ever shed tears. And Darcy wondered what the man was like when called to the house of a dying parishioner. Who comforted whom?

Darcy found Lucas Mercantile ablaze with candles and Argand lamps as Charlotte, Maria, and Jacob were conducting inventory in preparation for the fall cleaning that preceded the winter season. With little to be done in the fields, people looked to their houses. Wood must be chopped, siding and shingles replaced, chimneys cleaned, rugs beaten, windows and mirrors washed, and draperies and curtains washed, ironed, and re-hung, and so Lucas Mercantile must have axes and axe handles, chimney brushes, rug beaters, borax and brushes, and irons on display.

As soon as Charlotte saw Mr. Darcy, she knew why he was there as Mr. Collins had mentioned that he might seek the advice of Lady Catherine's nephew. After welcoming Mr. Darcy, she invited him to join her in the back office for a cup of coffee.

"Thank you for coming, William. I was looking for an excuse to sit down. I have been on my feet since dawn. This is a particularly busy time for us as we must order everything that will be required for our Thanksgiving celebration on November 28th. It is the biggest holiday of the year."

After both had had their coffee and a piece of gingerbread, Darcy spoke to Charlotte about Mr. Collins's appointment at Hunsford Lodge. After acknowledging the compliment Lady Catherine had paid Mr. Collins by offering him the vicarship, Darcy felt compelled to mention that his aunt was also a tyrant.

"Her Ladyship is a most difficult person to get along with on the best of days, and she has few of those. You will be summoned to the manor house with no warning, and summarily dismissed when she has grown tired of your company. In addition to being imperious, abrupt, and impatient, she interferes in everyone's business, and there is nothing that is beneath her notice. She will have every shopkeeper in the village reporting on your purchases, allowing her to chastise you for buying a whole leg of lamb from the butcher or too much ribbon from the milliner. I could go on and on."

"William, I have been working in this store since I was ten years old. That is now seventeen years ago. In that period of time, I have seen it all. My father and mother have been greatly criticized for abandoning the store in favor of Albany, but for nearly thirty years, they stood where I now stand and endured so much from their customers. While the farmers accused my parents of charging outrageous prices, their wives complained that we had insufficient stock. Our axe handles split, our brushes disintegrated upon contact with nothing harsher than water, and our brooms fell apart after one sweeping. I, too, could go on and on, and although I appreciate the warning about your aunt, she would be nothing when compared to the Widow Vanderveer, who screeches like a scalded cat when she is angry, or Mr. McAllister, who roars like a lion when he is drunk and displeased. They also are tyrants."

"Well, it sounds as if you have been in training for many years to be the wife of my aunt's vicar," Darcy said with a smile. "So please allow me to summarize the situation. You *would* like to go to England with Mr. Collins; however, you feel your sister and brother will be unnecessarily burdened with the responsibilities of the store. Is that correct?" Charlotte nodded.

Darcy stood up and started to pace. It was obvious Miss Lucas wanted to go to England with Mr. Collins and that she wished to be free of the store as soon as possible. So what could be done on her behalf?

"It is my understanding that there is a movement afoot to have Tarrytown Harbor expanded so that it might accommodate steamboats," Darcy began. "If that is the case, then your trade will grow exponentially; therefore, I would suggest you write to your father telling him that it is necessary for you to hire a store manager to handle the added volume. There is a possibility that Richard Bingley would be available, and with his experience, you could not find a more qualified man. I know he has spoken to Mr. Bennet about managing his sloops, but I suspect he would prefer not to have to go back and forth to the city on a regular basis. This might be the perfect opportunity for him."

Darcy could see the wheels spinning, and after mulling it over for a few minutes, Charlotte nodded her head in agreement. "Well, William, you have given me a lot to think about. Regardless of my decision, it was very kind of you to come this evening."

"Think nothing of it. I often set out on similar missions when I am at my estate in Derbyshire. We may live on different sides of the Atlantic, but our problems are the same. I am happy to have been of service, and so I shall say good night."

Darcy was pleased that he had been able to make helpful suggestions, but in achieving the desired result, he had been less than candid. Although the problems of day-to-day living in their two countries might be the same, there were some larger issues that were widely divergent, England's rigid class structure for one. If someone, other than a relation, were to address him as William, they would be criticized and shunned for being so presumptuous. The idea of sitting down to dine with one's servants would never happen, and even though there was an increase in marriages between the gentry and those families involved in trade, those arrangements were looked upon with disfavor by England's elite.

There was no denying that for the common man things were better in America and the opportunities greater. But he also had to agree with Georgiana. America was a wonderful place to visit, but he was an Englishman and a master and such he would remain.

Chapter 25

As Darcy turned the pony trap in the direction of Richard's house, he was being serenaded by a thousand crickets that lay hidden in resting fields. He had noticed with the cooler temperatures the mosquitoes were less of a problem, and the swallows were doing an excellent job of further reducing their numbers. As he drew nearer to the Bennet residence, he wondered if Dirck Storm was still pestering Elizabeth. He might possibly be eating a grilled cheese sandwich in the kitchen at this very moment, and the thought of Elizabeth's specialty, with its oozing cheese, caused his stomach to rumble. Other than a half bowl of chowder, he had not had anything to eat all day. Surely, Elizabeth wouldn't mind making him a sandwich.

Darcy was relieved when the door was opened by his sister and not Mr. MacTavish, who often wore the same knowing smirk as his employer. But then he realized the MacTavishes were Methodists and would be attending worship services in the village.

"William, what a nice surprise," Georgiana said. "Please come in."

Darcy kissed his sister on her cheek. "Did you say anything to Elizabeth or Mary about Caroline's engagement?" he whispered.

Georgiana shook her head. "I thought it best not to say anything until the news could be shared with Mr. Richard."

"Is Elizabeth about?"

"She is in her father's study. That is where she does most of her writing."

"Would you please ask if I may speak with her?"

Elizabeth, with ink-stained fingers, soon appeared in the entryway and immediately teased him. "William, have you changed your mind about having a cheese sandwich?"

"Yes, I have as I am very nearly starved."

Darcy followed Lizzy down the back steps to the kitchen where Phillis and Lottie were playing manger cradle with yarn. After Phillis had made a cat's cradle, she passed it to Lottie, and back and forth they went. After watching the exhibition for several minutes, the girls were dismissed.

After looking at his weary countenance, Lizzy said, "I suspect you have more on your mind than a cheese sandwich, William." Darcy nodded. But first, Lizzy got about the business of feeding a hungry man.

"It is true I do have something on my mind. Caroline Bingley remains at West Point. It is her plan to return to Saratoga Springs, and once there, to accept an offer of marriage from Louis Beekman."

"What?" Lizzy said, her knife suspended in mid air. She was unsure which was greater: her relief that William would not be marrying Caroline or her surprise that Caroline was marrying Louis Beekman.

"Caroline told me that Mr. Beekman has been asking her to marry him since her return from England. She said that he was a cousin to your mother and that Mrs. Bennet likes him very much. Is this not true?"

"Yes, it is true he is my mother's cousin, and she does like him." *Or as much as one can like a ruthless man of business who crushes all opposition.* "It is my understanding that he called on my mother when she was last in the city with your sister and, as usual, was most hospitable."

"Caroline said that she had made arrangements to return to Saratoga Springs by sloop."

"Not just any sloop, William, but Louis's *The Croesus*, a vessel fit for a king. I once traveled on *The Croesus* and in one of Mr. Beekman's carriages, and I can assure you that Caroline will return to Saratoga Springs in the greatest of comfort and safety as Louis always travels with at least one man who carries a pistol. And as for her interval at West Point, I am equally sure she will be the guest of the Commandant as Mr. Williams is a friend of Mr. Beekman's, and she has mentioned their friendship to me."

"I feel a little better now, but I am still unsettled by this sudden engagement. Caroline said that her father will readily approve of the match, but if that is the case, then why did she hesitate to marry him in the first place?"

Lizzy wanted to say *because she is in love with you*, but she could not mention that minor detail. Obviously, Caroline's plans to secure Mr. Darcy during their visit to West Point had not come to fruition. She felt bad for Caroline, but not enough to have wished for a different outcome.

"Why did she not marry Mr. Beekman, you ask? I can think of a few reasons. To begin with, Louis is not the best looking man. He has a double chin, a rather large head, and a bit of a paunch," Lizzy said, patting her middle. "And he is rather short, probably the same height as Caroline. However, when they enter a room together, they will be well matched."

Obviously, Elizabeth was trying to avoid saying the word "ugly," so Darcy asked her if that were the case.

"Ugly? Oh, that is such a harsh word. It is just that my preferences are for someone who is… is more… different."

"And what are your preferences?" he asked with a glint in his eye.

"Well, a man with blonde hair, blue eyes, slender build, and a good dancer would come close to fitting the bill," she said, being careful to avoid mentioning any of William's physical traits.

"You have just described Charles Bingley."

"Good grief, no!" Then Lizzy realized how harsh that sounded. "That came out all wrong. What I meant to say was that Charles and Jane are perfect for each other as they see only sunny skies. I, on the other hand, prefer a cloudy day now and then, and because of my nature, I get them. I have fallen short of the glory of God on many occasions."

"For example?"

"I have been accused of being too eager to share my opinions, and there are many who think that a woman should not have opinions on matters other than those affecting the wellbeing of her family. But why, when I am subject to the same laws as men are, am I to have no say? It seems rather unfair to me."

"Are you proposing that women should have the right to vote?"

"Why not? I could have told Mr. Jefferson that his embargo would prove disastrous for merchants and shopkeepers, and if he had listened to me, it would not have been necessary for my father to engage in…"

"Engage in what?"

"It would not have been necessary for my father to have looked for other ways of selling his merchandise," Lizzy said with a grimace. Mr. Bennet had outfitted several of his sloops as privateers bringing in European goods to New York City from Nova Scotia.

Darcy started to laugh. The idea of a woman voting was funny enough, but Elizabeth's unsuccessful attempt to hide the fact that her father was a privateer was even more amusing.

"Before becoming my valet, Mercer drove a Royal Mail coach between Dover and London. As a result, he has associates who are able to provide him with excellent French brandy, laces, and perfumes, among other things, despite the wars with France."

"Mr. Mercer wears lace and uses perfume? How unique," Lizzy said with a grateful smile, Darcy having rescued her from her gaffe.

"By the way, Mercer is to marry Mrs. Haas, and why do you not look surprised?"

"My mother was the first to notice that Mr. Mercer was putting on weight, which meant he was spending a lot of time in the kitchen. It was rather obvious if one had the eyes to see it."

"To the crime of indifference, I plead 'not guilty.' If you had heard, as I have on many occasions, Mercer's opinion of marriage, you would not have foreseen a wedding. But to finish our conversation regarding Caroline, she will be all right, will she not?" Darcy asked.

"William, I can assure you that no matter how challenging the situation, Caroline always lands on her feet."

Chapter 26

The next morning, Mercer asked if he should prepare a bath for his master, but Darcy was in no mood to sit in a little tin tub while his manservant poured water over his head. He decided he would take Dirck Storm up on his offer to use his full-length tub.

While traveling the distance between Bingley's house and Storm Hall, he thought how everyone seemed to be paired up: Miss Lucas and Mr. Collins, Jane and Charles, and Georgiana and a host of adoring young men. With Mercer in the kitchen wooing Mrs. Haas, he was feeling very much alone, and he wondered if Elizabeth was *sweet* on Dirck Storm. With Jane shortly to be married to Charles, Elizabeth might decide to replace her sister with a husband, and the thought of Dirck and Elizabeth as husband and wife sent a cold shiver rippling through him.

When Darcy arrived at Storm Hall, he was greeted by their butler. Although he felt awkward in begging for a bath, he was too dirty not to make the request. Jamison suggested that Darcy wait in the rear parlor while preparations were made, and he was reading the newspaper when Dirck came bounding in.

"Glad to see you that you have decided to take me up on my offer, Darcy. You may have noticed that Richard bathes infrequently, as do most people in these parts, because they think it is bad for their health. Richard is quite content to use that old tin tub for his quarterly ablutions. But for a big man such as yourself, it really is uncomfortable."

"Thank you again for your offer. When I return to England, I am going to see about installing a bath-room, one in which the water is channeled to a particular room from a cistern as Mr. Bennet has done in his kitchen."

"We are doing the same thing here. In the spring, we are to add a separate bath-room to the rear of the house. We are buying the pipe from Tom Bennet, and his men will excavate for the cistern and do all the work. The man's a genius."

"Yes, he is."

"I have known the Bennets all my life. Lizzy and I have always been particularly close. We used to go down to the river and dig for oysters and crayfish during the summer and go ice skating or ice yachting in the winter. We also spent many a lazy summer's afternoon at a nearby fishing hole as well as hours sitting side by side in a walnut tree. We had been sweet on each other for the longest time, but then I went to Oxford."

Oxford, that explains it. I should have guessed as much. "And after you returned, you were no longer sweethearts?" Darcy asked.

"Oh, I wouldn't say that. Ah, here is Jamison. Your bath is ready."

After bathing, while Darcy was dressing, he could hear Dirck talking to a lady, and he recognized the voice as belonging to Elizabeth, and she was giggling. When he went into the foyer, he found Elizabeth had her hand on Dirck's face. After mumbling his thanks to Dirck, he immediately went out the front door.

Lizzy followed him out. Although she called after him, he kept walking. "William, please wait!"

Darcy finally stopped. When he turned around, Elizabeth could see that he was angry, and she could guess the reason.

"I was going to invite you for supper this evening."

"No, thank you."

"With Richard still in the city, I suspect Mrs. Haas will only make potato leek soup, so why should you not come to Longbourn?"

"I would not wish to interfere with any of your social engagements."

"Are you referring to Dirck?"

Darcy did not wish to answer. He had no claim on Elizabeth, and if she wanted to be with Dirck, that was her business, not his. But unlike his conversation with Caroline, in which he had wanted to say nothing, now he had so much that he wished to say.

"In English society, when a woman puts her hands on a man's face, it usually indicates that there are expectations."

"Expectations? Of what? Marriage? Is that what you are implying?" Darcy said nothing. "Well, what does one do in England when a man is standing right in front of woman and has strawberry jam on his face? Cannot a lady, who has known the gentleman for the whole of her life, remove it? Or are they expected to get married over a smidgen of jam? That seems a bit drastic, but it is in keeping with my experiences in England where small matters are turned into major events.

"Furthermore, I think you have been here long enough to know that Americans are more informal than Englishmen and are certainly more forgiving. If I make a misstep, I am not pilloried in public and in private. And although there are differences in our expressions, I would not call you vulgar or gossip behind your back because you do not speak as I do. In England, you do many things, a great many of which I do not like, but it would not prevent me from inviting you to take supper with me. Good day, Mr. Darcy."

Lizzy walked away, but quickly returned. "The reason I am at Storm Hall is because Mrs. Storm is expecting her first child and is experiencing nausea. Mrs. Kraft prepared a draught for her, and I brought it to her. That is all." She then walked back to her pony cart and was halfway down the drive before Darcy could think of a response.

* * *

The next day, Darcy gave Longbourn a wide berth as he knew he had messed up badly. After a long walk, he wondered if he should go to the house and apologize. But if he showed up at Longbourn, it might indicate that he presumed an intimacy where there was none. He decided that it would be better to wait. Let things cool down.

Besides, many of the things Elizabeth had mentioned had nothing to do with him. It was true she had said a few things that would not be mentioned in mixed company in England. A good example was when she had encouraged him to bathe in Longbourn's bath-room. But he had not repeated her comment to anyone else. He certainly had never gossiped behind her back, and he most definitely did not consider her to be vulgar. No, Elizabeth had offended someone during her time in England. By English standards, she had fallen short and had been punished for it. Caroline Bingley was right. London society was no place for someone as spontaneous and honest as Elizabeth Bennet, but that realization brought him cold comfort.

Chapter 27

As soon as Jane and Charles returned from the city, plans for the nuptials were discussed. But it was also necessary to think beyond the wedding to Jane's voyage to England, and such discussions usually went forward without Lizzy. Noting his daughter's distress at Jane's impending departure, Mr. Bennet recommended an excursion to Greenbrook Falls in New Jersey. Because the autumn colors would be near their peak, it would be the perfect time to go. There was also another reason for the proposed visit. Mrs. Bennet's half-brother, John Gardiner, owned a hotel in Alpine near a waterfall, and Aunt and Uncle Gardiner were great favorites of the Bennet daughters.

With everyone busily planning for the wedding, it looked as if only Mr. Bennet, Lizzy, and Ezekiel would be making the trip, that is, until Georgiana indicated she too would like to go, and Lizzy knew that Georgiana could not go without William. But it did not really matter to Lizzy. Although cordial when in each other's company, only pleasantries were exchanged. The discussions they had once enjoyed were a thing of the past.

After outfitting Georgiana for treks in the woods and walks along the cascading falls, the party crossed the Hudson by ferry to a landing at the foot of the palisades. From there, they traveled by coach until they arrived at the Gardiners' hotel. As soon as the conveyance had disgorged its passengers, they were met by Mr. and Mrs. Gardiner and three of their four children, the eldest, Nathaniel Greene

Gardiner, being absent as he was an ensign in the U.S. Navy serving on the *U.S.S. Constellation.*

Mr. Gardiner, a gangly six foot, three inches, was even taller than Darcy, while Mrs. Gardiner was shorter than Elizabeth. But what Mrs. Gardiner lacked in height, she made up in girth, an admirer of her own cooking. Both were outgoing souls who were thrilled to have the company.

"My goodness, you have come at the perfect time," Mrs. Gardiner said. "Until this very morning, every room was taken by the Wilderness Society of Paterson, and they were a hardy lot. Out early every morning, combing the wilderness for what they called 'specimens,' and back at night to discuss their finds and for a hearty meal, several tankards of Mr. Bennet's ale, and off to bed to begin again in the morning. But listen to me going on when I have not yet been introduced to your company."

After the introductions were made, Mr. Gardiner showed them to their rooms. The inn, a structure that was fifty-years old when the Gardiners had bought it ten years earlier, was built into a hillside, and so for every two steps up, they took one step down, with the innkeeper reminding Darcy to watch his head. Finally, when they arrived at their rooms, the reason for the circuitous route was apparent. Most rooms had a spectacular view of the falls.

"We had quite a storm two nights ago," Mr. Gardiner said, "and so the falls are running full out. Because of the heavy rain, the leaves have thinned out at the higher elevations, but at the base of the falls and on out to the river, they are gorgeous."

Both Georgiana and Darcy had commented on the beautiful colors of the palisades, but because of extensive logging, there were few large swaths left where the colors could truly be appreciated. But not here. The views were glorious, and it was the diversity of the woods that provided the panoply of colors.

"We have red oak, hickory, black birch, sugar maple, beech, and dogwood. The swamp areas are covered with red maple, sweet gum, elm, tupelo, and willow as well as laurel, blueberry, azalea, and grape. There is also witch hazel, and I know Annie will be wanting some for her medicine chest," Mr. Gardiner said to his brother-in-law. "And if any of you fancy songbirds, we have hundreds of them. There's a fellow who comes here in the spring and fall and draws them. One of his sketches of a scarlet tanager is in the parlor."

"Are there many animals about?" Georgiana asked as she had seen all manner of beasts in a book that Richard had in his library of the Lewis and Clark expedition.

"You might see a black bear or two looking for berries, but they will scoot as soon as they see you. Then there's deer, fox, skunk, chipmunk, rabbit, squirrel and its cousins, flying squirrels."

"A squirrel that flies?" Georgiana asked, and she wondered if Mr. Gardiner liked to tease as much as Mr. Bennet did.

"It doesn't really fly, but has webbing attached to its arms that allows it to coast in the air, and we have raccoons at night and bats, but you will not be out there after dark. You can't see ten feet in front of you."

Supper was venison stew, pumpkin pie, and strong coffee served up with animated conversation that covered a range of topics, including the news that a mountain climber had reached the apex of Jungfrau in the Bernese Alps. Because of their English visitors, the topic on most people's minds was avoided: another war with Britain.

Shortly after supper, the tired guests were ready for bed, but Aunt Gardiner asked to have a word with her niece as she was eager to hear news of her family from across the river.

Lizzy was pleased to report that everyone was in good

health. After a long summer's break, the school year had barely begun, and yet the twins were already tired of their lessons. Although Lydia and Kitty might protest, there would be no hope of escape until Thanksgiving. Lizzy also spoke of how Georgiana had easily found a place in the heart of the Bennet family and would be missed by all, but most especially Mary.

"It is amazing how much Mary's playing on the pianoforte has improved as a result of Georgiana's instruction. Every time Mary plays a new tune, we nod our heads in appreciation for Miss Darcy's efforts."

"And what of Jane and Mr. Bingley? Your mother writes that Jane has made an excellent match."

"Jane has found the perfect husband in Charles Bingley. Everyone who knows Charles loves him as he is a wonderful man with a kind heart. It is just the distance between America and England that I find hard to bear, but please let us speak of something else or I shall shed copious amounts of tears and embarrass myself."

"I understand you will miss your sister, but considering that Jane is marrying a man whom she loves very much, such news should be celebrated," Aunt Gardiner said, placing her hand on Elizabeth's. "Is there any other news you wish to share?"

"Charlotte Lucas is to marry Mr. Collins, the pastor at St. Matthew's, and they are to move to England as Mr. Collins is to return to the vicarage in Kent."

"Lizzy, are you deliberately avoiding mentioning Mr. Darcy?"

"Of course not," she answered, her voice cracking. "He is a very nice man, the perfect English gentleman, and in three weeks, Jane and Charles will marry, we will celebrate Thanksgiving, and after that, they will all board a ship for Liverpool and, hopefully, arrive in England in time to celebrate Twelfth Night by their own hearths."

"Mr. Darcy is very handsome."

"So it said by many."

"Are you among them?"

"He is attractive enough, but not handsome enough to tempt me," Lizzy said, hoping to avoid any further discussion about Mr. Darcy. But there was no getting around her aunt's probing looks, and she confessed all.

"Mr. Darcy and I were engaged in a bit of a flirtation, but quarreled over something stupid. Although he is all politeness, we rarely speak on any matter of consequence, which is best for both of us. If you want to know why he is here, it is because of his sister, not me."

"May I inquire as to the cause of your disagreement?"

Lizzy summarized the argument that had taken place at Storm Hall, and in the retelling, it sounded even pettier than the actual episode.

"It seems as if you both lost your tempers. Considering that the gentleman is to leave within the month, I would think you would want to resolve the matter before he goes. I am sure that at some point you will go to England to visit Jane, and because Mr. Darcy is such a close friend to Mr. Bingley, you will most definitely see him. Surely, you do not want your quarrel to fester and grow into something more serious. I would suggest that tomorrow when you walk to the falls that you bring it up, get it out into the open, and then it will be over and done with."

"You are right, and I shall take your advice," Lizzy said, kissing her aunt. "But now I must go to bed as Georgiana will be wondering where I am."

"We have a great horned owl that has nested nearby, and her brood can get quite noisy when they have had a successful hunt," Mrs. Gardiner explained. "I hope they will not disturb Miss Darcy."

Lizzy just laughed. "I can assure you they will not."

Chapter 28

Proceeding Indian style, the party made their way to the falls. While Georgiana required a good deal of assistance, Elizabeth was jumping over logs, climbing rocks, and returning bird calls. She was clearly in her element, and Darcy was enjoying watching her as she pointed out an indigo bunting above them or a ruffed grouse walking among the brush.

When they arrived at the base of the falls, Darcy wished to go higher, but Georgiana was showing signs of fatigue. After Mercer agreed to remain behind with her, Lizzy and Darcy proceeded, and their efforts were rewarded when they were so close to the falls that the spray covered their faces and clothes. This caused both of them to start laughing, and Lizzy saw it as a perfect time to apologize for her behavior at Storm Hall.

"Mr. Darcy, please allow me to apologize for…"

"Elizabeth, please do not say another word. You have no cause to apologize. I misjudged the situation entirely, and even if I had not, it was impertinent of me to comment. But I feel that you were not just addressing me, but an earlier injustice, possibly from your time in England."

"You see right through me, Mr. Darcy."

"Now that I have admitted my error and have apologized for it, may I be William again? We are friends, are we not?"

"Of course, we are friends, *William*."

"As a friend, will you confide in me and tell me what happened in England?"

"It is a very long story." Darcy gestured to a rock away from the fall's spray, and Lizzy and he sat down. "This unpleasantness happened toward the end of my stay in England. I say that because I want you to know that I very much enjoyed my time in your country, and it is but one unfortunate episode in an otherwise excellent adventure.

"After leaving Hertfordshire, my family had taken rooms in Bath, and despite the daily cloud bursts, we loved everything about that ancient Roman town. Our rooms were near to Sydney Gardens, and I walked every day of fine weather. One afternoon, while Jane and I were in the gardens, I met a gentleman who..."

"Does this gentleman have a name?"

"Mr. Edward Chamberlain of Buckinghamshire."

"I am not personally acquainted with the Chamberlains, but, occasionally, I have seen Edward in town. His father was recently knighted."

"Well, the elder Mr. Chamberlain was merely a member of the gentry when I met him. Maybe, he was elevated because of our association," and Lizzy smiled her winning smile. "Anyway, Edward, Jane, and I enjoyed a pleasant afternoon watching the various performers scattered about the grounds of the gardens. During our ramblings, Edward suggested I go to a ball being held in the Upper Rooms, which I did, and we danced two sets.

"I found Edward to be very good company, nothing more, and I had no idea he was entertaining a notion of making me an offer of marriage. When his parents came to Bath, I was invited to their rooms at the White Hart for tea. I know I made a few gaffes, but I was unaware that I was auditioning for the role of daughter-in-law. When I did say something that made his parents wince, Edward just laughed and referred to me as a 'pistol.' I took it as a compliment.

"The next morning I received a note from Lady Chamberlain asking that I go for a carriage ride with her. If I had known what was about to transpire, I would never have gotten in that carriage. Her complaints were so many I can hardly remember them all. This was 1808, an election year in the United States. My father was a Federalist in favor of Charles Pinckney who was running against Mr. Jefferson's hand-picked successor, James Madison. I thought it a timely discussion because Mr. Jefferson's embargo had devastated trade between England and America. Apparently, ladies do not discuss trade or politics in England. But that was nothing compared to her next complaint. She said I laced my speech with colloquialisms, many of which she suspected were vulgar."

Darcy took Lizzy's hand and squeezed it and shook his head indicating she was incapable of such an offense.

"Furthermore, Lady Chamberlain told me that I was attempting to quit the sphere into which I was born. In America, we do not have spheres. You may rise as high as opportunity and hard work allow. I did not have time to think about the meaning of her words because when I returned to our rooms, I learned that my grandfather had died. But on the ocean voyage home, I *did* have the time to think about it, and I realized how I had erred.

"To begin with, I shared an observation that British society is much more formal than American society. In England, there are so many rules, and so many ways to get in trouble, especially if you are female. But my greatest error was in speaking about the United States. I am proud of my country and its accomplishments, but Lady Chamberlain could not believe there was anything in America that was superior to what one would find in England."

Darcy now understood why Elizabeth had been criticized. Knowing of her enthusiasm for pointing out the benefits of being an American, Darcy had no doubt she had challenged Lady Chamberlain's narrow views with gusto.

"Lady Chamberlain's objections were petty and stated for the purpose of keeping you away from her son."

"Oh, I know that now, but at the time, I thought we were having a lively debate. Apparently not. That same afternoon, I received a note from Edward, telling me that an emergency required his immediate departure from Bath. But I am not convinced he even wrote the note, or if he did, I believe his mother was standing next to him dictating his response. After sending it on its way, I suspect poor Edward was bound and gagged by his parents, placed in a trunk, and sent home by coach before he could do any more harm to his family's aspirations."

Darcy laughed out loud at the vision of a bundled Edward Chamberlain, and his voice echoed off the hard rock and rose above the spray, his laughter a balm for Lizzy's old wound.

"As for you quitting your sphere," Darcy said, "you did no such thing as you are the daughter of a gentleman. And there is no excuse for Lady Chamberlain's rudeness. None. But I hope you will understand that our society is much older than yours. Over the centuries, we have had ample opportunity to make up all these rules, some of them ridiculous, but many others important for the wellbeing of society as a whole. But it is easy to understand why you would chafe at such encumbrances. They probably make little sense to you."

"I no longer care about what happened to me in Bath, but I am concerned about Jane. Will she be treated in the same manner as I was?"

"No, I really do not think so. Charles does not move in high society where such prejudices are on display."

"As the grandson of an earl, I imagine you *do* move amongst society's elite."

"Yes and no. The highest society consists of the coterie surrounding the Prince Regent, and I will have nothing to do with His Royal Highness or the baggage that follows him around."

"But as the grandson of an earl, you must have access to the social world of the aristocracy."

"I do have access," Darcy answered, "but I choose not to visit these elite venues."

"May I ask why?"

"I do not have a good relationship with my cousin, Lord Fitzwilliam, as he can usually be found losing money at his club or in London's gaming parlors. Because of his losses, he is mired in debt and spends a good deal of his time evading merchants and debt collectors. But he is certainly not unique in that regard."

Darcy realized that Lizzy must be wondering why he would choose to associate with such people, but he had no answer for her. Instead, he climbed down off the boulder, and while helping Lizzy, she slid off the rock, right into him. He looked into her eyes and reached up and pushed the hair off her face and tucked it back into her bonnet. As much as he wanted to kiss her, it would have been wrong to do so.

"Do I have a smidgen of jam on my face, William?"

Darcy merely shook his head, unable to utter a word, and they headed down the path to rejoin Mercer and Georgiana.

Chapter 29

With November upon them, the nights had grown cold, but inside the common room of the inn, all were comfortable as there were two cast iron stoves giving off sufficient heat to warm the Bennets and their friends. Tom Bennet could not resist crowing about the thermal output of his Pennsylvania stoves, and he was soon engaged in a conversation with guests of the inn as to the obvious advantages of his product in the ongoing battle of stove versus open hearth.

Darcy relished his time in this woodland oasis. It also afforded an opportunity for Darcy to quiz Mr. Bennet on the particulars of the prospectus presented to him by Stephen Van Rensselaer regarding the building of the canal. Mr. Bennet had much to say on the matter, and although he could see there would be hurdles, his general opinion was that "the thing will be built."

In addition to Tom Bennet, he particularly enjoyed the company of Mr. and Mrs. Gardiner. Mrs. Gardiner reminded Darcy of Mrs. Bennet, someone in possession of an abundance of common sense and basic goodness, and like Tom Bennet, Mr. Gardiner, a veteran of the Revolution, enjoyed telling stories. When he was asked by Georgiana if he had always been an innkeeper, he had responded in supreme understatement that he had once been a lawyer practicing in New York City, "but retired from that profession to earn an honest living."

At the urging of his children, Mr. Gardiner shared some

of his more famous cases, including the gruesome murder of a young Quaker girl, Gulielma Sands, who was last seen stepping into a sleigh with an unknown gentleman in front of her boarding house and who was found a few days later at the bottom of a well.

"I was one of four lawyers who successfully defended the accused, Levi Weeks. But the trial turned into a circus with crowds outside the courthouse baying for Levi's blood. Shortly after his acquittal, I bought this inn."

"But, Papa, you did not tell Miss Darcy that Gulielma's corpse was put on display by her guardians for four days so that anyone with information concerning her murder might come forward," twelve-year old Daniel said.

"Yes, all Elias and Catherine Ring cared about was obtaining justice for their ward," Mr. Gardiner said bitterly of the gruesome exhibition. "But there is a lesson for every child in that unfortunate girl's story. Gulielma left the boarding house without telling her guardians where she was going and with whom. So what is to be learned from this poor girl's murder? If you do not listen to your parents, the bogeyman will get you." He then pointed at each of his three children, and they pretended to be frightened.

"I will tell our visitors that this part of the country there are many gifted storytellers. There is a particularly good story about a headless horseman who roams the countryside carrying his head under his arm. The rider is believed to be a Hessian soldier, who lost his head to a cannonball during the Revolutionary War. When he is not terrorizing the populace with his midnight rides, he is in his grave at the cemetery in the Old Dutch Church in Tarrytown."

"In Tarrytown!" Georgiana exclaimed, "But that is very near to where Mr. Bennet lives. We pass it every time we go into the village."

Darcy had heard his share of grisly tales from his fishing guide during his foray into the countryside near

West Point. According to Prickly Van Riper, the county abounded in ghouls and ghosts who stalked the night looking for their missing appendages. When he had returned to Tarrytown, he had shared some of the less offensive stories with his sister. Apparently, Georgiana was one of those people who enjoyed being frightened—something he never understood. From her expression, Darcy could tell that he would soon be visiting the cemetery at the Old Dutch Church in search of the grave of a nameless Hessian.

Darcy continued to enjoy this sylvan retreat, especially since it had provided him with an opportunity to mend fences with Elizabeth. Every time he thought about his childish display at Storm Hall, a wave of embarrassment came over him. Because there was no Dirck Storm to distract him, Elizabeth and he had spent an agreeable evening playing backgammon, and he was looking forward to another three or four worry-free days.

* * *

When Darcy came down to breakfast, he found another visitor at the table. Joshua Lucas had arrived from West Point. As much as Darcy liked the young man, his presence created problems for him. Although Georgiana continued to insist she had no romantic interest in Joshua, nothing in their words or deeds spoke of a platonic relationship, so Darcy used another walk to the falls as an opportunity to discuss the problem with Elizabeth.

"What am I to do about Joshua and Georgiana?" Darcy asked. "We are scheduled to leave in three weeks' time. I can just imagine an emotional Georgiana crying for her lover as we pull away from the dock."

Lizzy could easily picture such a scene and thought that Georgiana would not be the only one who would be crying. In addition to saying goodbye to a most beloved sister, she must part with Georgiana, whom she had grown to love as a sister, and then there was William. Since their discussion at the falls, her feelings for him had returned, stronger than ever. He was all that a man should be: strong, kind, attentive, and willing to overlook her foibles, but one who was soon to leave her.

"I agree that tears will flow, but once Georgiana returns to England, she will be so busy in preparing for her debut that Joshua will become a pleasant memory."

"You sound so sure. Why?"

"Because it is like you and me. You must admit that we have had a bit of a flirtation." Lizzy looked at Darcy for confirmation, and he nodded. "But it is harmless and will soon be forgotten once you are back in the midst of London society."

Darcy did not like this turn of conversation. He did not want to think Elizabeth would soon forget him as he knew he would *never* forget her. In fact, when he had placed his hand on her face, he knew beyond a doubt that he was in love. Although their coming together was impossible, he did not want to think he would be remembered as a "harmless flirtation," a mere pleasant memory.

Darcy could not remember a time when he was more confused. He loved Elizabeth Bennet, but was love enough? As a reasonable man, he must look at the facts. Although he considered Tom Bennet to be a gentleman, thus making Elizabeth a gentleman's daughter, there were many in England who considered America to be a land peopled by ruffians. Americans were held in contempt by London society as an inferior breed, a group of people who had failed to recognize the value of being citizens of the greatest empire on earth. And the very thing that Darcy admired in Elizabeth, her willingness, actually her compunction, to say what was on her mind, would be ridiculed. His friends might very well regard her as a "pistol," but it would *not* be a compliment. There was also the matter of Caroline's warning to him. If he married Elizabeth and threw her into the maelstrom of London society, he would be doing her a great injustice.

"William, if you do not concentrate on where you are walking, you will slip and fall," Lizzy cautioned him.

"Thank you for your interest in my safety."

"Oh, I wasn't thinking of you. If you fall, you might land on me." And there was that smile again.

Georgiana, who had found the climb to the falls too fatiguing just two days earlier, was clambering up the hillside as she made her way to the top where the cataract would begin its descent to the Hudson. As she made her assent, Georgiana found it necessary to take hold of Joshua so that she might not slip and fall, and Darcy doubted that his sister's need was genuine.

"William, stop frowning. It makes you look like a curmudgeon, and you are worrying unnecessarily," Lizzy said, scolding him. "Your sister knows she cannot stay in America, and Joshua can most definitely not go to England as he is shortly to be commissioned."

"When did this happen?"

"He spoke of it this morning at breakfast. And I ask you, will your worrying about Georgiana and Joshua change one thing? No, so you had best make use of your time to enjoy your stay."

Darcy nodded in agreement. There were falls to be enjoyed, rocks to be climbed, landscapes to be admired, and a picnic lunch to be eaten. "Lead on, Elizabeth!"

Chapter 30

The day of Jane's wedding was quickly approaching, but she would not be the only November bride. While Lizzy had been in New Jersey, her dearest friend, Charlotte Lucas, had become Mrs. William Collins. Charlotte and Mr. Collins had quietly slipped into the city and had been married by the Episcopal bishop of New York. The couple had spent the first three days of their married life together in the Beekman townhouse.

"Shortly after the excursion to West Point," Charlotte explained to Lizzy, "Caroline wrote to offer her congratulations. You look surprised that I had a letter from her when I have never had one before, but no more than I. In her letter, she offered the townhouse for our honeymoon, insisting that Louis and she would not be in the city until December. She wrote that they are to marry in the spring, and from her description of the preparations and a list of the guests, including President and Mrs. Madison and Governor and Mrs. Tompkins, it will be the wedding of the year."

"Caroline never does anything by half measures," Lizzy said, "but I wish her well."

"Really?" During their childhood in Tarrytown, Caroline had been rather unpleasant to every girl in the neighborhood, but had been particularly nasty to Elizabeth, probably because Lizzy would not defer to her in all things. "Do you wish Caroline well because she is marrying Louis Beekman or because Mr. Darcy broke her heart?"

"Who said anything about Mr. Darcy breaking her heart?"

"No one had to say it. At Storm Hall, it was rather obvious that Caroline was in love with Mr. Darcy. I am quite certain she thought that upon her return from West Point, she would announce her engagement. She did. It was just to a different man. I hope Caroline's heart will be the only one to be broken by that gentleman."

"You have no worries, Charlotte. William is shortly to return to England, and our flirtation will come to an end. I never thought it would be otherwise."

* * *

Mercer, who had spent a good part of his adult life avoiding marriage, could not wait to be called husband. After securing the permission of Mr. Darcy to marry, he had approached Mr. Collins about waiving the necessity of publishing banns of marriage so that Mrs. Haas and he might travel to England as man and wife. Because the bishop had just done that very thing for him, the minister was willing to unite Mercer and Mrs. Haas in marriage if Mr. Darcy would sign an affidavit declaring that he knew Mercer to have no living wife. In doing so, Darcy learned that Mercer's Christian name was not John, but Augustus.

"My mother had high hopes for me," Mercer explained with a sheepish grin, "but Hilda prefers to call me John. She doesn't want me to get a big head."

"I am beginning to suspect there is much that I do not know about you, Augustus," Darcy said, and Mercer answered with a smile.

Three days before Jane and Charles were to be united in marriage, Hilda Haas and Augustus John Mercer were joined in holy wedlock.

* * *

The day of the wedding arrived, and Longbourn was in turmoil. With Jane's four sisters serving as her bridesmaids, there were chemises, stays, dresses, ribbons, and bows in every upstairs room. To avoid the chaos, Mr. Bennet beat a hasty retreat to Richard's house where he found a calm Charles and an anxious Darcy, which puzzled him greatly.

Darcy *was* agitated. In addition to being surrounded by couples in love, Joshua Lucas had come down by sloop from West Point. Granted, he was captain of the guard and that rank had its privileges, but this was getting ridiculous. Darcy was not looking forward to the return voyage. A crying sibling and the company of three merry pairs of newlyweds might prove intolerable. Maybe it was a good thing that it was a near certainty he would be confined to his cabin for most of the voyage.

Kitty and Lydia were the first to walk down the aisle and looked adorable in their yellow dresses with white pantaloons, and Mary Bennet had never looked lovelier. But then Elizabeth appeared. She was wearing a pale green dress that made her look like a woodland goddess, and her beautiful tresses were adorned with jeweled pins that looked like stars plucked from a night sky. Darcy thought of Romeo's exclamation, "She doth teach the torches to burn bright," and he took a deep breath to calm his beating heart. When Elizabeth reached the altar, she smiled at him, and Darcy felt such longing he had to look away or she would see right through him.

Jane looked radiant, and for a second, Darcy thought an overeager Charles might run down the aisle to meet his bride. In order to avoid such a scene, he had placed his hand on Charles's sleeve, and the distracted groom, covered Darcy's hand with his own and left it there.

Before beginning the ceremony, Mrs. MacTavish came forward and placed a basket woven of white oak containing a quilt on the altar as a wedding gift, and tears appeared in

Jane's eyes in gratitude.

After the wedding, Darcy escorted Elizabeth down the aisle, and while they waited outside for the bride and groom, Lizzy complimented Darcy on how handsome he looked, but he was too overwhelmed by her beauty to respond. When he finally found his voice, he told her that she looked more beautiful than any woman he had ever seen. Lizzy, at a loss for words, nodded her thanks.

The reception for Mr. and Mrs. Charles Bingley was done on a grand scale. Guests came from near and far, traveling by carriage, coach, and sloop. Both the exterior and interior of Longbourn had been decorated with pine garland and sprigs of holly. Red ribbons were woven in and out of the banisters of the staircase in the foyer, and pine boughs hung from every light fixture. Musicians were brought in from New York City, and all the furniture was removed from the entryway and rear parlor for the dancing. Tables groaned under the weight of the food, and guests appeared elegantly attired and ready to eat and dance.

Mr. Bennet asked everyone to join him in a toast for the bride and groom, but then said nothing.

"Everyone, please make note of the date," Richard Bingley said. "This is the day on which Thomas Bennet was at a loss for words." The men laughed, but the women sighed their understanding. After all, a father was bidding farewell to his daughter.

"Weddings symbolize the end of one chapter in our lives and the beginning of another," Mr. Bennet began. "Today, my dear Jane has become a wife and now owes her allegiance to Charles, and that is as it should be. I am confident in saying that she begins this journey with a fine man, and how do I know this? During his months here, I have tested Charles to see if he really is as agreeable as he seems to be, and by Jove, he is." Once again, the guests started laughing. "So everyone be upstanding and please join me in raising a glass to Mr. and Mrs. Charles Bingley."

During the toast, Mrs. Bennet and Lizzy had been holding hands. At its conclusion, mother and daughter hugged each other, and Mrs. Bennet could feel the dampness on Lizzy's cheek. With her handkerchief, Mrs. Bennet dried Lizzy's eyes. "No tears today, my love. This is Jane's day, and we will rejoice and be glad in it," and Lizzy nodded. "There is a gentleman standing over there," Mrs. Bennet said, directing Lizzy's attention to William Darcy, "who looks as if he needs either a drink or a dance. I suggest the two of you dance." But when Lizzy turned around, William was gone.

* * *

Darcy asked the server for a tall glass of wine, and after a healthy drink, he wove his way through the crowd until he managed to squeeze through the front door and on to the veranda. Upon his return from Alpine Lodge, a letter from his cousin, Colonel Fitzwilliam had been waiting for him. Richard had written that his regiment had been ordered to return to England from Spain for redeployment to British North America. Richard was an artillery officer, and the thought of him training his guns on American targets made him ill. But with a president eager for war and the War Hawks in power in Congress, engagement between the two nations seemed inevitable. As a result, he felt completely adrift, with no hand to steady him.

"Well, Darcy, you look perfectly miserable," Dirck Storm said as he climbed the stairs of the veranda with drink in hand. "One would have thought you were the groom instead of Charles Bingley."

Darcy shook Dirck's extended hand, but in his mind, he pictured tossing him over the railing. But he probably would have survived the fall as the man was already in his cups.

"Have you heard the news from the Indiana Territory?"

Dirck asked. "It is in all the newspapers."

Because he was deliberately avoiding reading any additional news about a possible conflict between the Americans and British, Darcy had not seen a paper in days.

"General William Henry Harrison has defeated Tecumseh and the Shawnees at Tippecanoe. People are saying the British incited the savages to violence and supplied them with firearms."

"Dirck, although an Englishman, I am not a representative of the British government, but a guest in your country. This is a day for celebrating, and talk of war has no place here. So if you will excuse me." Darcy brushed past him and went in search of a dance partner.

With his mind in a state of discomposure, Darcy was most happy to have his thoughts diverted by dancing with Mrs. Charles Bingley, Katrina Van Wart, and Mrs. Collins, and without thinking about her misshapen foot, he had even asked Mary to dance, all in an attempt to avoid dancing with the one person he wanted: Elizabeth Bennet.

* * *

"I think we can comfortably say, 'And a good time was had by all,'" Mr. Bennet said to his wife as they stood back and watched their guests.

"Yes, the reception has been a big success," his wife agreed.

Looking in Darcy's direction, Mr. Bennet added, "At the beginning of the evening, I thought we might have another wedding in our near future. But now I am not so sure. What do *you* think about Mr. Darcy, Annie?"

"I think the gentleman is very unsettled," his wife answered without hesitation. "He received a letter from his cousin, who is a colonel in the British army. Upon reading it, Richard tells me that Darcy's mood altered immediately.

I can easily guess its contents."

"Every generation must have its war," Mr. Bennet said, with all humor gone from his voice. "We learn nothing from our forefathers."

"Tom, we shall speak of this tomorrow. There is nothing to be done tonight, and we have guests to entertain." Mrs. Bennet ran her fingers along her husband's cheek and pinched his chin before leaving him.

* * *

"Well, William, you have successfully avoided dancing with me. Is it your intention to avoid me all during the supper hour as well?" Lizzy asked Darcy as he stood staring at the stove in the rear parlor.

"I did not mean to..."

"Oh, yes, you did." But then Lizzy studied the gentleman's features, and she could see he was distressed. "Is there something wrong? Yes, I can see that there is. Please go into my father's study, and I will join you there shortly."

When Lizzy went into the study, there was only one oil lamp burning, and she had to wait for her eyes to adjust to the dark before locating William. When she did, she found him at the window staring at a half moon hovering over the river.

"William, what is wrong?"

Darcy turned to face her, and when he did, he saw a woman he longed to take into his arms, to kiss, and to caress. But, instead, he answered her question. "I have had a letter from my cousin, Colonel Fitzwilliam, but I am not at liberty to reveal its contents because if I do, I must ask myself, am I betraying my country? And if I do not, am I betraying my friends?"

Lizzy placed her hand on William's arm. "You said it

yourself. These things are decided in Congress and in Parliament, and I am sure there is nothing in that letter that is not already known in Washington. All we can do is pray that reason will prevail." But her words failed to soothe him, and so she sought to change the topic. "You must think of other things as you will only be here for another two weeks, and my family has so many things planned for our English visitors to keep them amused. A week from Thursday is Thanksgiving Day, the biggest holiday of the year. You will be wined and dined and royally entertained. There will be more apple pie than even you can eat, and we will give you a joyful sendoff."

Darcy grabbed Elizabeth by her two arms and pulled her to him, their lips nearly touching. "Do you really think I want to leave here? If you do, you do not understand me at all." After releasing her, he turned on his heel and left the room.

Lizzy, stunned by his outburst, cried out to an empty room, "No, I do not understand you at all."

* * *

After regaining his composure, Darcy brought Elizabeth a peace offering of a peach cobbler, her favorite, and sat so close to her that a knife could not have passed between them. Lizzy thought to break the ice by discussing the upcoming feast of Thanksgiving, traditionally celebrated in the Northeast on the last Thursday of November.

Darcy, who loved watching the ships moving up and down the Hudson, had noticed an increase in traffic. While sloops sailed north from the port of New York carrying Jamaica Rum, French and cider brandy, molasses, loaf and brown sugars, Hyson-Souchong and Bohea teas, various spices, dried fruits, coffee, and chocolate, barges filled to overflowing with cages containing live poultry and suckling pigs were arriving from Upstate New York at Tarrytown

Harbor. The topic succeeded in smoothing ruffled feathers.

Darcy engaged Elizabeth for the last two dances, thus preventing Dirck Storm from dancing with her. Lizzy would have loved to have asked William why he even cared about Dirck or any other gentleman who might be interested in her. He would soon be in far-off England, most likely looking for a bride of his own. Of what importance to him were the romantic inclinations of his colonial sister?

* * *

Because Jane and Charles were spending their wedding night in Lizzy and Jane's shared bedroom, Lizzy found herself relegated to a trundle bed in Lydia and Kitty's room. She listened as the twins speculated as to what the newlyweds were "talking" about, and that topic had the two of them dissolving into fits of giggling.

Unlike Lydia and Kitty, Lizzy was not thinking about Jane and Charles's lovemaking. She was struggling to make sense of the scene in the study. What did William mean when he had asked, "Do you really think I want to leave here?"

There was ample evidence to support her conclusion that William was ready to return to England and his estate in Derbyshire. First, he was growing increasingly unhappy with the relationship between Joshua and Georgiana, and their romance was a sticky wicket, to use his phrase, that would require much finesse, something William seemed to lack. Additionally, he had been completely broadsided by Mercer's marriage to Mrs. Haas. William did not like complications and having your manservant married was exactly that. Fortunately, Mrs. Haas was too old to bear children, thus avoiding that mare's nest.

Considering all these distractions, the man had a right to long for his home. It was understandable that he would want to go somewhere peaceful, and the ideal place for him to sort things out would be at Pemberley. The only reason he would *not* want to leave New York was if he was in love with her, and if that were the case, why had he not declared himself?

"Lizzy, you already know the answer to that," she said out loud. "He is afraid I will embarrass myself in society, and in doing so, embarrass him as well. My colloquialisms and independence of thought that he finds so endearing on this side of the Atlantic would invite ridicule in England. His friends would judge me in the same way Edward Chamberlain's parents did."

Both Lydia and Kitty climbed to the bottom of the bed and peered over the footboard. "Are Goodness and Mercy in here with you, Lizzy?" Lydia asked.

"No one is here. I am all alone." She rolled on her side and went to sleep.

Chapter 31

Signs of the approaching holiday were everywhere. While tailors, milliners, and mantua makers rushed to complete their orders, in Lucas Mercantile, there was an increased demand for laces, ribbons, and dancing pumps. Farmers harvested their pumpkins, gathered their eggs, fatted their pigs, and selected the best turkeys and chickens for slaughter.

When Mr. Bennet was not in his study working on his Thanksgiving Day proclamation, he was at the landing supervising the off loading of his sloops with all the essentials that the women of Tarrytown would need to make Thanksgiving dinner a resounding success. In the Bennet kitchen, Mrs. Kraft, Mrs. MacTavish, and Mrs. Wesley were busy baking pies with every possible fruit filling, including Marlborough pies, brimming with apple and lemon custard. The five Bennet daughters and all the help were either assisting in the baking or at Mrs. Bennet's beck and call running back and forth from the pantry cupboard, springhouse, or woodpile bringing needed ingredients to the bakers or kindling to those tending the fires.

After Mrs. Bennet was convinced that everyone knew what to do, she took off her apron, washed her hands, and put on her cloak and bonnet. There were more important things than apple pies, and the man who enjoyed hers more than anyone was in need of some attention. With that in mind, she set off for Richard Bingley's house.

When Mrs. Bennet arrived, William Darcy had just finished breakfast. Because he had not bothered to shave, he knew that he looked as if he was recovering from a night of drinking, but the reason for his haggard, unkempt appearance was that he had barely slept at all, having awakened from a dream, his brow covered with perspiration, and despite the coolness of the room, with his shirt clinging to him with sweat. In his dream, Elizabeth and he were aboard a ship, sailing to England, when she had declared she could not continue the journey and had jumped overboard. He had not had a nightmare since he was a boy, and the dream had rattled him to his very core.

With Mr. and Mrs. Augustus Mercer asleep in his bedroom, Darcy now occupied the room where Georgiana had stayed when they had first arrived in Tarrytown. After tossing and turning for hours, he had opened the door leading to the exterior staircase and sat on the top stair. He needed to regain the equilibrium that had been shattered by his feelings for Elizabeth and his inability to do anything about them. But there was no cure for the hurt raging inside him.

Looking at Mrs. Bennet, he had to wonder what pressing business brought her here when he knew the entire village was busily engaged in preparations for Thanksgiving Day. Did Elizabeth say something to her mother about his inexplicable behavior at Jane's wedding reception?

Mrs. Bennet removed her cloak and bonnet and then took a seat by the cast iron stove and held out her hands in front of it to warm them. "When I lived in this house as a young bride, we did not have these stoves, and I can tell you there were times when any liquid would freeze if it were farther than three feet from the hearth, and one year a bottle of wine exploded."

"I understand you spent your early years in Albany. It must have been even colder there."

"It *was* colder there. My mother used to keep me bundled up to the point where I could hardly move my arms and legs, but then we moved to the lower Hudson Valley. It is a rather interesting story if you care to hear it." After Darcy assured her of his interest, she began.

"My father was Hendrick Schuyler, and my mother was Martha Beekman. Along with the Van Rensselaers, the Schuylers are one of the most prominent families in the northern Hudson Valley, and the Beekmans and Livingstons are the same for the mid Hudson Valley. When I was eight, my father died. Everything was left to me with Mama serving as custodian of the estate until I turned twenty-one.

"It was my father's wish that when I reached the age of fourteen I was to marry Anton Van Rensselaer, who lived across the river in Rensselaerwyck, and who was, at that time, twenty-eight years old. But my mother had other ideas. Shortly after we buried Papa and the legal questions were settled, Mama told her relations that she was going to visit her cousin in Tarrytown. Everyone assumed the visit would be of short duration, but my mother never had any intention of returning to Albany where she would be under the thumb of her husband's relations."

"I gather that a streak of independence passes through the female line and is now making its appearance in the third generation of Schuyler women," Darcy said, thinking of Elizabeth.

"You are correct, William. My female ancestors had a role to play in establishing a civilization in the midst of a wilderness. They would have bristled at the idea of serving as mere ornaments in a drawing room and other rooms as well."

"I understand."

"William, you must keep in mind that I was now an heiress with properties spanning the length of the Hudson, so you can imagine how unhappy Anton's family was when they figured out that he would not be marrying me and getting his hands on all my money. Bitter words were exchanged before Anton's father sued my mother for a breach of trust. Of course, as a result of the lawsuit, my mother needed to hire an attorney, and she found one in Horatio Gardiner, who would eventually become my stepfather.

"Once Anton's family lost in court, every bachelor in the Hudson Valley, and many from the city as well, came calling on me. But once I met Mr. Bennet, I knew I would never marry another. When Tom and I finally did marry, and everyone realized that all my money was going to someone outside of God's anointed few, my mother and I were shunned for many, many years. But neither of us cared. I was very much in love with Tom, and my mother was very happy with Mr. Gardiner, and if there is a lesson in that story, I shall leave you to decide what it is.

"Now, as to a matter concerning your sister. When I first met Georgiana, she seemed to me to be a frightened sparrow, and I felt something had happened in England that had greatly unsettled her and was possibly the reason why you brought her to America. But in the time she has been here, I have seen that little bird spread her wings and fly. She came as a child and will return home an adult.

"I have also watched you. You were charged at a young age with the care of your sister, and you have done a most admirable job. However, you must now step back, and I can assure you that it is a difficult thing to do. That is not to say she will not need your wise counsel. But if Georgiana is to be happy, then she must make her own decisions, and her decisions may not be in accord with your own."

"Mrs. Bennet, are you saying that if Georgiana wants to remain in America I should allow it?" Darcy asked, thinking of Joshua Lucas.

"No, you will not have to suffer a separation from your

sister. I know from listening to her conversations with my daughters that Georgiana does not want to live in America permanently. However, that does not mean she will not be sad to leave. I can tell you from personal experience that girls of Georgiana's age can be very dramatic, so prepare yourself for some gut-wrenching scenes, especially since she fancies herself to be in love with Joshua Lucas. But she will get over him, and when she is older, she will look back with great fondness at this first flutter of love. What I *am* suggesting is that she may fall in love with someone in England who is not in her so-called 'sphere.' In order to be fair to your sister, you must judge any such suitor by his character not his rank in society."

"I can promise you that I will follow your advice, ma'am. Apparently, independence of thought is contagious, and Georgiana has contracted the American version of it."

"I am leaving you with a lot to think about, but our time together is short," Mrs. Bennet said, rising from her chair. "You come from ancient lineage, as do I, and there is value in that. But such considerations should not be the only things that guide you. Reason, intuition, faith, love, and loyalty should play equal parts in making any decision. The most important thing I can say to you is that you are the master of your own destiny. You are at the helm, and you will set the course for the direction your life will take.

"Now, I have finished preaching, and I must return to my kitchen as there are pies to be baked. For this most special of holidays, we cook for three families. In addition to my own family, the MacTavishes and the Wesleys have large families, and because of that, it is impossible to accommodate so many people in our dining room. However, in the evening, we all come together for coffee and dessert, and we play games and sing songs. There is a new game called The Farmer's Cat in which you must have an excellent knowledge of descriptives. You might want to study Mr. Webster's dictionary in preparation. I expect our

Lizzy will give everyone a run for their money. After Mr. Bennet, she is the family's greatest reader and our best writer, and she is always looking through the dictionary for the best word to use in her stories."

Before leaving, Mrs. Bennet gave Darcy two bottles, one containing small pellets of ground oyster shells mixed with sugar and another with powdered molasses. "If you are feeling seasick, reconstitute the molasses with some liquid, preferably a cider. However, if your stomach or chest is burning, then swallow a few of the oyster pellets. They should help. But, remember, despite what you may have heard from a certain member of my family, everyone gets seasick."

Darcy offered to walk with Mrs. Bennet to Longbourn, an offer she declined, but as she walked down the lane toward her home, Darcy knew he had spent a morning with a very wise woman.

Chapter 32

Before sunrise, Mrs. Bennet was in the kitchen seeing to the last minute details for today was Thanksgiving Day. After she was satisfied that everything was ready, she went upstairs to join the others who were waiting to leave for worship service. On their way to St. Matthew's, they waved to Mrs. Kraft who was walking to the Quaker meeting house and shouted greetings to the MacTavishes and the Wesleys, who worshiped with other Methodists at Cornelia Van Cortlandt's home. Once they arrived at St. Matthew's, Ezekiel dropped the family off and went in search of a place to leave the wagon during the service.

This was to be Mr. Collins's first—and last—Thanksgiving Day in America, and he was aware of the importance placed on the holiday by his parishioners. Charlotte had shared with Lizzy that he had spent a good part of the previous week writing his sermon, and she thought it would be the best homily he had ever delivered. Lizzy, in Christian charity, refrained from making comment about the quality of Mr. Collins's sermons as she had grown rather fond of the preacher. She especially liked how he frequently deferred to his wife when his thoughts were muddled, which was often.

As was the custom, matters of great political importance were mentioned in the Thanksgiving Day sermon, and Mr. Collins knew his audience. There were few in the pews who supported a war with Britain as many of the congregants bore physical, emotional, and financial scars from that war, and they did not want another one.

There was also the matter of trade with Britain and its colonies. Hudson River Valley wheat, corn, and cider were prized in the British West Indies, as well as its lumber, iron, and bricks. Conversely, Lucas Mercantile relied on finished goods from Britain for its store, especially textiles, and there wasn't a sewing needle manufactured in any of Britain's former colonies. But there was little Mr. Collins could do about such great matters other than lead his congregation in prayer for their political leaders.

After the sermon, a collection was made with monies designated for the poor of the parish, and great hymns of praise were sung. After a benediction, everyone gathered outside the church and complimented the Reverend Collins on his sermon. But there would be no lingering this day as there were chicken pies, hams, and roast turkeys to be eaten and apple and peach pies to be consumed.

There were fourteen seated at the Bennet's dining table: Mr. and Mrs. Bennet and their four unmarried daughters, Mr. and Mrs. Charles Bingley, Mr. and Mrs. Mercer, Mr. Darcy and Miss Darcy, Mrs. Kraft, and Dirck Storm, who had sent word asking if he could join the Bennets for supper as he had done when he was a youth.

After Mr. Bennet had finished saying grace and had read his proclamation, he began to carve the turkey, and everyone waited in anticipation as the bird was dismembered and the first slices fell onto the meat platter. Plates were heaped with potatoes, sweet potatoes, squash pies, plum pudding, and vegetables, and everyone was encouraged to gorge themselves. The second course of pickled oysters, cheese, grapes, jellies, dried fruits, and nuts was eaten with relish, and everyone admitted that a break was necessary before enjoying the desserts.

When it was suggested that all of the young people

adjourn to the rear parlor for charades, Joshua and Georgiana asked to be excused so that they might visit on the veranda. Knowing looks, accompanied by sly smiles, passed among all those present.

After everyone had had a turn at charades, Lizzy recommended the group try a new game, The Farmer's Cat. While explaining the rules, she provided a demonstration for the clapping that went along with the game. Lizzy started with "The farmer's cat is an *adorable* cat," which Jane followed with "The farmer's cat is an *attractive* cat." Lizzy saw signs of trouble with William's *angry* cat, and his second turn with an *aggressive* cat and noticed that all his efforts were directed toward Dirck Storm. Things did not improve with a *belligerent* and *bellicose* cat or a *cunning* and *callous* cat. By the time they had arrived at the letter "g," Lydia, Kitty, and Charles had been forced to drop out. Jane did not get beyond "h," and Dirck was bested by the letter "j," which caused Darcy to compliment "an Oxford man" for getting as far as he did. But Lizzy demolished William with keen, knowledgeable, kingly, and knotty. By that time, the MacTavishes and Wesleys had come to join them for dessert.

After everyone had eaten their fill and could not eat another bite, Georgiana and Mary played tunes so that all might dance, and the elders watched with amusement as Dirck and William vied for Lizzy's attention. But with Darcy leaving in a week, there were puzzled expressions to go with the smiles. If the gentleman was so interested in Elizabeth, then why had he not done something about it? Even though it was after midnight before the last of the guests had gone home, there would be no answer that night.

Chapter 33

The first sign of the impending exodus appeared when Georgiana's trunks were brought out of storage from Richard's owl-free attic and delivered to Longbourn. The second was when the same task was performed for Jane Bennet Bingley, but Lizzy could hardly bear to see her sister gathering up her possessions and begged to be allowed to visit Aunt and Uncle Gardiner.

"I know it will be difficult to say goodbye, but if you are not here, I think I would not have the courage to leave," Jane said, pleading with her sister to stay. Lizzy remained and watched as her sister packed articles of clothing they had shared or asked if she might take a certain book they had enjoyed reading together.

Georgiana's first bout of crying was a result of her brother telling her that she must begin to pack her things and that he would see to anything she had left behind at Mr. Richard's house. As she placed different articles of clothing in the trunk, she realized how much she had changed. In the chest of drawers were formal gloves with pearl buttons, fancy combs, and an exquisite Spanish shawl she had forgotten she had brought with her. Her everyday frocks, made by the village dressmaker, lay next to her beautiful dresses sewn by a French *modiste* in London, but that she had worn only once or twice. None of those things had been required in order for her to enjoy herself.

When Darcy told his sister it would be best for everyone

if she spent the night before their departure at Richard's house, there were more tears, and when she arrived at the house, she ran past her brother and up the stairs to her former bedroom. Darcy followed and found her sitting on her bed toying with an oyster-shell necklace Mrs. MacTavish had given to her as a symbol of their friendship. But the primary reason for her tears was that she had thought Joshua Lucas would be at Longbourn to say goodbye to her. Darcy explained that it was unrealistic for her to expect that Joshua would be able to come to Tarrytown after having so recently been granted leave to come home for Thanksgiving. But a plate full of reality was not on Georgiana's menu.

Even though he knew his news would cause his sister additional distress, Darcy revealed for the first time that Colonel Fitzwilliam was being sent to Nova Scotia in preparation for a war with the United States. It nearly broke his heart to see the confusion on his sister's face. Why must she choose between her American friends and her dearest cousin? But instead of the expected tears, Georgiana nodded her head in acknowledgment of the realities of the situation. As a loyal subject of the Crown, she had no choice in the matter but to leave.

Darcy watched as his sister placed those essentials in a valise that she would use for their short stay at the Beacon Tavern, and then she held up a book to show her brother what she would be reading, *An Innocent in Albion* by E. A. Leyden.

"Elizabeth Bennet wrote this book," she told her brother. "Lizzy is Elizabeth Anetje Leyden. Leyden is the village in Holland where her mother's ancestors were from. I bought it in a bookstore in New York City. I meant to give it to you, but I had forgotten. It is a series of essays from her time in England, and there are other books as well. Here is a collection of short stories about the Hudson River Valley and another documenting the capture of Major John André.

I cannot believe I forgot to show you her work as her writing is excellent.

After taking *An Innocent in Albion* from Georgiana's hand, Darcy kissed his sister on the top of her head and bid her goodnight. But he did not take to his bed. Enveloped in his great coat, he sat on the top stair of the exterior staircase. While thinking of all that he had seen and done, Darcy remembered the words of Heraclitus, "No man can step into the same river twice for both the man and the river have changed." He was living proof of the truth of that poetic metaphor.

His heart was filled to overflowing with the generosity of his hosts. Even with the drumbeat of war growing, he had been treated with nothing but kindness, and no disparaging remark about his being an Englishman had reached his ears. In his musings, he wished that Elizabeth had received better treatment when she had been in England so that she might love England and Englishmen as much as he loved America and Americans.

Darcy glanced at the title of her book, *An Innocent in Albion*. Did Elizabeth mean to imply that innocence was naiveté, and that she had traveled across a vast ocean to a country where she was snubbed and mocked by its citizens? Seeking warmth, he went down to the kitchen. After pulling a chair over to the hearth, he opened the book, scanning its contents, until he found an essay entitled "The Two Elizabeths" with an illustration by Jane of a young Elizabeth Bennet standing on the steps of the Tower of London where Princess Elizabeth had once stood, refusing to move because she did not want to enter the Tower by the Traitors' Gate.

In moments when I feel the weakness attributed to the female of the species, I call to mind the great Elizabeth's speech at Tilbury. She had come to address those men who would man the ships that would face the Spanish Armada. There was no king to spur them to victory, and they needed none as they looked to their queen for inspiration. She gave them courage and stirred their hearts with her words because in their hands rested the future of the kingdom:

Let tyrants fear. I have always so behaved myself that under God I have placed my chiefest strength and safeguard in the loyal hearts and good will of my subjects. I am come amongst you, being resolved in the midst of heat of the battle, to live or die amongst you all, to lay down for my God and for my kingdom and for my people, my honour and my blood even in the dust. I know I have the body but of a weak and feeble woman, but I have the heart and stomach of a king, and a King of England too.

Although I am an American, the great Elizabeth's words inspire me as do the plays of Shakespeare, the poems of Marlowe, and the writings of the Venerable Bede, Thomas More, John Locke, Hannah More, and Edmund Burke. There are those who choose to point out the differences between us, but I prefer to emphasize our commonality because we share more than a language. Our governments acknowledge the primacy of the Constitution and the welfare of its people. We are governed by a set of laws established for the good of the least amongst us so that we might protect the minority from the tyranny of the majority.

Critics will say that brother nations do not come to blows, but in all families, there are disagreements. We must work so that the sword will never again be unsheathed because we are family, and those things that bind us together are greater than our differences. After all, I was named after an English queen.

Darcy was so overcome by her words that he felt tears forming. He reached in his pocket looking for a handkerchief, but he had given them all away.

* * *

The group waiting to board the sloop *Tom B* was a somber one; even the newlyweds were quiet. The gray skies matched their mood, and the cold had them huddling in silence. Knowing he would soon be saying goodbye to Jane for God only knew how long, Mr. Bennet paced up and down the pier. He needed to keep moving or he might resort to weeping, much like his family at Longbourn had done, with Mary in a particularly bad way. For all of her life, she had drawn strength from her two older sisters, and now one of her sisters was leaving her, and Georgiana, the only true friend she had ever had, was sailing away as well.

Darcy sat alone and apart, reading and rereading Elizabeth's words from *An Innocent in Albion*: *Those things that bind us together are greater than our differences. After all, I was named after an English queen*, and he cradled the book against his breast. He looked up to find Georgiana staring at him, but he shook his head, warning her not to ask for him to put into words what he was thinking. If she did, he was at risk of falling apart.

Lizzy had stood stoically on Longbourn's veranda, barely uttering a word, but as the wagon pulled away from the manor house, her father could see her walking toward the river with her mother right behind her. They would climb to the highest point on the property so they might see the sloop as it made its way down the river for a last glimpse of Jane and Charles.

With a stiff wind blowing from the north, the sloop's journey to the city would move at a clip, but that would be small comfort to Lizzy and Mrs. Bennet who were sitting on a bench waiting for the ship to pass. It was nearly an hour before Lizzy sighted the *Tom B*, and with arms waving wildly, she shouted her goodbyes, calling out Jane's name. When even the top mast could no longer be seen, she turned to her mother and said, "Oh, Mama, what am I to do without my dear Jane to comfort me?" and she dissolved into heartbreaking sobs. But there was nothing her mother could say that would be of comfort because she knew that she cried not just for Jane, but for William Darcy as well.

Chapter 34

When Lizzy returned from the river, she avoided the manor house. The idea of going back to a room she had shared with her sister since she was ten years old was unbearable to her. Since there were no words that could provide solace for so much hurt, she went to the barn to brush Timber. In the past week, the pony had been doing better, but with everyone showering him with so much attention, he had grown lazy and stubbornly refused to exercise. When Lizzy entered his stall, she found him lying on his side. After giving her one long look, he placed his head back on the straw and yawned.

"Oh, no you don't. Everyone earns his keep in the Bennet household," Lizzy said. But all efforts to get Timber up failed. "I know just how you feel." After sitting down next to him, she rested her head against his neck. "Some days it just isn't worth the effort."

"Is Timber unwell?" a voice asked, and Lizzy shot up.

"Who is there?" Lizzy said, her heart exploding out of her chest.

"Hello, Elizabeth," Darcy answered as he peered into the stall.

Lizzy sat staring at what was clearly an apparition. In the past few days, she had slept little, eaten less, but had cried buckets of tears. She was emotionally spent, and now she was having visions.

"It is I, Fitzwilliam Darcy. Don't tell me you have forgotten me already?"

"I do not understand. I saw the sloop go down the river."

"Yes, you did, and Charles and your sister are on their way to Manhattan with Mr. and Mrs. Collins and Mr. and Mrs. Mercer. Obviously, I was not on the ship."

"William, I know how much you were dreading the return voyage, but there is no other way to get back to England except by sea. You are not a bird; you cannot fly."

Darcy came and sat in the straw next to Elizabeth and ran his hands over the pony's mane before taking Lizzy's hand in his. "I did not want to make that awful trip twice, and if I left without you, it would be necessary for me to return as I must have you come to England with me." Lizzy's look spoke of extreme confusion, and Darcy's heart ached to see her tear-stained face drained of all emotion. "I could not leave because I love you. You are as much a part of me as the heart beating in my chest."

"But if that is how you felt, then why did you not say something sooner? What has changed?" Lizzy asked, the tears already beginning to pool.

"I read this." And he showed Lizzy Georgiana's copy of *An Innocent in Albion.* "I was leaving you behind because I had misjudged… I had misinterpreted everything. Your vociferous declarations of the superiority of America led me to believe that if I asked you to come and live with me in England, you would either refuse me or you would be miserable. I thought you harbored an implacable resentment against a society that created such small-minded people as the Chamberlains."

"But you should know I do not run from a fight, but toward it," Lizzy said, wiping her tears on her cloak. "Yours is a nation in need of education as to the virtues of Americans, and I am perfectly willing to provide it."

Darcy's smile provided the necessary encouragement for her to continue. "As for the Chamberlains, I forgave them for their pettiness a long time ago. Although Americans are quick to anger, we are also quick to forgive."

"Yes, I can personally attest to your capacity to forgive," Darcy said, squeezing Lizzy's hand.

"You said my book changed everything," Lizzy said, pointing to the title, "but when did you read it?"

"I read it for the first time last night. But it was while I was sitting on the dock waiting for the *Tom B* to finish loading its cargo that I fully grasped its meaning, and with that understanding, everything changed. The impossible became possible." Darcy felt tears welling up in his eyes, and tiny rivers appeared on his cheeks.

Not knowing how to comfort a weeping man, Lizzy stared at the formidable form of Fitzwilliam Darcy, but then he looked at her and asked, "Do you not hug in America?"

"We most certainly do." After inching closer to him, she fell into his arms, pushing him back onto the straw, and he held her tightly against him until he could feel her heart beating with his. After placing his hand on her face, he brought his lips to hers, but sweet kisses soon gave way to pent-up passion. With no resistance from Elizabeth, he feared he would devour her. After a few minutes of ardent kissing, he whispered in her ear, "I love you Elizabeth Bennet, and I am asking you to be my wife."

Lizzy nodded her assent, and then both sat up, but quickly resumed their kissing. The results were to be expected. Darcy asked if this was not the perfect time to consider reinstating the practice of bundling to its former prominence in the rituals of courtship.

"Like the Puritans, I take this marriage business very seriously," Darcy said with mock sincerity, "and I would be willing to share a bed with you so that we might see if we get on. Of course, there will be a bundling sack, but I shall come prepared with a knife. However, knowing your father, I will more likely encounter a sturdier bundling board, so I shall also bring an axe. I predict we will get along famously."

Lizzy burst out laughing. "Despite your unselfish gesture, I doubt your idea would pass muster with my mother even though her ancestors *did* practice queesting. As for my father, who is neither Dutch nor a Puritan, you have no hope of gaining his consent, bundling board or not."

"If you knew how I ached for you," he said, standing up and pulling her to her feet.

Lizzy, who had been in misery just minutes earlier, now was in the mood to make Darcy suffer a little. She rubbed his neck and ran her fingers through his hair, and after kissing him deeply, she teasingly pushed him away. But he was not yet done and pulled her back, and when he thrust his leg hard against her pelvis, she did not resist and surrendered to his rhythm. But their romantic interval came to an end when Lizzy heard her mother calling her name.

When Mrs. Bennet came into the barn, Darcy and Elizabeth were standing side by side with Darcy's arm firmly about her daughter's waist.

"William, I see you have found Elizabeth," Mrs. Bennet said, ignoring the straw clinging to their clothes. "Lizzy, William came to the house and told me in a most animated fashion that he needed to find you immediately, and I pointed him in the direction of the barn. Actually, I think he has been looking for you for quite some time now."

"You are again correct, ma'am, and it was you who turned me in the right direction."

Lizzy looked at Darcy for an explanation.

"Last week, your mother paid me a visit at Richard's house and told me that I should stop being a mule and to start thinking for myself. She suggested there was a possibility that I was bound to some traditions that might no longer make any sense and that I might possibly be placing too much importance on the opinions of others."

"Of course, William is paraphrasing my words," Mrs. Bennet said, but she nodded at him, acknowledging that he had understood the parable.

"When I was sitting on a bench at the landing, perfectly miserable, your mother's wise counsel finally penetrated my thick skull. Although my mind was overwhelmed with a hundred different thoughts, in one thing there was clarity: I loved Elizabeth Bennet. When your father called out for me to come aboard, I knew I would not.

"What happened after that is a blur. I recall your father ordering Ezekiel to take Georgiana and me back to Longbourn post haste, and as the *Tom B* pulled away, he yelled that by the time he returned from Manhattan I had better be an engaged man, 'unless she does not want you, and that is a possibility as she is a sensible girl.'"

Lizzy shook her head. It was exactly what she would expect from her father.

Turning to Mrs. Bennet, Darcy said, "I wish I could tell you that I will stay here in America for a good while longer. But ill winds are blowing, and I have a responsibility to see my sister safely back to England. I am not sure exactly what I shouted to Mr. Bennet, but I do believe I asked him to check ship schedules to Liverpool and to see if two berths could be reserved. If none is available, there is the possibility I can use my influence to gain passage on a British military packet ship, but we shall know more when Mr. Bennet returns."

"And when do you plan to marry?" Mrs. Bennet asked.

"Is tomorrow too soon?" Darcy said, laughing, with his arm still encircling Lizzy's waist.

"Oh, no! We cannot marry tomorrow," Lizzy said.

"With Mr. Collins gone, there is no minister at St. Matthew's, and I know that Pastor Smith would never marry someone unless the banns were announced on three consecutive Sundays. He is a stickler for such things."

"It is my understanding that a ship's captain can marry a couple;" Darcy suggested. "Will that satisfy, Mrs. Bennet?"

"There are few benefits in having lived through a war, William, but one of them is that a person must learn to adapt to unexpected events. So if you wish to be married by a ship's captain, it is a lawful means of achieving that end."

"Elizabeth, if you do not mind such an arrangement, it would allow us to exchange vows at St. Margaret's in London where my parents were married."

"I think that would be perfect," she answered and stood up on her toes and kissed his cheek.

"Well, why don't the two of you come up to the house, and we may discuss these things in front of a warm fire. Shall I expect you in about ten minutes?" Mrs. Bennet asked as she pulled a piece of straw out of Lizzy's hair, and she left the couple alone. Before she was out of the barn, the two were in each other's arms, pledging their love and getting to know each other a little better.

* * *

Although Elizabeth and Darcy were agreeable to being married by a ship's captain, their families, neighbors, and friends would not be denied a party. A letter was written to the Episcopal bishop in New York asking that a minister be sent to Tarrytown for the purpose of marrying Elizabeth Bennet, the granddaughter of Hendrick Schuyler of Albany, and Fitzwilliam Darcy, cousin of Antony, Earl Fitzwilliam. Reverend Heslip was quickly dispatched by his superior, who made note of the increase in marriages in their part of Westchester County, and presided over the marriage of Elizabeth Bennet and Fitzwilliam Darcy on December 8,

1811.

At the reception, Mr. Bennet was so overwhelmed at the thought of his favorite daughter being taken from him that for several minutes he found it impossible to make the toast, but finally, without embarrassment, and with tears glistening in his eyes, he said, "Mr. Darcy is a fine man, and you may believe my words because I could not have parted with my dearest Lizzy to anyone less worthy."

Dirck Storm immediately called for a second toast, wishing the couple joy and smooth sailing. When they had a moment alone, Dirck told Darcy that he knew he was in love with Elizabeth from the time of their encounter on Longbourn's veranda. Dirck had seen the fire in Darcy's eyes and understood its meaning.

"I can hardly account for Lizzy preferring you to me," Dirck began. "I must attribute it to your snobby accent and superior tailor. In my opinion, it is an error in judgment on her part."

"You failed to mention my being a Cambridge man," Darcy said, trying to ease the man's pain.

"Seriously, Darcy, despite my feelings for Lizzy, I would never stand in the way of her happiness. That evening, when you joined us on the porch, we were talking about you. I mentioned that despite your being English and a Cambridge man, you were a decent fellow." Dirck extended his hand, and Darcy grasped it. "You are a lucky man, Fitzwilliam Darcy. I hope you know that." With a firm handshake, Darcy acknowledged that he had misjudged the man, and no longer had any wish to throw him over the railing.

* * *

It was well past midnight when the couple waved to the last of their guests and were finally allowed to retire. The newlyweds, firmly in each other's embrace, looked out the window of Lizzy's bedroom that faced west toward the Hudson, and although they could not see the moon, they saw evidence of its presence reflected on the water, and the pair stood transfixed as they watched the sloops navigate the silvery estuary by moonlight.

Darcy commented that they would soon be on her father's sloop, traveling down the Hudson to Manhattan and a ship that would take them to England. But the person who would board that ship was a new man. Although he still believed that society had a role to play, he now saw it merely as a framework in which people of different persuasions lived their lives. Although there was value in his rank, it was not everything. In fact, it was not the most important thing. His wife and children would form the nucleus of his world. That was Darcy's promise to his wife.

Darcy took Elizabeth by the hand and led her to the bed and whispered the words that he had withheld for too long. "You are everything that is good, and I love you most ardently." After making love, the lovers lay in each other's arms discussing their extraordinary odyssey to becoming man and wife, a journey that had begun with a seasick Darcy arriving in Tarrytown Harbor. While they spoke of their future together in England, they could hear Kitty and Lydia giggling in the next room.

"They are wondering what we are 'talking' about," Lizzy whispered in her husband's ear.

"Talking? They think we are talking? Well, we can't have that," and Lizzy soon felt the full weight of the man she loved. With the sound of the wind in the pines and a new moon suspended above the Hudson River, they made love, proving that at least one Englishman and one American could get along quite well.

Chapter 35

Two weeks after their marriage, Elizabeth, William, and Georgiana sailed on *HMS Valiant* as guests of Admiral Trent of His Majesty's Navy. Shortly after the *Valiant* had sailed out of the Narrows and into the Atlantic, Darcy insisted to his bride that she would soon be a widow as he was convinced he was dying. He groaned that it would be a kindness if Elizabeth would help him up on deck so that he might be thrown overboard and put out of his misery. But his wife ignored his complaints and stayed by his side throughout the voyage, cooling his brow with damp towels, and plying him with a combination of oyster shell pills and reconstituted molasses. Her ministrations were effective, and before the coast of Ireland was sighted, Darcy was feeling well enough to join his wife and sister on deck where he declared that he was now an able seaman, a comment that caused both ladies to roll their eyes.

The weary travelers went first to Netherfield Park where Elizabeth and Jane were reunited. The Bingleys requested that the newlyweds and Georgiana remain with them for at least a fortnight before going on to Pemberley, a wish Mr. and Mrs. Darcy were happy to grant.

When the trio finally arrived at Pemberley, they were greeted by all the servants, dressed in starched uniforms or the Darcy livery, with Mercer standing next to the former Mrs. Haas. Pemberley's new pastry chef had won the approval of the staff by rising early each morning to make a batch of doughnuts for their breakfast. Her ability to make the best apple fritters in the world solidified her position with the staff.

Mrs. Darcy greeted each servant, and when she had been introduced to all of those who served above and below stairs, she made a speech in which she stated that she anticipated a continuation of the excellent service she had heard so much about from Mr. Darcy and Miss Darcy. The servants nodded their heads in approval at the speech, the unique accent of its speaker, and its brevity.

By the time the newlyweds had arrived at Pemberley, January had come and gone. Although Christmas was now a memory, at the direction of the housekeeper, Mrs. Reynolds, the manor house was decorated with sweeping boughs of pine garland and bright red holly berries on string. With such inspiration, Lizzy declared her first official role as mistress of the manor would be to host a belated Christmas feast, and the staff flew into action and produced a veritable banquet. The Darcys were hosts to the vicar of St. Michael's Church and his wife, the mayor of Lambton and his family, and members of the local gentry.

For dessert, Mrs. Mercer had worked her magic once again, and it was she who placed before Mr. Darcy a Dutch apple pie, followed by a peach cobbler, and the promise of a pumpkin pie for the celebration of the first Thanksgiving at Pemberley the following November.

The staff was rewarded for their efforts with gifts from their master and mistress, and everyone adjoined to the drawing room where Georgiana played Christmas music, carols were sung by all, and the staff was introduced to American-style cookies and other confectionary delights. It was an auspicious start for Mr. and Mrs. Darcy, an omen of good things to come.

After the newlyweds had seen their guests safely on their way and had said good night to Georgiana, the couple went out onto the balcony outside their bedroom and looked into a night sky punctured by a thousand "blessed candles of the night."

"Look, Lizzy," Darcy said, pointing to a crescent moon resting on the top of Pemberley's woods. "The crescent moon is a symbol of a fresh start, a new beginning, in a new land."

"How lovely," Lizzy said as she burrowed deeper into her husband's encircling arms. "Do you have any suggestions as how best to celebrate the appearance of such a promising sign?"

"Yes, but it will be the same suggestion I have offered every night since our arrival in England."

"And that is?"

"Most glorious night! Thou wert not sent for slumber! To bed, woman."

"Did you compose that yourself?" Lizzy asked.

"No, the first part I borrowed from Lord Byron, but the 'to bed' part is mine." The two of them laughed until they fell into bed and were soon in each other's arms, the only sound accompanying their lovemaking was the hooting of an owl.

Epilogue

For Elizabeth, the challenges of London society were great, and so she turned her attention away from the cattiness and ennui of the London salons to politics. The Darcy townhouse became a meeting place for supporters of the moderate Lord Liverpool, who had succeeded the assassinated Lord Perceval as Prime Minister. Although Liverpool had directed the British Navy to avoid clashes with American ships, his efforts to avoid an armed conflict had failed, and President Madison declared war on Great Britain in June 1812.

At the start of the conflict, Elizabeth served as a voice of hope for the quick conclusion to the war as she continued to insist that England and the United States were brother nations, and the bloodshed was a betrayal of their shared history and the rule of law. She penned numerous essays on the subject, garnering the attention of people of influence. As a result, Mr. and Mrs. Darcy were often guests in the home of those who, in the coming years, would serve in the highest echelons of British governmentl. Such attention did not go unnoticed by London society.

The orders for Colonel Fitzwilliam's regiment to be sent to British North America were rescinded by the Duke of Wellington as their services were required in the assault on Ciudad Rodrigo in the Peninsular Campaign. He never saw service in North America.

An agreement on "a Treaty of Peace and Amity between His Britannic Majesty and the United States of America" was reached on December 24, 1814 at Ghent and concluded the unfortunate War of 1812. Although an uneasy peace would follow for a good part of the century, the two nations were never again to unsheathe their swords.

The delay in the Darcys' departure from New York had allowed Second Lieutenant Joshua Lucas one last opportunity to visit with Georgiana. On his way to his first appointment at Fort McHenry in Baltimore Harbor, he had stopped at Longbourn to say goodbye to the young lady who had completely captivated him. Their time together was spent in long walks along the Hudson, and before he left her, Georgiana received her first kiss, which she was to treasure for all of her days.

Georgiana's return voyage to England was made easier by the employment of a new lady's maid. Darcy had petitioned the elder Storm to free Esther from bondage, and he had agreed to do so for the sum of two hundred dollars, an amount Darcy gladly paid. Two years after her American sojourn, Georgiana married Daniel Winston, a man who had made a significant fortune in trade and whose wealth funded his wife's activities in working toward the abolition of slavery in Great Britain and its colonies in 1833.

Many times, over the years, the Darcy family would visit their relations in the Hudson River Valley, their passage made easier with the advent of the swift clipper ships and, soon thereafter, reliable steamship service between Liverpool and New York. During their long ocean voyages, their four children would be entertained with stories of hardy Dutch pioneers who had settled the length of the Hudson River Valley trading finished goods with the Mohicans, members of a noble tribe, who had come to the frontier town of Albany bearing a bounty of beaver skins, some of them six feet in length.

When the English conquered New Nederland, the era of the patroons came to an end, but the Englishmen who replaced them would soon find themselves sitting down at a Dutchman's table eating cole slaw, waffles, pancakes, and cookies. The houses of the Dutch were easily identifiable with their stepped gable ends facing the street and the occasional owl holes, and some traditions would survive, including Sinter Klaas and ice yachts racing across a frozen Hudson.

A special treat for the young Darcys, Thomas, Anne, Fitzwilliam, and Hannah, was when their mother would read to them from her autographed copy of Washington Irving's *The Legend of Sleepy Hollow,* in which schoolmaster, Ichabod Crane encountered a headless horsemen crossing a wooden bridge in Tarrytown, very near to the home of their Bennet grandparents.

The Darcy children would bear witness to the closing days of the sloops negotiating their way through the Narrows and on the broad expanses of the Tappan Zee. The sleek vessels, with their rigs and masts, had long since yielded primacy of the river to steamships belching black smoke on their way to Albany, the eastern terminus of the Erie Canal. As predicted by Tom Bennet, the canal brought untold wealth to its investors, including Fitzwilliam Darcy and Charles Bingley, as well as New York's merchants (and an increase in the sales of cast iron stoves) and had opened the Upper Midwest to settlement, just in time for an onslaught of immigrants fleeing a famine in Ireland, and they would settle in cities unknown to Tom Bennet: Cleveland, Toledo, Chicago, Milwaukee, Duluth, and a hundred towns in between.

After a lengthy visit with their grandparents and Aunts Mary, Lydia, and Kitty and their families, they would board a ship for their return voyage to Liverpool. Shortly after their arrival at Pemberley, they would be joined by their Aunt Georgiana and her brood of five, and they would tell tales about what they had seen in America. On occasion, Aunt Georgiana would share her latest letter from Joshua

Lucas. The major, who was serving at Fort Vancouver on the Columbia River, had crossed the vast American continent, traveling in the footsteps of the explorers, Lewis and Clark, and in his correspondence, he wrote eloquently of the majesty of America's Pacific Northwest. And after the tales were told, all would agree that their families had the best of both worlds as both British and American blood ran in their veins.

THE END

Chapter Notes

Chapter 1

Sloops (from the Dutch word *sloep*): Sloops continued to ply their trade on the Hudson River for decades after the arrival in 1807 of Robert Fulton's steamship, *North River* (aka *Clermont*). However, their days were numbered. Unlike the rigged sloops, steamships were not at the mercy of the wind, and with the convenience of scheduled arrivals and departures, they provided reliable transportation between New York City and Albany.

Frederick Philipse: The vast properties of Loyalist, Frederick Philipse of Philipsburg Manor in Westchester County, were confiscated by the Continental Congress in 1779 and were sold at auction in 1786. The British Parliament ultimately indemnified a large number of Loyalists in an amount exceeding £3 million.

Chapter 2

Dutch Cooking: Information on the Dutch cooking and customs in Holland and America were obtained from *Food, Drink and Celebrations of the Hudson Valley Dutch* by Peter G. Rose, a woman.

Chapter 4

Reverend Thomas Q. Smith and his wife, Jemima Allen of the Old Dutch Church: "The Rev. Thomas Q. Smith had a great affliction in a termagant wife. She sometimes locked him in the house when it was time for him to go to church... Sometimes, while he was preaching, she would enjoy herself by driving his horse up and down the road. When she came to church she always carried a pillow. And she was always loud and unceasing in her complaints to the church and its officers of the faults and shortcomings of her husband." *Two Hundredth Anniversary of the Old Dutch Church (1697 – 1897) De Vinne Press for the Consistory of the Dutch Reformed Church*

Chapter 5

The Thomas Bennet Home: The Bennet home is modeled on *Boscobel*, the home of States Morris Dyckman and his wife, Elizabeth Corne. The house was originally sited on a 250-acre piece of riverfront property in Montrose, New York. The mansion had been scheduled for demolition in 1955, when a group of conservationists, including Lila Acheson Wallace, the wife of the founder of *Reader's Digest*, intervened. It has been meticulously restored on a site in Garrison and is an excellent example of Federal architecture in the Hudson Valley.

Chapter 7

Dutch Influence in New York: During the staging of this story, there were few Dutch speakers remaining in the lower Hudson River Valley. However, it was still spoken in the upper Hudson Valley near Albany. An excellent example of colonial Dutch architecture can be seen at the Pieter Bronck house in Coxsachie, New York where owl holes are visible, and the outdoor kitchen is painted blue to ward off flies and other insects.

Names of Supporting Characters: All of the names of the supporting cast, including Dirck Storm, Beekman, Van Tassel, Van Wart, etc. were taken from the gravestones found in Sleepy Hollow Cemetery in Sleepy Hollow, New York.

Angelica Schuyler Church: Angelica was the eldest

daughter of Philip Schuyler and Catharine Van Rensselaer, prominent members of the New World Dutch aristocracy. Angelica eloped in 1777 with John Barker Church, a British-born merchant, who had made a fortune during the Revolutionary War. There were rumors that Angelica had an affair with Alexander Hamilton, the husband of her sister Elizabeth. Hamilton biographer Ron Chernow notes that: "The attraction between Hamilton and Angelica was so potent and obvious that many people assumed they were lovers. At the very least, theirs was a friendship of unusual ardor." *Alexander Hamilton* by Ron Chernow, The Penguin Press, New York, 2004, p. 133.

Food for the Continentals at Valley Forge: Fearing mutiny and desertion because of the lack of food, in the winter of 1777-78, George Washington wrote to General George Clinton of New York asking that he send cattle to Valley Forge. Clinton sent 100 head of cattle as well as grain and pork. Washington later wrote to Clinton: "Your assistance has prevented many souls from starvation... It has been one of the forgotten instances of the Revolution that with the assistance of Old Ulster, your native country [county], you more than one time saved my army in our darkest hours of this long struggle."

Chapter 8

Slavery: Most prominent families in the Hudson Valley owned slaves, including Robert L. Livingston, who served on the committee to draft the Declaration of Independence, as he considered it to be "an economic necessity." John Jay, the founder of the New York Manumission Society, was also a slaveholder.

Chapter 10

The Burning of the Livingston Estate: On October 19, 1777, British troops, under the command of General John Vaughan, burnt *Clermont* to the ground in response to the surrender of the British forces by General Burgoyne at nearby Saratoga. Even before the war had ended, "Margaret Beekman Livingston [Widow of Robert the Judge Livingston] rebuilt *Clermont* on the same Georgian plan. In order to get workmen, she wrote to Governor George Clinton requesting that he exempt skilled tenants, masons, carpenters, plasterers, etc. from military service to work on the house. By 1782, she was able to entertain General and Martha Washington in her new home, the British forever gone from the Hudson River Valley." http://www.friendsofclermont.org.

Chapter 11

Capture of Major John André: "The fate of Major André became the subject of a heated dispute between Alexander Hamilton and George Washington over whether he had acted as a spy or as a liaison officer between the British command and Benedict Arnold... If André was a spy, he would hang from the gallows like a common criminal; whereas if he was merely an unlucky officer, he would be shot like a gentleman... Washington was adamant that André's mission could have doomed the patriotic cause and feared that anything less than summary execution would imply some lack of conviction about his guilt." *Alexander Hamilton,* Ron Chernow, p. 143.

Servants v. The Help: According to Englishwoman Mrs. Frances Trollope, who spent three years in the United States, "The greatest difficulty in organizing a family establishment in Ohio is getting servants, or, as it is there called, 'getting help.' For it is more than petty treason to the Republic to call a free citizen a servant." In 1832, Mrs. Trollope's *Domestic Manners of Americans* created a sensation on both sides of the Atlantic by reinforcing unflattering British stereotypes of Americans.

Chapter 12

Delft Tiles: Delftware was originally created as a response by Dutch tile makers to the importation of vast amounts of Chinese porcelain into Holland in the early 1600s.

Campeachy Chairs: The chairs were named for the port city of Campeche on the Yucatán Peninsula. These reclining chairs were most popular in the South among those who suffered from lung complaints, which were common among people who lived in smoke-filled houses and who used tobacco products. In his later years, Thomas Jefferson, who suffered from rheumatism, purchased a Campeachy chair.

Chapter 13

Washington Irving: In late 1809, Irving completed work on his first major book, *A History of New-York from the Beginning of the World to the End of the Dutch Dynasty by Diedrich Knickerbocker*, a satire on self-important local history and contemporary politics. Today, the surname Knickerbocker has become a nickname for Manhattan residents in general and one basketball team in particular.

Chapter 14

Apotheosis of George Washington: When George Washington died in 1799, the nation was plunged into a period of prolonged mourning that took many forms, including thousands of reproductions of an engraving by John James Barralet of George Washington in his grave clothes ascending to heaven with the assistance of Immortality and Father Time.

Chapter 20

Boterberg Hill: The name Boterberg Hill or Butter Hill was changed to Storm King Mountain in the 1830s at the urging of artists and writers who had found inspiration in the Hudson Highlands.

Erie Canal: The canal was begun on July 4, 1817 and completed in 1824. With the repeal of the Corn Lawns in 1846 in Britain, there was a huge increase in exports of Midwestern wheat to Britain, binding the two nations through trade. Much of this trade flowed along the Erie Canal.

Chapter 22

The Duel between Hamilton and Burr: "During the election year of 1804, Aaron Burr's character was savagely attacked by Hamilton. After the election, Burr challenged Hamilton to a duel. On July 11, 1804, the combatants met at the dueling grounds near Weehawken, New Jersey. Burr shot Hamilton in the stomach, and the bullet lodged next to his spine. Hamilton was taken back to New York and died the next afternoon. The nation was outraged by the killing of a man as eminent as Alexander Hamilton. Charged with murder in New York and New Jersey, Burr returned to Washington, D.C. where he finished his term as Vice President to Thomas Jefferson, immune from prosecution." *History.com, This Day in History.* Elizabeth Schuyler Hamilton, Alexander's widow, lived another fifty years, much of which was spent in preserving and polishing her husband's memory.

Chapter 28

The Trial of Levi Weeks: "On December 22, 1799, Gulielma Sands left the boarding house where she resided with her Quaker relatives, Catherine and Elias Ring. It was believed that she had gone off to marry her fiancé, Levi Weeks, who was also a tenant. On January 2, her corpse was fished from a wooden well owned by the Manhattan Company. Perhaps because he had founded the company, Aaron Burr joined with Alexander Hamilton and Brockholst Livingston to defend Levi Weeks against a murder charge... A verdict of not guilty was returned after five minutes of deliberation." *Alexander Hamilton* by Ron Chernow, p. 606.

Chapter 30

Thanksgiving Day: Most of the information on Thanksgiving Day traditions was taken from *Our Own Snug Fireside, Images of the New England Home, 1760-1860*, by Jane C. Nylander, Yale University Press, 1994. Although the importance of Christmas would increase throughout the Victorian Era, during the Federal Era, Thanksgiving was the biggest holiday celebrated by Americans.

The Farmer's Cat: This is actually a rip-off of the Victorian parlor game, The Minister's Cat. Liberties were taken.

Chapter 31

Webster's Dictionary: In 1806, Noah Webster published his first dictionary: *A Compendious Dictionary of the English Language*. A year later, he began compiling a comprehensive dictionary which took 27 years to complete. He hoped to standardize American speech and to simplify spelling. It was he who dropped the superfluous vowels in words such as colour and labour and the redundant "k" in picnick.

Epilogue

War of 1812: "The War of 1812 was an indecisive military conflict fought between 1812 and 1815 between the forces of the United States and the British Empire. The issues in dispute included trade restrictions, impressment of U.S. personnel into the Royal Navy, and British support of Native American tribes along the frontier in their fight against American expansion. Britain, which had regarded the war as a sideshow to the Napoleonic Wars raging in Europe, welcomed an era of peaceful relations and trade with the United States." (Wikipedia)